SUCKERS

Book 2

Raising A Vampire

Jacky Dahlhaus

Folla Fiction Publishing

First edition published in March 2016
Second edition published in March 2017

ISBN 978-0-9956719-1-1

jackydahlhaus.com

Books written by Jacky Dahlhaus:

Releasing A Vampire

Living Like A Vampire

Raising A Vampire

Killing A Vampire

Short Shockers

jackydahlhaus.com

Contents

Black October

My life changed forever during Black October 2004. It was an apocalyptic event during which a genetically enhanced virus escaped the Army Medical Research Institute of Infectious Diseases, infecting people all over the world. The affected people acted like vampires as the infection made them UV-sensitive and, most importantly, made them lust for human blood. If they didn't drain you of all your life juices, you lived and changed into a sucker yourself.

That was the name we had given them. Suckers. At first we called them vampires, and it was funny how the media adopted vampire terms from modern books and movies. If only these monsters glittered in sunlight and were vegan. A bioscientist interviewed on TV during Black October had explained that these so-called vampires weren't the living dead. They were still alive and human, just not the same person they had been before the infection. Hence, they had named the virus *Succedaneum* as it meant 'substitute.' From then on, everybody called the infected 'suckers.'

During that world-devastating event, I had become a daywalker, a sucker who could walk in daylight without any ill effect. With the help of my blood, the army was able to create a vaccination against the disease. They got on top of the suckers 'invasion' and vaccinated everyone. As far as we knew, no sucker roamed the planet anymore and everyone was safe again.

Not soon after Black October, I had found out I was pregnant. Charlie and I became a family. We named our daughter Sue, to honor the friend we had lost.

So, many years later, life was good. Good, but not great as we were hiding a terrible secret.

A Dark Day

It was a wet and dreary October Thursday, ten years after Black October. I wasn't teaching at Bullsbrook High anymore. Instead, I was homeschooling my daughter, Sue, and my friend Rhona's twin girls, Maddy and Milly. To make up for the loss of income, I worked early hours as a cleaner at the school where Charlie still had a job as the industrial arts teacher. I had just finished work and was about to walk outside when I noticed rain was bucketing down.

"Oh no," I said to nobody in particular as I stared through the doors' windows.

"What's up?" John, my manager, asked as he walked up to me, ready to leave as well.

"It's raining cats and dogs, and I forgot to bring my umbrella." I sighed. "It's not far to my house, but with this torrential rain, I'll get soaked."

"Can't you just wait until it clears a bit?" John suggested as he zipped up his jacket.

"No, I can't. I have to get back in time, so Charlie can get to work. My daughter will still be asleep, but I don't want to leave her alone in the house."

"Yeah, I understand," John said. "Kids can be such troublemakers. You can never trust them."

I frowned and glanced sideways at John. Ten years ago, he had applied for the job as Arts teacher at the school. Luckily, for us, the job had been given to Charlie, and John had to settle for the position as cleaners' manager. I found his remark strange for somebody who had wanted to work with kids but didn't say anything.

"I'll tell you what," he said. "How about I give you a ride?"

I looked at John. He'd been nice to me since he hired me for the job, but we'd never exchanged more than the necessary communication: 'clean the upper floor,' 'don't forget the waste bins,' and the like. His attitude toward me had certainly changed these last few weeks, and now this offer of a ride. I couldn't help but like the change. It was nice to have someone to talk to outside the house.

"Would you? That'd be great. Thanks, John." I looked out at the rain again and was glad I didn't have to get completely soaked. I hated the feeling of wet clothes on my body. It brought back dark memories of Black October, of when Charlie and I were nearly lynched during a downpour.

John smiled at me and put his hands on the door.

"Let's run on the count of three. One, two, three!"

Together, we dashed for his car. We still got wet but not soaked. Once inside his car, we laughed and wiped the water from our faces.

"Phew, we made it! Now, where's your home?" he asked as he started the car.

I gave him directions, and within a few minutes, he parked in front of my house.

"Thanks, John. I owe you," I said as I unbuckled myself.

"I could do with a cup of coffee."

My breathing halted as he said it. Since Sue was born, I had never invited a stranger into my home. John smiled a sweet smile. Surely there was no harm in letting him come inside for a coffee? It would be a small token of gratitude for saving me from the rain. One cup of coffee, and he would be off again. Sue could hold off on breakfast until he left. Wasn't it a normal thing to do? I smiled back.

"Okay, come on in then."

We ran through the rain to the front porch. As we entered, Charlie came into the living room from the kitchen, holding his lunch bag.

"Hi, honey. You're back early," he said.

As soon as he saw John following me inside, he stopped in his tracks. The happy, surprised look on his face changed into one of weariness. I caught his eyes and didn't miss the anxiety in them.

"The rain's torrential, so John offered me a ride," I explained and threw my keys onto the dish on the sideboard. In trying to act as nonchalantly as possible, I missed. The keys slid over the top of the sideboard and hit the floor on the far side.

"Is it still raining?" Charlie asked.

Do you want John out of the house, or are you fishing for a ride to school from him?

"Um, I just offered John a cup of coffee," I said as I picked up my keys and put them onto the dish where I had intended them to be.

Charlie walked to the front window where he peeked through the still-drawn curtains.

"It's okay. It's stopped." There was a flash of disappointment on his face as he turned around, but he forced a smile as he walked over to John and stuck his hand out.

"Nice to finally meet you," he said.

"Likewise," John replied as he shook Charlie's hand.

Awkward.

John tried to take his hand back, but Charlie held on to it.

"No hard feelings?" Charlie asked.

John's Adam's apple bobbed up and down.

"No, no hard feelings. I like the job I've got now. You can keep yours. I have more free time than I would've had if I'd gotten your job." His smile was half-hearted.

When Charlie finally let go, John couldn't get his hand away fast enough and put it into his pocket. Charlie gave him a chummy pat on the arm and turned to me.

"See you later, honey," he said and gave me a kiss. He squeezed my hand which he also held a bit longer than normal, his gaze emitting a warning. Reluctant to let go of me, he left for work.

I waited until the door was shut.

"Coffee?" I said as I turned to John.

"That would be great." He smiled and took off his wet jacket. There had been a tension palpable in the room before, but it had left with Charlie.

"Just hang it behind the door," I said to him as I indicated the coat hanger and walked into the kitchen. There, I got out of my own coat and threw it over a dining chair.

"My aunt sends her regards," I heard John say from the living room.

I frowned as I put the kettle on. I took two mugs from the cupboard and spooned the instant coffee into the mugs.

"Does she now?" I called back to John.

I recalled the time Fiona, the history teacher, had come uninvited and unwanted into my home when Sue was only a week old. She had been a real pain in the ass, and Charlie had politely gotten rid of her, but our relationship had never been a friendly one after that. I wondered why she suddenly sent me her regards now. It must have been just superficial conversation from John. While waiting for the kettle to boil, I stared out of the kitchen window. My thoughts about Fiona disappeared into the rain puddles that had formed in the garden. The dark water reminded me of the time during Black October when Charlie and I were nearly executed in the next village.

'We were with Harry!'

Four little words had saved our lives that day. The water was about to boil when I heard John come into the kitchen. I turned around.

"You look great, Kate," John said as he walked toward me.

"Um, thanks," I said. I wiped a wet string of hair out of my face.

What a strange comment. I'm sure I look like a drowned cat.

"No, truly, I mean it. You look great." He stood within an inch of me.

Somebody's playing space invaders.

I heard the kettle switch itself off.

"Coffee's nearly done, John." I turned to get the kettle and away from him.

Before I could get a hold of the kettle handle, John put his hand under my chin, turned my face back to him, and kissed me.

What the...?

I averted my face, resisted the urge to wipe my mouth. I didn't want him to know I was disgusted.

"John, please. What are you doing? I don't want this. I'm with Charlie." I kept my voice quiet as I didn't want to wake up Sue. John put both his hands on the bench-top beside me and locked me in. There was nowhere I could go. I looked this way and that, like a caged animal trying to find a way out.

"Come on, Kate. Don't play games. Charlie's not here, and your kid's asleep, so it's fine." His eyes looked hungry, and his stare dropped to my chest. He lifted one hand, slid it over my waist and up and put it on my left breast. He licked his lips. Was he going to drool?

Holy shit, this is for real.

There was nothing I had done to lead him on. Was there?

Offering someone a coffee's not the same as offering them your body nowadays, is it?

After an ultra-fast check of my past behavior toward John, a wave of anger flowed through me. I had been nothing but professional toward him. How dare he come in and assume I wanted this? How dare he touch my body without my permission? I swiped his hand off me.

"No, it's not fine."

John immediately tried to touch me again.

"Come on, Kate. We haven't got time for games," he said.

Is he panting?

John wasn't taking no for an answer. I pushed his arms off me, and before he could put them back, I pushed his body away from me. He stumbled against the kitchen table. The heavy wood screeched over the kitchen floor.

"I said, it's not okay," I hissed. "I don't want this. Get out!" and I pointed toward the front door.

John's eyes became dark. Before I knew what was happening, he grabbed me and threw me onto the kitchen floor. I hit it hard. Cups may bounce when you drop them on vinyl, but I didn't. Upon impact, pain radiated from my right hip and shoulder. I found myself on my back, stuck between the cupboards and the dining table. John was immediately on top of me, putting his filthy mouth on mine and ripping my shirt open with his eager claws.

"Sure... you want... this," he was saying in between breaths while groping me all over. I desperately tried to get my mouth away from his. His mouth now moved from my face to my neck, licking it. "Besides, you owe me something," he said as he looked me in the eye. "Your little man got my job, and I had to make do with the janitor's job. This is just a little something in return." He then continued to grope my breast and kissing me. I tried with all my might to push his hands off me, but as soon as I had one off, it would come straight back. "I don't know why you object. You've done it before... with your doctor friend Harry... Everybody knows it... Just look at your daughter."

My actions to get this weasel off me stopped for a split second as I realized why I was in this situation.

Holy Moly! That's what this is about. He thinks Sue is Harry's child because they both have long canines.

And that I do it with anybody.

I bet Fiona's behind this.

Once I was over the shock of his words, I forced myself to focus on how to get John's groping hands and heavy body off of mine. I tried to grab his throat, but he took one of my hands and pinned it to the floor. He was so much stronger than I was. I felt his other hand slide into my pants. I screamed. I frantically tried to push his body off me again with my free arm and kicked out, but my feet hit nothing but the cupboards. Desperate, I tried to grab a chair. It appeared too heavy to lift with one hand.

"Mom, what's going on?" I heard Sue say, her voice sleepy.

Tilting my head back, I saw her bare feet in the kitchen doorway. There was a sudden ache of despair in the pit of my stomach.

Oh no, Sue. Get out. I don't want you to see this.

John gave Sue a quick glance.

"Your mother and I are just having a bit of fun. Go back to bed, girl," John said, breathing heavily.

"Mom?" Sue asked.

"Sue, call for help!" I yelled.

John hit me in the face. The sting of it burned on my skin, and there was a dull ache in my jaw.

Next thing I knew, the kitchen table seemed to

levitate. Chairs fell. The table crashed on its side and Sue flew through the air in her white nightgown.

My little angel.

She clawed at John's shoulders. I could see a flash of her fangs and that look in her eyes I knew all too well.

Oh my god, she wouldn't?

"No! Sue, don't! Please don't!" I screamed, but Sue lifted John off me as if he was a rag doll and pushed him against the cupboards. As I feared, she sunk her fangs into his neck. John screamed like a pig being slaughtered.

Nooo!

I scrambled up and tried to pull Sue off John, the attacker turned victim.

"Sue, don't! You can't kill him! Don't!"

I knew I wasn't strong enough to stop Sue from doing whatever she wanted. Harry had explained the *Succedaneum* virus in my body had changed Sue's genetics when she was conceived. Even though she officially was only eight years old, Sue had matured twice as fast as a normal human and was now a sixteen-year-old. Being born a half-blood sucker also meant she was a lot stronger than a normal person. I had to try to stop her for John's sake.

Finally, the urgency in my continued screaming compelled her to listen to me. She let go of John and stepped back. Blood dripped from her mouth onto her white nightgown. She spat the blood in her mouth onto the floor.

"He tastes disgusting anyway," she said and spat out some more blood.

John sank to the floor. His hand went to his neck.

"She bit me!" he screamed as he looked at the blood on his hand. He scrambled into the corner to get away from Sue. "She fucking bit me!" he cried again. He put his hand back on his neck, trying to stop the bleeding.

Shih Tzu! What have you done?

I pulled Sue close and hugged her. She was trembling. I didn't know if it was from excitement or fear.

"It's okay. It's okay," I said to her as I caressed her hair.

"It's fucking not okay!" John screamed from his corner.

I knew things were far from okay but wanted Sue to know she didn't do anything wrong. It had been a matter of self-defense.

Well, mother-defense.

At that moment, we heard Rhona and her girls come in. Of all days, they had to arrive early for their homeschooling lessons today.

Understandings

"What's going on?" Rhona asked from the living room. She must have spotted the chaos in the kitchen through the doorway. Still wearing her coat, she walked in and stopped in her tracks. As I struggled to find the words to say, I saw her eyes scan the fallen chairs, the upturned kitchen table, my disheveled state. I watched her take in my ripped shirt, the blood dripping from Sue's mouth, and John, whining in the corner of the kitchen, bleeding like a wounded animal.

Like a pig.

Disgust appeared on her face as her stare lingered on John.

"What are we going to do with him?" Her question was directed at me.

"What are we going to do with whom?" Milly asked as she stuck her head through the kitchen doorway. Maddy wormed herself past Milly and Rhona, but her mother held her back from going any further. Rhona was looking at me now, her eyes as cold as ice.

No Italian warmth in there at the moment.

"Holy moly, Sue. What have you done?" Maddy said.

Sue wiped the blood from her mouth on her sleeve

and looked at me. Tears appeared in her eyes and her lips began to quiver.

Having her friends judge her actions must have made her realize the gravity of the situation. Seeing a daughter this distressed was every mother's nightmare. She was my child and she needed me, yet I didn't know what to say or do to make her feel better. She had bitten John. Nothing could change that. Rhona's presence wasn't helping. I knew that for sure. What I needed was time to think. I also needed to have a shower to get the stink of that pig off me and out of my mouth. It would have to wait as Sue needing me was more pressing. Besides, I didn't dare to leave the girls alone with John. I feared what they might do to him once they realized what he had done, and I wouldn't be here to protect him.

I looked down at the pathetic life form that John was. He was still whimpering and clutching his neck, his eyes in a daze, staring in front of him. His neck needed to be bandaged. He probably needed to be vaccinated as well, just to be on the safe side. We didn't want another sucker epidemic. I looked at Sue, whose eyes were pleading for me to tell her what to say.

Pulling Sue into a hug again, I said, "Let's get this table and chairs up first, so I can sit and think."

While I was turning a chair back up, my mind was already racing through the possible scenarios. I really wanted Charlie here for emotional support, but then again, I didn't want him to find out what had happened. He wouldn't let me go back to work, and we needed the money. I wanted Sue to have a shower, to get the blood off her, but I didn't dare to send her upstairs on her own.

We had never anticipated something like this happening. Charlie and I never thought Sue would be capable of doing something so horrible to a human, not with the education we had given her. We had always stressed that she wasn't to hurt anyone. How wrong had we been to be so naïve. How could we have been so stupid to ignore instinct? I needed to explain to Sue that she was okay. That what she was was okay. It was important she wouldn't feel guilty about what she'd done. After all, he had been committing a crime, and she had stopped him.

On top of all this, I didn't want John to find out that Rhona's girls were suckers as well. It was very likely that John would think so, with them having fangs like Sue's. Somehow, we needed to find a way to ensure John would keep his mouth shut about Sue but get him vaccinated all the same.

When the chairs and tables were back into position, I turned to Sue.

"Go upstairs, honey. Maddy, Milly, please go upstairs and stay with Sue. Only come down when we tell you to."

Rhona had been keeping an eye on John. When the

girls had left the kitchen, her stare shifted to me.

"So, what are we going to do with him?" she repeated.

I pulled out a chair and sat down. "I don't know." My hand went through my hair. I felt like pulling it out.

"We can't let him go, Kate," Rhona said. "He'll tell on Sue."

"I don't think he will." I looked at John. "Because he knows what will happen if he does." As I said this, I tried to make eye contact with the man, trying to establish if he registered what I meant. "Don't you, John?"

"What?" he said as he lifted his head, his eyes focused on infinity.

Great, he's in shock.

"We have to tend to his wounds." I stood up to get the first-aid kit.

"You don't have to," Rhona said as she put her hand on my chest and stopped me in my tracks. I knew exactly what she was implying.

"Rhona, what you're thinking is wrong," I whispered, hoping John couldn't hear what we were discussing here.

"What *he* did was wrong," she hissed back as she pointed at John.

"Not wrong enough to die for!"

I wouldn't allow her to kill this man, regardless of how wrong and revolting his actions might have been.

"Think of what will happen to Sue, Kate. They'll take her from you," Rhona continued, now gripping my arm. "Don't you want her to be safe?"

I recognized the motherly fear in her eyes and realized she was worried about the consequences of my actions, about losing her own girls.

"Of course I do, but I won't murder someone in cold blood. I wouldn't be able to live with that. I'll have to take my chances." I shook myself loose from her grip. Opening a kitchen cupboard, I reached in and grabbed the first-aid kit. I slammed it on the kitchen table.

"Okay, if that's how you feel about it," Rhona said, her tone zero degrees Kelvin now. She walked out of the kitchen and into the hallway. "Maddy, Milly, get downstairs. We're leaving!"

"Rhona, please listen! Think about it..." I tried to convince her.

"I have, and I've heard enough. We're going." She guided her daughters toward the front door. I followed them.

"Please, Rhona. Don't do this."

"Thank you for teaching my girls. Have a nice life." Without looking back, she closed the door behind her.

I stood alone in the living room. I had John's blood smeared on my face from hugging Sue, my shirt was torn, my body violated, and I had just watched my best friend walk out of my life.

What have I ever done to deserve this?

I felt like crawling into a deep, dark cave and not coming out for a few years. Somehow, I didn't cry. Crying wouldn't help. John's wounds needed tending to, and I wanted to get back to Sue as soon as possible. When I walked back into the kitchen, I immediately noticed the missing first-aid kit and the open back door. I spun my head to where John had been sitting and found an empty space.

Fuck!

Finding Out

I couldn't handle this crisis on my own, so I wasted no time and called Charlie on my cell phone. There was no point keeping him out of this any longer as he was going to find out what had happened one way or another. Biting the skin of my thumb, I counted every ringtone.

Please don't go to voicemail. Please. Not now.

"Yo, whazzup?" Charlie's voice finally said.

"I need you to come home. Now."

"Why? Can't it wait? I'm in the middle of a class. You know that," he replied.

"Charlie, please. I need you to come home. I'll tell you what happened when you get here." Before he could object, I hung up on him. I had never asked Charlie to come home during class before and hoped he figured I probably had a good reason to do so.

I hurried upstairs to Sue and found her having a shower.

"Are you okay?" I said to the shower curtain.

"Yes, I'm better now," Sue's voice came from behind the curtain.

I was relieved to hear no anxiety in her voice.

"That's good to hear, Little Smudge. I'll be waiting for you in your room."

Once there, I sat on her bed and let my gaze wander around the room. It was a typical young girl's room with unicorn wallpaper and fluffy toys everywhere. As Sue hadn't been that young girl for a while now, a year or two ago I had offered to change it into something more appropriate for a teenager. She hadn't been able to find a wallpaper she liked, and we had forgotten about it. She was such an easy-going child. I picked up a teddy bear and hugged it. I let out a deep sigh.

So much for the illusion of having a normal life.

After the stresses of what happened downstairs, the silence of Sue's room calmed me. In my solitude, I relived the moment of my discovery that Sue was no ordinary girl.

I gave birth to Sue in Portland Hospital after an eight-month pregnancy, and the doctor had been amazed at how fully developed and healthy Sue was. The birth had gone well and, as Sue had healthy diaper fillings and drank the formula, we could go home the next day. Charlie and I had both agreed I wouldn't breastfeed, so I could go back to work as soon as possible. I didn't want to give up my teaching career. Sue didn't want to drink the powdered milk at first, but as she became hungry after a while, she finally drank it. It had pleased the pediatrician, and he had signed her release form.

Charlie appeared to have my sisters, Maxine and

Julie, on speed-dial, and they were over for a visit. It was a lovely surprise when I arrived home as I hadn't seen them in a long time.

We were sitting at the kitchen table, halfway through lunch, when Sue cried. We all looked up at the sound coming from the cradle in the living room. I was half out of my seat when Charlie told me to stay put.

"You relax and finish your lunch, love. I'll give Sue her bottle." He was already out of his chair to prepare the formula.

Maxine stared at me with a perplexed look on her face.

"Where did you get him?" she said after finishing her mouthful. "Are there any more like him? I may swap my husband for one."

"Unfortunately, ladies, there's only one Adonis, and I'm already head-over-heels in love with your sister." Charlie beamed a broad smile. He threw me a kiss while he was waiting for the milk to warm. I pretended to catch the kiss and threw him one back. I had no problem showing my love for Charlie anywhere, anytime.

Not anyhow, though.

Both Maxine and Julie pretended to throw up at the open display of love between Charlie and me. Charlie pursed his lips and frowned.

"Don't you worry, honey," I said to him. "It's not your food. They're just jealous they can't have you."

"That's what you think. You don't know what I put in the quiche," Charlie said as he walked past us and into the living room with Sue's bottle. He had a huge grin on his face. Both Maxine's and Julie's heads turned to scan the food on their plates, and I giggled.

My sisters and I finished lunch and set out to do the dishes. I excused myself for a moment to check up on Charlie and Sue. Charlie held Sue on his lap as he was sitting on the couch. My heart warmed at the sight of my two loved ones. When I sat down next to Charlie, I saw the bottle was still as full as it had been before. It had been a while since he began feeding Sue, and I found myself annoyed.

"Smudge, you must be doing something wrong. She's not drinking," I said and moved to take Sue from him. To my surprise, Charlie held Sue away from me, making it impossible for me to get a hold of our daughter. I frowned at him.

Surely, a mother knows best.

Charlie nodded his head in Sue's direction.

"Kate, she is drinking," he whispered. "Look!"

Charlie now held Sue closer to me. I studied our daughter again and saw her chubby cheeks move with sucking motions.

How odd.

I lowered the blanket Sue was wrapped in to have a better view. What I hadn't seen before was that she didn't have her mouth on the teat of the bottle but on

Charlie's thumb.

"I sliced my thumb cutting the veggies for the quiche," he continued to whisper. "She doesn't want the milk. I kept trying to put the teat in her mouth, but she keeps going for my thumb!"

Holy shit! Oh my god! No!

My hand grabbed my stomach in an attempt to stop the nausea that washed over me. I turned to Charlie, hoping to find support. All I found was a look of resignation on his face. This wasn't what I wanted. I wanted a normal child and the 'they lived happily ever after' story. I wasn't sure if I was ready to accept what I had just seen. Looking at Sue again, watching her sucking on Charlie's thumb, my heart sank.

Our daughter was a baby sucker.

Charlie and I put up a show for our visitors and pretended nothing was wrong for the rest of the afternoon. After I had downed the awful-tasting formula milk when I was sure my sisters weren't watching, I even told them how proud I was Sue had finished all of her milk. When Maxine and Julie had left and Sue was asleep in her cradle, I went to our bedroom to have a lie-down. Charlie joined me, and I sought comfort in his embrace. This was supposed to be one of the happiest times of my life, but I cried.

So much had happened since that day. With the help of Harry, who was Rhona's husband, our family doctor, and our dear friend since Black October, we had made a great discovery. When Sue was four months old, we found out that she, being a half-blood, could eat meat. It had made our lives so much easier as Charlie and I had been feeding Sue our own blood. From that moment on, we could give Sue a relatively normal life.

There were slip-ups though. When Sue was a toddler, she had killed a kitten, sucked it completely dry. We had been shocked and began teaching her it was wrong to bite animals or humans. She didn't bite anything or anyone after that. We believed it was safe to let Sue go to kindergarten. Unfortunately, Sue, along with Rhona's half-blood girls, had bullied and traumatized the other children on their first day in school, proving to be too aggressive for the teacher to handle. That's when we had decided I would home-school the girls.

We'd also noticed that Sue and the twins appeared to grow faster than the average child. Harry had told us to tell anyone who noted it that it was due to a growth hormone condition. So far, nobody had questioned the explanation.

Charlie and I were careful to keep Sue away from the outside world as much as possible after the incident with the kitten and the kindergarten experience. It was great to have friends like Harry and Rhona, particularly as they were in the same boat with Maddy and Milly. Rhona had also been a sucker when she fell pregnant with the girls. I tutored the twins in return for Rhona helping me with my housework. Over the years, Rhona and I had become very close friends. Her leaving me now, when I needed her most, felt like a stab in the back.

I'm sure she feels the same about me.

A stab of pain made me look at my thumb. I had bitten the skin until it bled, and I sighed.

I really need to stop this self-destructive habit one day.

Sirens

I heard the front door open and Charlie come home. As I stood up to go downstairs, I caught my reflection in the mirror of Sue's dresser. My disheveled state wasn't a good sight. I quickly tucked in my shirt and with a tissue wiped the blood from my face as well as I could. I didn't want to make it look any worse than it was. There was a redness on my cheek I couldn't get off. As I realized what had caused it, my eyes closed, and a shiver went down my spine.

"Where are you guys?" I heard Charlie call from downstairs.

Staring into the mirror, I thought of what to say to Charlie.

The truth, the whole truth, or nothing but the condensed version?

"We're upstairs," I yelled.

I went to the bathroom, knocked on the door, and told Sue her father was home. She replied she was already getting dressed.

Charlie and I were both just on the stairs when he saw me. His eyes went from the buttons missing on my shirt to my face. I wondered if it was John's mark he saw or if I'd missed wiping off some of the blood.

"You okay?" He raced up toward me.

"I'm fine, Smudge," I said. I took his hand and tried to pull him downstairs with me.

"What about Sue," Charlie asked. He resisted my pull and remained standing on the stairs.

"That, my love, is a different matter." I sighed.

Sue came out of the bathroom and saw her father.

"Dad!" she called as she ran to greet him. He stumbled down a few steps in her boisterous hug.

"Careful, Little Smudge. You okay? What happened?"

It always made me smile to see Charlie hug his 'Little Smudge,' who was so much taller than her dwarf-father.

Charlie's words made Sue's smile disappear from her face, which made mine a short-lived one as well.

"We better sit down first," I said.

The three of us went into the living room where Sue and I sat down on the couch. Charlie remained standing, his eyes shifting between Sue and me, hands on his hips. I couldn't hide my worry but didn't know where to start. Which version did I tell him?

"Please tell me what happened," Charlie said as he sat on the edge of the coffee table. He leaned forward in anticipation.

I took a deep breath and told him everything that had happened since he had left for work. I didn't know if I could trust John to keep his mouth shut and had to prepare Charlie for the worst. Together, we had to prepare Sue for what might happen. I didn't think she understood what the exact implications of her actions could be.

When I had finished my account, Charlie rubbed his face with his hands. He stood up and hugged me. His embrace became tighter and his body shook. I wasn't sure whether he was crying because of what John had done to me or because of what Sue had done to John or both but seeing him this upset made me cry with him.

A shared pain is half the pain.

Doesn't feel that way now. More like double.

Charlie motioned for Sue to come closer. She dropped to her knees next to us and we both hugged her.

"It's okay, Dad. I didn't kill him. I only warned him. I didn't kill him," she whispered.

My heart bled for my little girl. She was trying to make her father feel better while she was the one who needed help.

"I wish it was that simple, Little Smudge," I said.

Charlie took Sue's head in his hands and kissed her forehead.

"You were very brave to protect your mother, girl, but she's right. It isn't as simple as that," he said. Sue didn't question him. She watched and waited for Charlie to continue. "You shouldn't have bitten him. That was wrong. We always told you not to hurt anyone. Now John knows what you are. He may tell on you, and they may come and take you away from us. That's why we're so sad. We don't want to lose you, Little Smudge."

Sue sat back, blinking. I could almost see her brain working the cogs in that head of hers. She frowned.

"I'll kill him if he tells on me," she said. Just like that.

Horror shivered through my body.

What part of 'don't hurt anyone' doesn't she understand?

"No, Sue. You can't," I said with more force than Charlie had just used. "You can't go around killing people. Remember what we taught you. Hurting and killing are wrong. There are serious consequences for that." I didn't know how else to put it so she would understand. Sue tilted her head and frowned. I looked at Charlie and my eyes pleaded for help.

"But he was wrong, Mom!" Sue cried. "He attacked and hit you. Why should I be punished for that?"

"That may be so, Little Smudge," Charlie said, "but biting and killing isn't a proper punishment for hitting or telling on people. Yes, he hit your mother, but you bit him, and that's far worse than hitting."

"He was molesting Mom! I couldn't let him do that, could I?" Sue yelled and jumped to her feet.

I could see her point of view and wondered how I could best explain the concept of excessive force. Sue was normally very rational, but was lately acting like a typical teenager, letting her emotions overtake rational thought. She was doing it now, and it wasn't helping.

"No, Little Smudge. You did right to stop him. Come here." I got up and took her into a hug. Seeing her so upset broke my heart.

"I tried to help you. He was hurting you. I didn't want to see you hurt," Sue cried.

"It's okay. We love you. It's okay, Little Smudge." I wiped the tears from her face and looked into her eyes. They were so much like Charlie's. "You came to my defense, and I'm glad you stopped him. We'll just have to wait and see what happens. Maybe John won't say a word about it, who knows?" I kept my fingers crossed he had indeed gotten the message.

Sue nodded, and I hugged her again. When I smiled encouragingly at Sue, she smiled back. It made me hope the whole affair wasn't as dark as I thought it was.

"If you don't mind, I'll go upstairs and have a shower now," I said.

Sue nodded. Charlie put his hand on my back. "Good idea."

***

I turned the warm water tap open further than usual. The hot water cascading over my body made my skin tingle to the point I felt like a lobster being cooked. It was a welcome pain. I imagined the filth of John being boiled off me. It took great effort to get out of the shower as I couldn't imagine ever getting clean, but the urge to be with my loved ones was greater.

Sue and Charlie were sitting on the couch together when I entered the living room. The TV was on. A newsreader was telling a story about some politician or other. I assumed they were anticipating a news report on a man bitten in the neck by a sucker girl.

"You want a coffee?" I asked Charlie. I so could do with one as I still hadn't had my morning cup.

"Sure. You sit, and I'll make it," he said as he moved off the couch.

Charlie always took care of me. It was one of the many reasons I loved him so much. He also knew me well enough to know I would want to be close to Sue right now. As we passed each other, Charlie hugged me. He put his hand on the side of my face.

"You okay?" he whispered.

"I'm fine," I replied and kissed his hand. There was no point letting Charlie worry about me. I wasn't sure myself how to deal with the fact that someone had tried to violate my body. John didn't get to third base and what had happened to me seemed trivial compared to what had happened to him. I would have to deal with my issues later. There were more important things to think of right now.

I sat down next to Sue and put my arm around her, and she rested her head on my shoulder. When I heard

the sirens outside, I knew they were coming for Sue.
No cup of coffee again, then.

Taken

Charlie hurried into the living room. One look at him, and I knew he was as worried as I was.

I turned to Sue and brushed a lock of hair behind her ear.

"Little Smudge, whatever happens, never lie, but don't tell anybody about Maddy and Milly," I said to her.

"Mom, I'm scared!" she said.

She didn't need to tell me as the fear in her eyes was obvious. I wished I could take it away, but I didn't know what future lay ahead. It scared me as well.

"Don't be, Little Smudge. I'll be with you always," I said. "I'll never let them take you away from me."

Sue, Charlie, and I were standing in the middle of the living room when soldiers barged through our front door.

Soldiers? Why not the police?

"Step away from each other and put your hands on your head!" one soldier yelled.

The soldiers were wearing thick, padded armor, especially around their necks, and their guns had black lights attached. More soldiers entered the living room from the kitchen, surrounding us. We did as we were told, but I stayed close to Sue. She was holding my hand. Her grip was cutting off the blood supply to my fingers. Subconsciously I patted her hand. I breathed again when Sue released her grip. I hoped she wouldn't do anything foolish. We put our hands on our heads.

"You!" the soldier addressed me. "Step away from the sucker!"

When he said the word 'sucker,' the hairs on my neck rose. I had never liked the word, but it never sounded as horrid as it did when he said it.

"This sucker is called Sue," I said. "She's my daughter. I'm not leaving her side." I took my hands off my head, grabbed Sue's hand and let our arms swing down. The soldiers began yelling to put my hands back on my head. Most soldiers took a step backward. The one who had been yelling instructions at us hadn't. Instead, he had taken a step forward. He aimed his gun alternatively at our heads. I couldn't help the corner of my mouth lifting as I admired his courage.

"Put your hands back on your head! Now!" he yelled at me when everybody else fell quiet.

There's nothing wrong with my hearing, you know.

I felt Sue wanting to let go of my hand to obey him, but I kept a firm hold of her.

"Look, we'll come with you without a struggle if you let us stay with Sue," I said to the soldier. "Even though she's a sucker, she's still a minor, and it'll be over my dead body you're taking her away without us." My whole body trembled with anxiety. Glancing at Charlie, I saw him look at me with a hint of admiration. I hitched up one shoulder.

It's a mothers' instinct, I guess.

The soldier hadn't expected my reply. He blinked a few times and took a moment to process my words. I hoped he knew that when you push a wild animal far enough into a corner, you'll provoke it to attack. It would be better to give us some space if he wanted to keep us friendly.

"Okay, but you'll still be restrained," he finally said and motioned for his colleague to do so.

First, Sue was handcuffed. The soldier then produced a half-mask and moved to put it over Sue's face, to cover her mouth. They sure weren't taking any chances. Sue moved her head away from the contraption.

"Mom?" she said with that fearful look on her face again.

It pained me so much she had to experience this. She wasn't a dangerous serial killer at all, just a frightened teenager who had acted upon instinct.

"It's okay, Little Smudge. Let them put that thing on you. They'll feel safer that way," I soothed her.

Before the soldier could grab my hand to handcuff me, I hooked one arm through Sue's, and then offered my wrists to him. Sue's eyes went wide, and I winked at her.

"I told you I wouldn't let them take you away from me," I said. Sue smiled with gratitude.

After I'd been cuffed and chained to Sue, Charlie was cuffed as well. They escorted the three of us outside. I saw neighbors in doorways staring at the spectacle. Heads were put together to exchange whispers. Some people got out their cell phones and took pictures. I could imagine the headline in the local newspaper tomorrow; 'Sucker family apprehended.' I couldn't care less. Over the years, I had avoided all contact with my neighbors, and we had established a mutual agreement of privacy. Now, at last, they knew why.

In the van, they attached our cuffs with chains to the floor. The soldiers sat surrounding us and they kept their guns within easy reach. They had learned a hard lesson during Black October, I presumed.

I had no idea where they were taking us or even in which direction we were going. There were no windows in the van. We drove in silence for hours.

When we stopped and they let us out, a pleasant, warm breeze greeted us. I inspected my surroundings to find a clue about our location. We were at some out-of-the-way, high-security facility, surrounded by empty space as far as the eye could see. Around the buildings were high, double fences, topped with barbed wire. They carried yellow signs, warning of electric shock. There were towers in between the fences with huge lights mounted on them. The lights faced the interior of the compound. As they pushed me forward, I studied the single-story buildings. There were many, most of them connected by enclosed walkways. As soon as I noticed none of them had any windows, I realized who it was they were trying to keep in here.

Once inside, we had to go through a metal detector. They patted us down and took our belts and cell phones. The soldiers lead us through a long corridor. Halfway, they ushered Sue and me through a door. Charlie and I exchanged worried looks before we were separated, and I wondered how long it would be before I saw him again. The room we found ourselves in looked like an interrogation room. It had a table and a few chairs in it, no other furniture. A large window of mirrored glass took up most of one wall. I wondered who was watching us from behind the other side.

We were seated facing the mirror. They took off our cuffs and Sue's mask. A soldier positioned himself next to the door. They left us waiting for a long time.

Come on, guys. I could do with a coffee here.

Prisoners

At first, Sue and I didn't talk. I knew the people behind the mirror would probably record everything we'd say. I didn't want them to catch something that could be used against us. So we sat there, exchanging glances now and again. I was so glad I could be there for Sue even though we weren't talking. We waited and waited, but nothing happened. When I couldn't stand it any longer, I got off my chair and walked over to the mirror. I put my hand over my eyes and tried to see through it.

"Hellooo," I said as I knocked on the glass.

"Do you know where we are?" Sue asked.

"I don't know where, Little Smudge," I said as I kept looking at the mirror. "But I have an idea of what sort of a facility this is. I think you're not the only special person here."

I turned around to Sue. She copied my weak smile. I glanced at the soldier near the door and walked over to him.

"This is a sucker prison, isn't it?" I asked him. The soldier kept staring straight ahead. "Okay, can you at least tell us where we are?"

I saw his glance flicker toward the mirror, but he remained silent. I sat down next to Sue again and began humming a popular tune while staring at the mirror.

The door of the room opened, and Sue and I both turned our heads. Major Moore walked into the room. I couldn't say Maddy and Milly's grandfather was the person I least expected to show up, but it still surprised me to see him. I hadn't seen the man since he put our world back in order so many years ago. Harry had broken all contact with his father soon after the girls were born as he didn't want his father to find out about Maddy and Milly being half-bloods. Harry had explained to us that his father was an extremely conscientious military man.

Another man followed Moore into the room. He wore a lab coat. Moore took the chair opposite me, his back to the mirror. The other man sat next to him and arranged paperwork on the table.

Damn, Moore. Why you? This complicates things.

How was I going to explain to Moore how Sue was conceived without him finding out that his own granddaughters were half-blood suckers?

"Kate, we meet again," Moore said. His blue eyes still had that sparkle, and his smile was forever hiding behind that huge mustache of his.

"Major Moore," was all I said. My brain was going warp speed on finding a way out of this situation.

"This is Dr. Greene," Moore said, introducing the other guy. "He replaced Dr. Haley not so long ago. My head turned to Dr. Greene.

I had liked Dr. Haley. He had taken my blood and with it created the *Succedaneum* virus vaccine which had saved the human race from the pandemic. I wasn't sure if I liked Dr. Greene. He appeared too young to be a doctor. His face was round, like an apple. I thought it was too wide for a normal human face, making his eyes look too close together. His eyes looked even more alien as they were enlarged by his round, gold-rimmed glasses of which the sides pressed into the skin. If the man didn't have ears all, I presumed his glasses would stay put by pressure alone. I nodded to him.

"And you have a daughter," Moore continued, smiling behind his mustache at Sue.

"Her name is Sue," I said.

Please don't talk about her as if she is an object or something.

I wanted him to know Sue was a human being, with feelings and rights. Particularly rights.

"Nice to meet you, Sue," Major Moore said.

Sue said nothing. I had to put my hand on her knee to stop her leg from twitching.

"Cut the crap, Moore. What do you want from us?" I didn't have the patience to do niceties. I wanted him to tell me why we were being held at an Army facility. And for how long.

"We're here to meet Sue, Kate. That's all for now," he said.

"Well hello, nice to meet you, see you in a next life.

Now let us go," I said. Although I liked Moore as a person, I didn't like what he represented at this moment in time. "Please," I added after remembering our position.

"I didn't know you had a daughter. How old is Sue?" Major Moore asked.

Dr. Greene was still shuffling through his paperwork.

"She's eight," I said.

Dr. Greene now looked up and studied Sue. He took out his pen.

"How long ago was she bitten?" he asked after he wrote something on one of the papers.

"She was never bitten," I replied.

Dr. Greene looked at Moore who mimicked Greene's knowing stare, after which they both looked at Sue. It was Dr. Green's look that gave me the chills. My imagination made him resemble an alien who wanted to dissect my daughter. I held myself onto my chair and resisted the urge to put myself between him and Sue.

"What do you mean 'she was never bitten'?" Dr. Greene said, his eyes squinting at me through his glasses.

Here we go.

"Sue was conceived when I was still a sucker. Charlie's the father. Sue's a half-blood, so to speak." I hoped that the sooner we gave them what they wanted, the sooner they would let us go.

Nothing wrong with that.

Moore and Dr. Greene both leaned their bodies even more forward upon my words and seemed to study Sue more closely. I knew Sue appeared older than her eight years, but I got the feeling this wasn't why they were so interested in her.

"You're sure Charlie's the father?" Moore asked.

"Yes, of course I'm sure. I was there, wasn't I?"

"And he was unbitten at the time of conception?"

"That's right."

Moore wiped his mustache. I heard Dr. Greene's sharp intake of breath. I hated not knowing what was going on.

"And you were a daywalker?" Dr. Greene continued.

"Yes."

"And Sue's a daywalker?"

"Obviously."

"So she can walk in daylight?"

"Duh."

"And she drinks blood?"

"No, she eats meat. You could say she's a carnivore."

Moore and Dr. Greene exchanged glances. Dr. Greene looked like a kid in front of a candy store.

"Which reminds me, we haven't eaten at all today, and we would really appreciate it if you could give us something to eat." I moved my eyes from Sue's mouth back to their necks.

You *would really appreciate it if you want to live longer than today.*

"What do you mean 'she eats meat'?" Dr. Greene asked after he had nervously licked his lips while taking lots of notes. The guy gave me the creeps.

"Exactly what I said. She eats meat; ground meat, steaks, blood sausages. She'll eat anything that has raw meat or blood in it." I couldn't believe the look on their faces. The both of them now looked like little kids *in* a candy store, with money in their hands.

"So... she has never drunk any... blood?" Dr. Greene continued. He had tilted his head and there was this infatuated look upon his face as he regarded Sue. He couldn't get his eyes off her. The vision made bile rise in my throat.

"Not until this morning, no," I said.

Unfortunately.

"Actually, that isn't true," I corrected myself. "We fed her blood as a baby, laced her bottles of milk with it. We put her onto solids when she turned four months old as I began to get fainting spells." For a moment, Dr. Greene looked puzzled at me. "We'd been feeding her our own blood," I added. He wrote it all down. When he finished, he sat back.

"This is very exciting news," he exclaimed, looking at Sue again. "I'd like to examine your daughter. To find out what makes her tick, so to speak," he said. He had turned his head toward me long before his eyes left Sue.

Over my dead body will you cut her open!

I sat there, staring at him. When it became obvious I wasn't going to say anything, he looked at Moore.

I looked at Moore as well, who returned my stare with raised eyebrows and a hidden smile, awaiting a reply from me.

Damn, man, I need time to think.

"What if I don't agree?" I said.

Moore's smile vanished. "We'll charge Sue with aggravated assault," he replied, "which means immediate solitary confinement and a harsh sentence due to the fact she's a sucker. Times have changed since Black October."

There was no remorse in his voice. He didn't look at Sue though.

So much for having a choice.

I turned to Sue, and she gave me an anxious look. The words formed in my head as I gave Moore my answer.

"As long as this study's not done in a mortuary, I suppose I could agree to this. I do have a few conditions though. One: I get to stay with her at all times. Two: Nothing is done she doesn't like. She's still an American citizen with rights after all. Three: No handcuffs or mask. Four: You'll arrange for Charlie to have unlimited access to us. Five: When the tests are over, we are free to go home, without persecution or any criminal record for Sue. And I want all of this written on paper. No wishy-washy verbal agreements you guys can worm your way out of."

I sat back and watched Moore. He had been quiet during my speech but had listened attentively. For a moment, I wondered why they hadn't written down any of my words. Then I remembered the mirror.

"I'll see what I can do," Moore said. The two men rose and left the room.

"Don't forget to feed us!" I yelled before they closed the door.

The soldier on guard took a slightly stronger grip on his gun.

Contract

As soon as the door was shut, Sue turned to me.

"Was that true?" she said.

"Was what true?" Too many things were going through my mind right now.

"That you fed me your blood."

"It's true, but we didn't do it for long."

"Still, it's pretty cool. Tell me more about it." Sue had this excitement on her face she always had when I was about to teach her something new.

Charlie and I had never told Sue she had drunk blood as a baby. We never had a reason to do so. At first, we hadn't planned to tell her how special she was at all. We had hoped there would never be a reason. When she asked about her meat diet, we had explained it was due to an unknown illness of her digestive tract, that she couldn't eat anything else.

Unfortunately, when Sue's fangs began to grow, she figured out herself that she was different. She had taken me by surprise with a question after a shopping trip. We were unpacking the groceries when she told me she had heard people talking behind our backs about her fangs. She had asked me if Harry, who had naturally long canines, was her father. I had told her not to believe such nonsense, but Charlie and I had sat her down that evening and told her why she had fangs, told her what she really was.

Obviously, she had refused to believe it at first. She had insisted she wasn't a sucker as she ate meat. When we had explained to her she could because she was a half-blood, she had finally believed us. And as children do, she had just taken it in her stride.

I sighed. I guessed now was as good a time as any to tell her how it all began.

"We found out you were a sucker the day after you were born. Your father had cut his thumb when cutting the veggies for the quiche for lunch. Auntie Maxine and Auntie Julie were visiting at the time. As I hadn't seen them for a long time, your father fed you your bottle of milk while I caught up with my sisters. When I went to check on you two, it appeared you preferred to suck blood from his thumb above drinking milk from the bottle."

"No way!" Sue exclaimed.

"Yes, way!" I said and chuckled. "That same evening, I had an idea."

"What was it?" Sue was hanging on my every word.

"We had fed you blood during the day, but it worried me. Apart from the fact we had to hide it from your aunties and everybody else in the future, of course. I knew we couldn't keep feeding you blood. You'd soon need more than we would be able to give you. So that evening, when your aunties had left, I cut one of my fingers with a knife and let the blood drip into your milk bottle until it turned a nice shade of pink. I suppose it wasn't the color that made you drink it, more likely the smell, but you drank it eagerly, which was the most important thing at the time. It was funny. As I was feeding you with the blood-laced milk, your father mentioned he couldn't believe I'd cut myself." I smiled as my memory took me back to the astonishment on Charlie's face that day.

"Why not?" Sue asked.

"Because I hadn't been able to do it when we were pretending to be suckers during Black October, and my life had depended on it. I told your father this was different, that *your* life depended on it now. He replied he would never understand women."

I chuckled, and Sue grinned.

"It was a sad day, though," I said, my face serious again.

"Oh. Why? Weren't you happy with me?" Sue asked before I could explain. She leaned back when she said it. It was as if someone had stuck a dagger into my heart.

"No! Of course we were happy with you, Little Smudge. We were over the moon!" I took her hand in mine.

"We were sad because we realized we wouldn't be able to offer you a normal life. You couldn't go to daycare as we had planned. You wouldn't be able to have any friends to play with. We would have to hide your eating habits from everybody. We didn't know about Maddy and Milly then. They were born a week later. But from that day on, we lived in fear you would be taken away from us. Today, our fears have been realized." My eyes brimmed with tears as I stroked Sue's hair.

"You'll never lose me, Mom," she said and gave me a big hug.

With all my heart, I hope not.

"Whatever happens, Little Smudge, know that Dad and I want nothing but the best for you, and that we love you very, very much." I held her in a tight embrace and wished I could hold on to her forever.

***

After they had brought us a meal, and I finally got a coffee, they showed me the paperwork. I read it thoroughly and was happy to find all of my wishes had been granted. I signed the agreement.

Next, they brought Charlie into the room. After some hugs, I recounted what I had discussed with Moore and told him about the agreement. As soon as I said I had signed it, Charlie jumped from his chair and paced the room. He rubbed his face with both hands, but it remained set in thunderstorm mode.

"Why did you sign it? Why didn't you ask to talk to

me first or to a lawyer at least? They aren't going to let Sue go that easily, Kate, which means she's their prisoner now. I don't know if I'm ever going to see her again." Charlie strode around the room, not looking at either of us. Sue was silent and subdued. She had never seen her father so upset.

"No, that's not true," I said first to Sue, then directing my words to Charlie. "I told you, they will only keep us here until the tests are done. Besides, you have unlimited access to us."

"Kate, we are hours away from home. How in heaven's name am I going to visit you every day?"

Oops, you have a point there.

I lowered my eyes and picked the skin off my thumb. I swallowed hard as I realized how stupid I had been.

"Charlie, it'll only be temporary," I said to calm him. "What else was I supposed to do? Let Sue go to prison? At least we know there's an end to this and soon we will be able to live our normal lives again."

"I hope you're right, Kate. I sure hope you're right." Charlie stopped his pacing and sighed. He took my hand in his and with his other hand caressed the side of my face. The skin of his fingers was rough from the woodwork he did at school, but he touched me tenderly. Being away from Charlie wasn't my choice either, but I needed to be with Sue more than anything else right now. I knew Charlie would cope. I wasn't sure if Sue would if she had to face all of this on her own.

"Maybe they'll find a cure for Sue," I whispered. This had been my main motive to agree with the tests. I would do anything for our girl to have a normal life.

"Fingers crossed," Charlie said and gave me a weak smile.

I pulled his head against mine. "I love you," I murmured.

Charlie lifted my chin and kissed me. "I'll miss you two so much." His eyes were full of sorrow.

I tried to smile. "Maybe I can organize a computer, so we can keep in contact that way," I said. "But they've taken our cell phones, so I'm not so sure if they'll let us."

"It's the least they can do," Charlie grumped.

There was a knock on the door and two soldiers announced they were taking Charlie home. We walked with him as far as we could. Sue wasn't allowed to go past the security point, so we said our goodbyes there. When Charlie hugged her, Sue cried. He reminded her not to be too sad as he would be back on the weekend. Sue and I waved goodbye until the army van left the compound. A sigh escaped me as I turned around.

I hope I'm right too, Smudge.

New Accommodation

When Charlie was gone, the soldiers brought us to our new temporary living quarters. They were two adjacent rooms in a long corridor. Sue took the left room; I got the right one. As the soldiers let us in, they asked us for our sizes. I asked them sizes for what. They told us we were getting uniforms. Before they left, they warned us not to leave our rooms.

"Are we going to be locked up?" I asked.

"No," the shorter soldier said, "but you'll get lost if you try to wander off on your own."

They said they'd come back with the clothing, and after we'd changed, they'd show us the rest of the complex.

Great, we'll be getting a grand tour.

They closed the door behind them. True to their word, I didn't hear them lock it. As I took in my new surroundings, I thought about getting the uniforms. I'd never thought I'd ever wear a soldier's uniform, but, from a practical point of view, I was glad we were going to get them. We hadn't been given the opportunity to bring anything from home and, if we were going to stay here for a while, I guessed they better supply us with all of our needs.

I sat on the single bed in the far-right corner of the

room. A desk with a chair and a shelf above it occupied the left corner. A wardrobe stood against the wall on the corridor side, a TV hanging from a bracket high above it. Every item had a Spartan look about it. I sat and bounced on the bed. It was sturdy and functional, yet it was as minimalistic as they came. I wondered how long they expected us to stay here. I certainly couldn't call this place home. There was green linoleum on the floor, which reflected off the white walls, and it matched the bed linen.

Relaxing green tones.

Somehow the atmosphere in this room didn't make me relaxed at all. My glance fell on a door in the middle of the left wall, next to the desk, and I hoped it would lead me to Sue's room. I got up and opened it. I had mixed feelings when it appeared to lead to a small en suite bathroom running the length of the room. There was a shower to the left, a toilet to the right. I winked at myself in the mirror above the sink.

Here I am, stuck in the middle with you.

Well, at least I don't have to share a bathroom with strangers.

I knocked three times on the tiled wall next to the mirror. I didn't have to wait long before there were three knocks back. I smiled. Three sudden knocks on the door leading to the corridor made me jump. When I opened it, one of the soldiers handed me a stack of clothing. He told me to come out when I had changed.

I looked to my right and saw Sue sticking her head out of her door. She was receiving her stack of clothing.

"Knock, knock," I said to her.

"I already know who's there," she laughed.

No fooling you, smart ass.

We disappeared into our rooms again. I threw the pile of clothing onto my bed and picked up the first item. It was a top. I couldn't call it a shirt. It resembled the tops hospital nurses wore. Also in a relaxing, green tone. It had short sleeves and two pockets on the front bottom. I dropped it next to the pile on the bed and picked up the next two items. These were white. At first, I thought they were flannels or something. Then I realized they were underwear. They were huge.

Thank goodness Charlie won't see me in these.

Next on the pile were pants. Like the top, they were also made of the thinnest, green-dyed cotton. It had elastic sewn into the waist band which couldn't be adjusted. I stretched it around the front of my waist. I guessed it would fit. Left on my bed were white socks and green rubber clogs. Disappointed, I plumped myself on the desk chair and stared at my new outfit. I was sure I would have looked much better in a proper soldier's uniform. Remembering the soldier waiting outside my door, I got up again and changed into my new clothes. When done, I inspected my appearance in the bathroom mirror, turning this way and that. Definitely not the dashing uniform look I had hoped for.

Sue stepped out of her room dressed in the same colored outfit and her 'joy' mirrored mine. The soldiers asked us to follow them. While we were walking through the corridors, I thought I'd better make the most of their presence.

"What is this place?" I asked.

"This is a research and training facility," the tall one replied. I didn't need to ask who they were researching. I did wonder what sort of training they were getting.

"How big is it?"

"What do you mean?" the soldier asked. He didn't look at me. He kept walking and staring ahead of him.

"I mean, how many suckers are being researched here?"

The tall soldier glanced over his shoulder at me and then at his partner. "That's classified information," he said.

"Okay, I get that." His answer didn't stop me on my quest for information. I winked at Sue. "So, how long do these suckers take part in this research on average?" I asked. I was dying to know how long we were going to be stuck out here.

This time I received a reaction from both soldiers, but it wasn't what I had expected. They avoided looking at each other while trying not to laugh.

"That, too, is classified information," the short one finally said.

I huffed. These suckers were here forever. I got it. I didn't know what to think of it. I understood suckers couldn't roam around the world freely, but somehow, at the same time, I felt sorry for them for being locked up here. Most of them probably hadn't asked to be bitten. Would they have asked to stay bitten? I avoided eye contact with Sue. Charlie's words repeated themselves in my mind and they made me feel more and more uncomfortable.

We arrived in a bigger corridor with more foot traffic. The people walking around wore either the hospital-style uniform or the army uniform. It was clear who were suckers and who were not.

We were literally given the grand tour. This place was huge. There were several lounges, some including games like table tennis, pool, and air soccer. There were multiple large gyms, steam rooms, saunas, an Olympic-size swimming pool, two theaters, one large canteen, and several smaller ones. Our last stop was a cross between a department store and a supermarket. It felt weird because it looked like a supermarket, but it didn't have sections for household stuff or pet food. The soldiers told us we didn't need money to get anything. Sue and I were both given a card we could use for payment. I told Sue not to go overboard, and we each disappeared into the aisles.

What a shame they don't have my favorite deodorant.

When we were done, the soldiers guided us back to our rooms. They told us about the daily cleaning and laundry services and that we were free to go where we wanted. Our payment cards were also keys. If a door didn't open with our card, it meant we weren't supposed to go through it. They left, and I invited Sue over to my room. She didn't feel like integrating either, so we stayed in my room and watched TV from my bed.

***

The next day, a soldier picked us up early and brought us to the large canteen. It was as busy as a bee hive. After breakfast, we were taken to a room similar to the interrogation room but without a mirror. Dr. Greene arrived shortly after us and began with a thorough questioning. He wanted to know everything about Sue. I had to answer questions about the pregnancy, the birth, and Sue growing up. I answered him as well as I could but had forgotten most of the little details. After all, it had happened a long time ago. The session was tedious, with lots of irrelevant questions to which I gave him irrelevant answers. One question caught me off guard.

"Did you have Sue vaccinated against the *Succedaneum* virus?" Dr. Greene asked.

"We did, but it didn't work out," I answered. "Immediately after the injection, Sue stopped breathing and nearly died. Harry revived her just in time." I smiled at Sue, remembering how glad I had been when she was breathing again. My gratitude for Harry's quick action was eternal.

Dr. Greene looked up from his paperwork and took off his glasses. With his now tiny eyes, he stared at me. His eyes reminded me of pigs' eyes.

Oink, oink.

"Who's Harry?" he asked.

Realizing what I had done, I felt the blood drain from my head.

Shit.

The Greater Good

It was the first time I had mentioned Harry during the questioning. His name had slipped out in an unguarded moment.

"Mom?!" Sue said as she, too, had realized my grave mistake.

I had no choice, I couldn't lie. It didn't mean I exposed Maddy or Milly by mentioning Harry, I rationalized.

"Harry's our family doctor," I said as I squeezed Sue's hand.

"So he knows about Sue?" Dr. Greene asked. His eyes had a new gleam in them upon hearing a medical professional had been involved in Sue's upbringing. He put his glasses back on and continued scribbling on his paper.

"Yes, he does," I answered truthfully.

"Yet he didn't report Sue?" He looked at me with his over-large, spectacled eyes, accusing Harry as well as me.

"Harry's a dear friend of ours. He respects our wishes to give Sue a normal life," I said. I had stuck my nose in the air and talked down to Greene. Of course, I didn't know if Harry's 'dear friend' status would still be mutual after the episode with Rhona yesterday. I kept my fingers crossed that mentioning Harry's name wasn't going to make things even worse. "I can get Sue's records for you if you want," I offered, trying to prevent Dr. Greene from getting Harry's details.

"No, that's fine. Just give me his name, and I'll get in touch with him myself," he said. He awaited my answer with his pen ready. I sighed. Even if I refused, they would be able to get Harry's details. It was better to cooperate.

"It's Harry Moore, from the Bullsbrook Medical Center." My eyes flicked from Dr. Greene to the paper and back.

"Harry Moore," he said as he wrote the words. As the doctor studied what he had written, I could hear the penny drop. "That's not Major Moore's son by any chance, is it?" he asked as he looked up at me.

"Yes, it is," I confirmed, looking away from both Dr. Green and Sue.

Before I could judge his reaction, Dr. Greene picked up his paperwork and left the room. All this time, Sue had kept quiet. As soon as the doctor had closed the door, she turned toward me.

"Mom, why did you give him Uncle Harry's name? You told me not to expose Maddy and Milly, and now they're going to find out about them," she chided.

"I know, Little Smudge. It slipped out. Hopefully, it doesn't make a difference," I said.

And pigs can fly.

I squeezed her hand again and began biting my nails on my other hand. I knew Moore wasn't born yesterday. We didn't have to wait too long before he opened the door of the room. Dr. Greene wasn't with him.

"Kate, let's go for a walk," he said.

I glanced at Sue as I got up. She tried to keep a hold of my hand.

"It's okay, Sweetie. I'll be back shortly." I let my hand slip from hers.

Moore led me through a maze of corridors until we were in front of a door with a yellow triangular danger sign on it. It didn't state what the danger was. Moore opened the door with his key card and indicated for me to go first. I stepped into an enclosed courtyard. A bench stood in the middle, surrounded by a couple of bushes, and it had a trashcan next to it which contained lots of cigarette stubs in the sandy top part.

"I guess you figured it out," I said to Moore as I turned around to face him.

"I always had my doubts. Harry was very cool toward his mother and me after the girls were born. He soon broke all contact. It broke his mother's heart. He'd said it was because of my work. He told us that, as someone who was trained to save lives, he didn't want to have any contact with someone who was trained to kill."

Moore motioned for me to sit on the bench.

"Harry's the best actor I've ever met. You've got to give him that," I confessed to Moore. Moore didn't smile back as he sat down next to me. Instead, the pain on his face was vivid. I could only imagine how much it hurt him. "It was a shame he did what he did, cutting you out of his life, out of the girls' lives, but he was protecting them, as he was protecting my Sue."

"The girls are a health hazard, enemies of the state," Moore said without a hint of emotion.

Oh, hell no!

His words raised the hairs on the back of my neck. I sucked my lungs full of air.

"They are *not* enemies of anybody, and you know it. Sue only attacked John in self-defense, in my defense. The moron was trying to rape me. Sue has never bitten anyone else in her entire life, ever. Nor have Maddy and Milly. The three of them aren't enemies of anybody. This is the biggest bullshit I have ever heard!" I had gradually raised my voice and was now yelling at him. My whole body trembled with anger. I held my breath, waiting for Moore's reaction. When my lungs burned, I took deep breaths through my nose to calm myself. Saying Sue had never bitten anyone made me think of Kitty.

Kitty doesn't count. She wasn't a human being.

Moore still kept silent. I waited to speak again until I had calmed down.

"If you care for your granddaughters, you'll let them be. They don't need to be dragged into this... this... whatever you're doing here. They can have a normal life, like I want Sue to have after these tests are completed. Do whatever you need to do on Sue. You don't need Maddy and Milly. Nobody has to know. I won't tell if you won't." I watched Moore, waiting for an answer.

Moore looked at me for a moment before turning his face away. He leaned forward, elbows on knees, seemingly contemplating my words.

"I'm sorry, but I can't do that," he said eventually.

What?

Apparently, blood isn't thicker than water for Moore.

I couldn't believe Moore wanted to drag his own granddaughters into this. I had given him a choice to leave them out of the picture, and he had bluntly refused.

"Why not?" I asked.

"Look," he said, "Sue bit this guy, for whatever reason. If Maddy and Milly also went about biting people as soon as they had a hissy fit, we could have another Black October on our hands before we know it. Worse even, as I'm assuming they are daywalkers like Sue. I know Rhona was. I just can't risk it. I'm sorry."

I could understand where he was coming from. During Black October, I had been ready to give my life to prevent a daywalking sucker epidemic. I knew nobody would be safe if suckers could walk the streets in daylight. But since Sue, I wasn't so convinced suckers were such a threat.

Whatever my own thoughts on the matter, I realized I couldn't change Moore's. It made me wonder what the hell I was doing here. There was no point.

"If you have already made up your mind, then why are we having this conversation?"

Moore regarded me with those piercing blue eyes of his.

"I wanted you to know I'm not taking this decision lightly."

I studied the old man. Lines wrinkled his skin, which showed liver spots against a pale background. He looked tired. The twinkle I had seen in his eyes yesterday was gone. Decisions like these must take their toll. I couldn't help but respect him. Although I still didn't think it was for the right reasons, Moore was sacrificing his own family for the greater good.

He rose and indicated for me to go inside again. There was nothing more to be said.

Big Brother is Watching You

As Moore took me back to the interrogation room in silence, I went over our conversation in my head, and the memory of Kitty re-surged. Charlie and I had thought it was a good idea to get a pet when Sue was a toddler. It had been the worst idea ever. She had played nicely with it until dinner time. Then she had put her teeth into the poor creature and sucked it dry. Charlie and I had been shocked, but we had used the incident to teach Sue not to kill anyone or anything. We thought we had done right as she hadn't since then. Until this morning.

If only I had been stricter with Sue. If only I hadn't invited John into our home. If only I had reminded Sue about Kitty as she grew up. Maybe, just maybe, Sue wouldn't have bitten John, and we wouldn't be in this ugly mess. It was all my fault.

Sue jumped up when I re-entered the interrogation room.

"Is everything okay?"

I shook my head. "No, I'm afraid everything's not okay."

How was I going to tell her? I hadn't explained to her yet why Rhona and the girls had left so suddenly that dreadful morning. I sat down next to Sue.

"Major Moore is Uncle Harry's father," I said. We had let Sue call Rhona and Harry 'Auntie' and 'Uncle' as we'd wanted her to have the idea she had family. Charlie had no living relatives, my parents had died during Black October, and my sisters were too busy living their own lives.

"Is he? Then why have I never met him before today? You never told me Uncle Harry had a father who's in the army. Why didn't you tell me? What does it matter anyway?" With my one sentence I had given Sue an information overload.

"Let me finish, Little Smudge. Please be patient. This is hard for me to say."

Sue pressed her lips shut like she always did when I told her to listen first and ask questions later when I was homeschooling her. I turned my chair, so I could face her, and took her hands in mine. I always felt more connected mentally when I also had physical contact. For a moment, I closed my eyes and took a deep breath.

"First of all, I need you to know I love you, more than anything in this world. Okay?"

"I know, Mom," and she pressed her lips shut again, waiting impatiently for me to explain.

"Okay. Now..." I still tried to find my words. "Major Moore appears not to be... 'friendly.' Uncle Harry has kept what Maddy and Milly are a secret from him. I guess it gave the twins a greater chance of having a normal life. Uncle Harry has also kept his knowledge of you a secret. Thanks to him, we have been able to lead the life we've had so far. All of this changed when you bit John."

I looked away from Sue and cleared my throat. I didn't want to say the next bit.

"Yeah, Mom, and...?" Sue prodded, trying to make eye contact.

"Auntie Rhona wanted to kill John, so he couldn't tell anyone about what you are. She knew that when people would find out about you, it wouldn't be long before they would also find out about Maddy and Milly. And now Major Moore knows." Goosebumps appeared on my skin.

I took a new breath to continue, but Sue cut in.

"Why didn't you let John die? We wouldn't be here if you had."

"Sue! Don't you ever talk like that," I said through clenched teeth. My knuckles turned white as I clenched her hands in mine. My feelings were strong about this matter. "We don't decide who's to live and who's to die. Taking a life isn't to be thought of lightly." My words came out fierce.

Sue was taken aback by my reaction. She tried to pull her hands away, but I kept holding on to them. I closed my eyes and calmed myself down, not wanting to create a distance between Sue and myself. Not now. I brought her hands to my mouth and kissed the back of them.

"Auntie Rhona didn't understand why I didn't want to have John dead. She didn't understand why I wanted to save his life and risk him spilling the beans about you, risk him exposing Maddy and Milly."

Sue looked at me with cold eyes.

"I don't understand it either," she said and jerked her hands out of my grip. I grabbed her wrists.

"Sue, you're not dying. You're not being killed or tortured here. They're just asking you some questions. Is that so bad? Should someone have died so you wouldn't have to be here?" I held her gaze. After a short moment, she looked down.

"No... I suppose not..." she finally said. I could still hear uncertainty in her voice.

"So, now Major Moore has figured out Maddy and Milly are the same as you. He will very likely bring them here." I watched Sue and let the information sink in for a moment. "Auntie Rhona's already angry with me for not doing something about John. I have no idea how she'll react when she's forced to come here, presuming she'll accompany the twins. I don't know how Maddy and Milly will react. They may not be nice to us anymore."

Sue's expression was dark, but I wasn't finished yet. I still had to tell her the worst news. I released my grip on Sue's wrists, and let my hands rest on her knees instead.

Better get it over and done with.

"Also... Major Moore told me he sees you and the twins as health hazards, as enemies of the state. They may not let you go after the tests are done."

"What? That's stupid!" Sue yelled. She jumped up, breaking our bond, and stormed to the corner of the room.

I'm so glad you haven't learned how to swear yet.

"I know, Sweetie. I totally agree," I said. "He doesn't know you yet, and this is how he sees you now. I still don't know exactly what the implications of his words are, but I thought it best to tell you. I know you are too young to deal with this, but you need to grow up, and fast. You need to try and change his mind about you in the time to come. If we want to get out of here, we must work together, Little Smudge." She turned toward me. I held my arms out to her and was relieved she walked back and hugged me. "I love you so much, Little Smudge!"

"I love you too, Mom," she said. From the way she said it, I knew she had just grown up a little more.

***

During meal times, it became clear there were lots and lots of other suckers held in the compound. There must have been hundreds of them. They were all blood drinkers as the variety on the canteen menu was extremely limited. I also never saw one sucker go outside. There were men and women, varying in age including seniors, and, to my surprise, children. These younger ones all looked about sixteen years of age, like Sue. I could only assume they were conceived during Black October or shortly afterward.

The large canteen was packed at dinner time. The only unoccupied chairs Sue and I could find were at a table where two male suckers were already seated.

"May we join you?" I asked them.

They looked at us, but the only reply we received was a grunt. I took it for a yes and indicated to Sue to have a seat opposite me. As I dug into my three-course meal, feeling a bit guilty for having such a variety in my diet, my curiosity got the better of me.

"So, how did you guys get here?" I asked the dark-haired one sitting next to Sue.

He looked at me, at his partner opposite him, and back at me again. I hadn't missed the warning look his friend had given him.

"By truck," he said.

Details, you're leaving out details like why and what for.

"What a coincidence, so did we," I chirped. "We arrived yesterday. How long have you been here?"

I noticed the man sitting next to me looking around uncomfortably. When I followed his stare, I noticed the cameras hanging from the ceiling in strategic places around the room. One of them was directly pointed at us.

Big brother is watching you.

"A while," the dark-haired one said.

"A while..." I repeated.

Sue kicked my shin under the table but was looking away from me, sipping her blood. I ignored her.

"That's a long time. Maybe as long as ten years." I studied my table mate and got my answer as he cast his eyes down but didn't say anything.

The guy sitting next to me stood up.

"Let's go," he said to his partner, and the both of them left.

"Well, that was an informative conversation. Not." My eyes followed the two guys who had dragged their chairs with them and sat down at another table. "They aren't the most social bunch. That's for sure." I couldn't get rid of the feeling they were afraid. But of what?

Company

On Saturday morning, Sue and I were notified that Charlie had arrived. We met him at the checkpoint and took him to the lounge with the red furniture. All the lounges had a color theme going for them. I liked the red one best as it was the only one which exuded a bit of warmth. The suckers didn't seem so fond of the color red which surprised me but suited us fine. Sue and I were elated to see Charlie again.

"You look tired, Smudge," I said as I stroked his face.

"Well, what do you expect? I got up at 4am to get here, so I can spend as much time as possible with you guys," Charlie replied.

"I'm so sorry, Smudge. Was it an easy ride?" I asked.

"Not too bad. Not much of a view, like the first time."

"So, where are we? We still don't know."

Charlie stared at the both of us. "They still haven't told you?"

"Nope, we know nothing. I tried to get more information from the soldiers and the suckers, but no luck so far. I think they've all been told to ignore us. At least, that's the feeling I get. The suckers seem afraid to talk to us; the soldiers just don't. There are cameras everywhere too." I pointed at the cameras in the corners of the lounge, and Charlie noted them. "My guess is these suckers have been here since Black October, but for what, I have no idea. What did you find out?"

"I'm afraid I haven't got much more information either. According to Google, this place doesn't exist. When you go to Google Maps, there's only one area where it could be that's a four-hour drive from us, but the map gets very fuzzy when you want to zoom in, no details at all. There's nothing about it on the Internet. Absolutely nothing."

As Charlie spoke the words, a chill ran down my spine. I could only deduce that whatever they were doing here couldn't be anything good.

"So, what have you been up to, Little Smudge?" Charlie asked Sue.

"Not much, really," Sue said. "It's been mostly Mom who's been answering all the questions so far. They wanted to know everything about me growing up. They were very interested in the fact I eat meat."

"I bet they were," Charlie said.

"Mom told them about Uncle Harry."

Charlie spun his head to me. "You didn't..."

"I'm sorry. It was a mistake. I accidentally mentioned his name as I spoke about Sue's vaccination. I totally screwed up. Moore has put two and two together." My stomach tightened up at the memory of my mistake and the possible consequences.

"What did he say?"

I was about to answer but stopped short when I saw the door to the room open and recognized the people who came through.

Speak of the devil.

Charlie and Sue turned around to see what had shocked me. Rhona, Maddy, and Milly had entered the lounge.

Rhona had stopped for a millisecond when our eyes met but continued to walk on and sat down at the far side of the room. Maddy and Milly followed her.

"Hi," Milly said shyly to Sue as she passed. She had always been the friendlier one.

"Hi," Sue said back to her.

I looked at Charlie, but he didn't give me any hint of what he thought other than that the situation was awkward. It didn't matter what he thought. This was something I had to deal with myself. I rose and walked over to Rhona and the girls. How I dreaded confrontations like these, but I had to do it.

"Hi, guys... I just want to say I'm really sorry for the way things have happened. I'm sorry you were dragged into this." My words were directed at the girls. I wanted to tell them how it was their grandfather's choice to get them here, and that I had tried to persuade him not to. Unfortunately, Rhona didn't give me that chance.

"Yeah, it's not as if you had a choice or anything," Rhona said without looking up. She had picked up a magazine and was pretending to read it.

"Look, Rhona," I turned to her, "I have my limits. I don't kill, you know," I said in my defense. Rhona made me extremely irritated with her attitude. I had tried to persuade Major Moore they didn't need to be here. Ultimately, I wasn't the one who had betrayed them. It had been Moore. I didn't know if it was the fact that Rhona had killed before as a sucker or whether it was her motherly instinct that made her want to kill John, but I hadn't been capable of making that decision.

Rhona lowered the magazine and looked me in the eye.

"No, instead you prefer to destroy three lives, including that of your own daughter."

I realized it was useless trying to change her mind. There was no convincing her of seeing it from my point of view.

"Besides," she continued, "you're a fucking hypocrite. You killed Caleb, remember?" She held the magazine up again, ending our conversation.

That. Was. An accident!

Rhona had pushed the wrong button. My blood pressure skyrocketed, and a headache instantaneously made itself present. I fought the urge to take her bait with everything I had. I bit the inside of my lower lip and focused on breathing through my nose, opening and clenching my fists in the meantime. When I was in control of myself again, I addressed Maddy and Milly.

"I'm sorry, girls. I truly am," I said.

Maddy ignored me, didn't look at me. I could tell she had taken her mother's side. Milly gave me a weak smile but said nothing. I had nothing more to say either, so I turned and strode back to Sue and Charlie.

"Come on, let's go," I said as I stormed past them. Charlie and Sue hurried to follow me.

As soon as we were in my room, Sue asked the question I had dreaded answering since Rhona mentioned his name.

"Who is this Caleb, and why did you kill him?"

It was an Accident

Sue appeared mesmerized with the news I had killed somebody. Her eyes were wide, and she begged me for more information. I sighed. I had wanted to avoid the topic of Caleb with Sue. I had wanted to avoid the topic of Caleb with anyone. For ten years, I hadn't talked about him, not even with Charlie. Charlie knew I still had nightmares about Black October, but I never told him the details of my dreams. In them, I was deeply in love with Caleb but pulled the trigger, killing him, seeing him die in front of my eyes over and over again. There really was no point talking about it. Caleb had died, and I had killed him. No use lingering over something I couldn't change. Yes, I had been in love with Caleb, but he appeared to have been nothing more than a cold-hearted sucker. When he had attacked me, the shock of our fall had made me accidentally pull the trigger. I had never meant to murder him in cold blood. Now how was I going to explain to my daughter I killed the man I had had a crush on but who had betrayed me, without it sounding like premeditated murder?

"Come on, tell me. Why did you kill him?" Sue prodded again.

"Your mother didn't kill him on purpose, Little

Smudge. It was an accident," Charlie said. He sat on the desk chair, swirling it to the left and right.

"But how did it happen?" Sue still wanted to know.

"Okay, I'll tell you the whole story, otherwise you won't understand," I said. I moved into a comfortable position in the corner of my bed, and Sue lay down on her belly, feet in the air and hands holding up her face, eagerly awaiting my storytelling.

I stuck to the facts, not telling her how deep my feelings for Caleb had been. How those feelings had turned into hate, and how all that hate had turned into love again when I looked into his eyes after I had pulled the trigger. I didn't tell her that whenever I visited my parents' graves and the memorial for Black October, I mourned for Caleb as well. I had never told Charlie. There was no use in torturing him with it.

A big sigh escaped me when I finished. Now Sue knew I had killed. I had done the very thing I was so aggressively against. Rhona had been right; I was a hypocrite. I was a failure as a parent. I was like a smoker who told her kid not to smoke, like an obese parent telling her daughter not to eat junk food. I was a killer telling Sue not to kill.

I waited for Sue's reaction, but she didn't say anything. I could only hope she had matured enough to see reason.

"Penny for your thoughts, Little Smudge," Charlie said after a while.

"It's... it was... an accident, like you said, Dad," Sue said, turning to Charlie.

"It was, Sweetie," I said. "I never meant to kill anybody. After the army brought everything under control, all the suckers were vaccinated and are now living a full life. But Caleb can't... because I killed him."

I lowered my eyes, trying to hide that they were filling up with tears. In my nightmares, Caleb's face in his final moments was so close to mine. Every time, I would see the hurt, the betrayal, and the love in them. Over and over again. His eyes were forever haunting me.

Charlie got up from the chair and sat next to me on the bed. He squeezed my hand as he realized how much effort it must have cost for me to recount the memory of killing Caleb. Sue put her hand on my foot.

"Mom, I'm so sorry..." she whispered. "Now I know why you're so passionately against taking a life."

Even though Sue was only eight years old, she was a sucker and had the body and mind of a sixteen-year-old. At this very moment I was glad she had matured to fast.

"Don't be sorry, darling. You didn't kill anybody," I tried to say, but I struggled to get the words out of my throat. I sounded like a crackling radio. We all laughed, and I wiped the tears from my eyes.

"Come on, let's go. Let's have lunch," I said.

Puppy Love

We went to the canteen and got in line for our meal. Sue grabbed herself a beaker of blood, like a normal sucker.

"You're not getting any meat here?" Charlie asked.

"No, I don't think they have raw meat," Sue said. "The blood's okay. It's animal blood. It doesn't taste like that jerk John did." Charlie let out a sigh of relief. "I don't mind the blood," Sue said with a grin, "but I miss putting my teeth into a nice juicy steak."

Sue had already told me the day before that the blood here tasted better than human blood, for which I was very grateful. It gave me some relief I didn't have to worry about her getting a taste for humans. I realized we had been very fortunate Sue could eat meat. Otherwise, our lives would have been a hell of a lot more difficult.

The canteen was filled to the brim. We could only find enough free chairs at a table already occupied by a young man.

"Do you mind if we join you?" Charlie asked.

"Of course not. Be my guest," he said and moved his chair an inch.

The boy was good-looking, about Sue's age. He

looked at her with interest.

"You must be Sue," he said.

The three of us looked at him in surprise.

"I am. And you are...?" Sue replied.

Don't tell me it's Ben.

My mind flashed back to the time Ben had courted me during Black October. Our introduction had gone exactly the same.

"I'm so sorry. I hadn't meant to be rude. My name's Alex, I'm number sixty-six," he said and stuck his hand out. Sue shook it.

"Nice to meet you, Alex," she said.

"Number sixty-six?" I asked as I sat down.

"Ah, you don't know. I am the sixty-sixth male child conceived, but instead of calling us a number they followed a list of names according to the alphabet. That's why my name's Alex," he smiled.

"That's just weird," Sue said.

"Could have been a lot weirder. If I had been number ninety-five for example." He laughed. "I prefer being called Alex over Augustus."

"Darn, I forgot to get salt and pepper. Anybody else want some?" Charlie got off his seat. Sue and I both shook our heads, and Charlie walked off.

"Are you a sucker?" Sue asked.

"Pretty obvious, I'd say," Alex said as he lifted his beaker to emphasize his answer.

He smiled at Sue and I saw a twinkle in his eyes. My

head turned to Sue, and I saw the same twinkle in hers. Instantly, I didn't like this boy. Charlie wasn't here to see the crucial exchange, so I took matters into my own hands.

"Sue, I think I see a table that's free, let's go and sit over there."

Sue frowned, tilting her head slightly. "Why, we're perfectly happy here."

A bit too happy for my liking, darling.

I ignored Sue's remark.

"Let's leave this young man alone. He probably wants to sit by himself."

In my haste to get Sue away, I clumsily knocked over my chair as I stood up. I juggled my serving tray in one hand to try to pick up the chair with my other.

"I'm not alone. Here's my father," Alex said, and his gaze went to someone behind me.

I turned around and saw a man pick up my chair. When he straightened up, I looked into the same deep, dark, brown eyes I knew all too well. His hair was still stylishly short and wavy, without a gray hair in sight. There were no lines on his face showing any signs of aging. And those eyes... Eyes that made time and space disappear. They were the eyes I had fallen in love with so many years ago. Eyes I had seen fade out when Caleb's body had collapsed lifelessly on top of me after I had shot him.

How can this be?

My mind tried to make sense of my memories and this visual contradiction. My heart seemed to have stopped beating and my knees buckled.

The man's eyes locked on mine.

"Kate, is that you?" he said.

I fainted.

Introductions

When I came to, I tried to steady my mind before opening my eyes. I heard Caleb say, "Kate, are you okay?"

Within no time I heard Charlie's voice, "Kate, Kate! You okay?"

Weird.

"Let me hold her," - Charlie.

"No, I've got her," - Caleb.

Awkward.

"How do you know my mother?" I heard Sue ask.

I opened my eyes and looked straight into those dark brown eyes, nearly making me faint again.

"Caleb," I whispered.

It really was him. There was no doubt about it. Feelings of love, hate, longing, guilt, and confusion rushed through me. Particularly confusion. Sitting on the floor, Caleb held me in an embrace. He must have caught me as I lost consciousness.

Twice before had he held me in an embrace. The first time had been sensual and arousing. He hadn't been able to finish his bite and had unknowingly vaccinated me against the photo-phobic effect of the virus. The second time I had feared for my life as he had nearly drained me of all my blood. That time, he had turned me into a true sucker. Well, not a *true* sucker, but a daywalker.

Now, for the third time, he held me in an embrace. This time he wasn't out for blood at all. He tenderly stroked my face, moving strands of hair aside. I became aware of Charlie standing next to him, looking extremely unhappy.

"Charlie," I said as I tore my eyes away from Caleb's.

"Kate, you okay?" Charlie asked again. He wasn't great with words, but I'd known him long enough to hear the frustration in his voice. He clenched the rim of the chair, his knuckles white.

I tried to get up. "Yes, I'm fine. I must have fainted."

"You sure did," Caleb chuckled as he helped me up and onto my chair.

The people around us who had gathered to see the commotion sat back down, minding their own business now that the excitement was over. A lady from the canteen came to clean up the spilled food which had fallen from my tray. Charlie took my hand and kissed it while he put his other arm around my shoulders. He made a show of us being a couple in case Caleb hadn't caught the hint yet.

"I'm fine, Charlie. Really," I said. I pulled my hand back into my lap, trying not to look at him or Caleb.

"Let's have you checked out anyway," he said.

Anything to get me away from Caleb.

"Honestly, I'm fine. I'll just get a new tray and we can finish having lunch."

"Sue, get your Mom a new lunch tray," Charlie said.

It was obvious he wasn't going to let me be alone with Caleb. Sue didn't move. She wasn't going to miss a thing either.

"Father, how do you know Sue's mom?" Alex asked.

Caleb hesitated in answering. There was an exchange between the two I couldn't place.

Hearing the question, Sue gasped. She hadn't noticed the exchange. "You mean you don't know?" she said.

Now you're a show-off, Little Smudge. You only just found out yourself.

Alex looked at her.

"She used to love your father, before she killed him," Sue said to Alex.

I had the sensation of oxygen being sucked from my lungs.

Oh no, don't say that. Not like that.

I so regretted telling Sue the story.

Why, why, why?

"What do you mean?" Alex said, and he looked at Caleb. "Father looks very much alive."

His words were hitting the nail on the head. I stared at Caleb.

"How are you alive? I shot you. You collapsed and died right on top of me. I put flowers on your grave."

From the corner of my eye, I saw Charlie's head turn toward me. I regretted saying it out loud, but I couldn't take my words back.

"You're only half-right. Your first shot was more than a flesh wound. After the gun went off the second time, I collapsed on top of you because I was losing a lot of blood. I must admit I thought I was a goner too, but I wasn't," Caleb explained as he grabbed a chair and sat down. "I blacked out. My wounds were serious but obviously not fatal. The army picked me up after the attack and airlifted me to a secure hospital. They operated on me and it was touch and go for more than a couple of weeks before I recovered. They had kept the vaccine from me as the doctors thought being a sucker would increase my chances of survival. Unfortunately, by the time I was out of danger, the vaccine didn't work anymore. I have been living here ever since." He indicated his surroundings.

I couldn't believe my ears. He had been alive, all this time.

"And you have a son," I looked at Alex.

"Well, I had not much to do with that, to be honest. Although I have no regrets," he smiled at Alex in a strange way. "As I lay unconscious in a hospital bed and they thought I wasn't going to make it, they took the liberty of extracting some... um... particular cells from me. Apparently, they thought I was a prime specimen, and they used my DNA in a procreation program. His mother is no longer with us. She... died."

He appeared sad when he said it, but not sad enough in my opinion. Then again, maybe he never had a relationship with the mother. According to him, Alex was conceived without Caleb's conscious involvement.

"And you have a daughter!" Caleb said cheerfully, changing the topic before I could ask more about Alex's mother.

His cheerfulness and mentioning Sue brought me back to the here and now, and it didn't seem right. It was as if we were best mates catching up on old times. I didn't answer immediately. I struggled to organize my thoughts. Charlie squeezed my arm and reminded me of his presence. I hadn't involved him in my conversation with Caleb.

"I... don't want to be rude, Caleb..." I said, "but I shot you for a reason. I don't think I want you in my life."

If I'm honest, I don't know what I want right now.

I knew I had said it to make Charlie feel better. He still held me in that awkward way, as if he was trying to prevent me flying into Caleb's arms. Was I annoyed Charlie didn't trust me? Was I ashamed of Charlie showing his love for me? I had never been ashamed of it before.

Why do I have these strange feelings?

Waking up in Caleb's arms and looking into his eyes, those dark eyes which apparently hadn't lost their effect on me, stirred emotions in me I hadn't felt for a long time. I kind of liked them, but I'd be a fool to tell Charlie.

"I'm so sorry," Caleb said. "I realize you need time to get used to the fact I'm still alive. Come on, Alex. Let's give Kate some space." He stood up, put his hand on Alex's shoulder, and together they wandered off.

Reaffirmation

When Caleb and Alex had left, Charlie told Sue we needed some time together.

"What was all that about?" Charlie muttered, agitated, as soon as we were in my room, alone.

"What do you mean, 'all that'?" I asked him, even though I knew exactly what he meant. I sat on my bed with my hands in my lap. My eyes followed Charlie's feet as he paced the little amount of floor in the room as if he were a caged tiger.

"You know very well what I mean, Kate. I know you, and I can see you're falling for that creep all over again. Don't you see he's using you?" Charlie almost yelled. Veins were standing out on his temples, and his fists were balled. I couldn't blame him for being angry with me. He may be right I was falling for Caleb again. If I were Charlie, I'd be angry, too. I didn't see how Caleb was using me though. Where was he getting that from? It had only been nice of Caleb to catch me when I fainted. Although I may have feelings for Caleb, he hadn't shown any obvious amorous advances towards me.

Charlie couldn't possibly have felt the sensuality in Caleb's touch when he stroked my face.

"I'm not falling for him, Smudge. Of course I'm not!" I said, trying to convince him of my innocence. I had to say it out loud to convince myself. "I was just shocked to find out Caleb was still alive. Remember, I shot him?" I pleaded, now trying to make eye contact.

"Yes, remember. You shot him." Charlie abruptly stopped walking and pointed his finger at me. "You had a very good reason. He's a cold-blooded killer."

As he became aware I was staring at his finger, he put his hand through his hair. He sighed heavily.

"Kate, I don't know what he's up to, but I'm telling you he's using you. Don't fall for his charming looks and sweet words. He'll only hurt you again. And I don't think I can go through that a second time," he added quietly. He rubbed his face with his hands. His last words made me blink.

"What do you mean?" I asked.

"Forget I said that," he answered as he waved his hands in the air. He walked up to me and gently took my face in his hands.

"Kate, I love you with all my heart. I would give the world for you. You know that."

His face was intense. I knew he spoke from the bottom of his heart, and I loved him back just as much. Our time together had been wonderful. We had built a life together after Black October. We had a beautiful daughter who wouldn't have been the same without Charlie as her father. I loved him for his devotion to us.

I had so much love for Charlie, and I didn't want to hurt him. That was the furthest thing on my mind. Much closer on my mind were Caleb's eyes.

What the...?

My thoughts scared the hell out of me, and to drive them away, I kissed Charlie, hard. I needed to touch him, feel him, to be close to him at that very moment. Anything to stop Caleb from invading my mind. I put my hands through his hair and all over his body. Charlie responded likewise. We fell on the bed but didn't stop kissing. We took our clothes off faster than if we had been sprinkled with itching powder and made love in a wild, raw, almost painful way. How I had missed having sex like this. These last few years our lovemaking had been sparse and tame, but this was different. This time, primal emotions were the drive of our actions. Longing made way for lust, tenderness made way for roughness, love made way for sex. I suppose you could compare it to getting a new toy, to getting high, to having a lover.

To having Caleb.

Thoughts of Caleb drove me mad and spurred me on to love Charlie even more, trying harder. Charlie didn't seem to mind in the least.

Afterward, I lay exhausted in Charlie's arms. He stroked my back gently. It made me shiver, but I loved it. We stayed in our embrace until our bodies felt cold. We pulled the sheets over us, and I cuddled up to

Charlie again. I nuzzled my face into the hollow on the side of his neck. It always felt like a perfect fit.

"I love you," I whispered.

Charlie didn't say anything. He didn't need to as he had already done so. Instead, he lifted my chin and kissed me tenderly.

"I'm so sorry for making you think otherwise, but I truly do love you," I said as I looked him in the eye. I had to say it. I wanted him to know I meant it. I wanted myself to know I meant it.

Invasive Testing

Charlie and I spent the rest of the weekend close together. I had arranged with Moore that our cards could open the courtyards. It was good to feel the sun on my skin and to breathe air that didn't come out of an air-conditioning unit.

Sleeping arrangements were cramped as Charlie and I had to sleep in the single bed provided. We didn't mind as we had plenty of experience in spooning. We had slept together in Charlie's single bed for a few weeks after Black October. The house I had rented before, with the double bed, had been immediately sold by my landlady's surviving children.

Early Sunday evening, Charlie had to leave again to be back in time for work on Monday. Sue said goodbye to him at the checkpoint. She still wasn't allowed to go into the parking lot. I was, though. They knew I would never leave without my daughter, and I, of course, wasn't the one being detained.

"I envy you," I said when I walked Charlie to the army truck that was going to drive him back home.

"Don't envy me, please," he said.

"Why not? You get to sleep in our bed, go to work, and have a normal life for at least five days of the week."

"I may sleep in our bed, but you're not with me, and that makes it feel extra big and lonely. Every day I come home to an empty house. I miss spending time with our Little Smudge in the afternoons. And as for work... things haven't been quite the same since you two left. Everybody knows Sue's a sucker now, and some people are not exactly friendly."

I hadn't realized how tough Charlie's situation was. I felt ashamed for complaining about mine. At least nobody was unfriendly to us here. Not that they were friendly either, but at least they weren't unfriendly.

"We think of you often if this helps a little. Let's hope the tests finish soon."

I wanted to add 'and that we can come home again,' but I was afraid this would give us false hope. I had told Charlie what Moore had said, and we both had no idea what was going to happen to Sue after the tests were completed.

Loneliness crept over me as I watched the truck leave the compound. I kept on waving even after I remembered Charlie couldn't see me. As I went back inside, I knew these next five days were going to be tough. They had told me they would begin physical tests on Sue at some point, but I also dreaded bumping into Rhona and the girls. Not to mention facing Caleb again. I knew I had to see him. There was no getting out of that one. I needed more questions answered. I had thought the wound of my short-lived love-hate affair with Caleb had healed over the past ten years. Seeing him alive and well, however, had painfully ripped it wide open.

Once inside and reunited with Sue, I put my arm through hers and together we strolled back to our rooms to have another quiet night in.

***

In the morning, we were brought to the same interrogation room where Dr. Greene was already sitting at the table, waiting for us.

"Good morning to you," he said. "I hope you had a nice weekend?"

The man said it in such a sleazy way. Anything he said sent shivers down my spine. He had done nothing wrong, apart from keeping us here, so I couldn't explain it.

"We've had better," I replied.

Dr. Greene pushed his glasses up his nose with his middle finger.

"I'd like to talk about Sue's current diet today. Please tell me how you switched her from blood to meat."

I looked at the ceiling and racked my brain for the memory file.

"One day when Sue was about four months old, Charlie found me unconscious on the hallway floor. I had fainted due to anemia and low blood pressure.

Charlie had freaked out as he was worried I would one day fall with Sue in my arms. He called Harry for advice and he told us to wean Sue of the blood-laced milk and try solids."

"That's early, but not unheard of," Dr. Greene said as he scribbled details on his notepad.

"Well, I thought it was too early, but we had to do something. Personally, I didn't think it was going to work, with Sue being a sucker and all, but I was willing to give it a try. I didn't want to faint and put Sue in danger. Anyway, Charlie immediately went out to get some meat. He came back with a whole shopping bag full.

"Hallelujah, did you think I was going to eat like a pig all of a sudden?" Sue giggled.

"No, your Dad just didn't know what to get and thought it would be better to get you as much choice as possible. The more choice, the more chance you'd like something."

"Good thinking," Sue said. I turned my attention to Dr. Greene again.

"We tried feeding her little bits of everything, one after the other. We began with the whitest meat first, but... she didn't like it. The only thing she would eat was the blood sausage and the raw steak. We were very happy with that. Of course, we also tried veggies and bread and the like, but we couldn't even get it near her mouth. We still fed her milk laced with blood, but before she was six months old, she completely refused those and was, from then on, a one-hundred percent carnivore."

I sat back and relaxed.

"That's amazing. Wonderful news!" Dr. Greene exclaimed. "You're quite extraordinary," he said to Sue.

I could tell Sue was pleased by the remark as she sat more upright, but she was looking at me for my approval to be happy with it or not. I squeezed her hand.

"She sure is," I said with a glow of pride which made her blush.

"I'd like to examine Sue's intestines," Dr. Greene said.

Excuse me?

"What?!" Sue and I said simultaneously.

I had visions of Sue lying on a mortuary slab and Dr. Greene pulling her insides out.

Over my dead body!

"Hold your horses," he said as soon as he saw our reaction. He chuckled and put his hands up. "It's not as bad as it sounds."

"It sounds horrible," Sue said. She hugged her sides while protecting her belly.

"It's an examination where we go in through your mouth with a tiny tube and take some tiny little bites from your intestines. You won't even feel it." He smiled. His face made me think of Dr. Bunsen, the scientist Muppet.

Sue didn't smile.

"It's a standard examination for people with bowel problems, nothing new." Dr. Greene looked at me. I saw a warning in his eyes that said 'or else.'

The hairs on the nape of my neck stood upright.

"Will she have wounds? Will she get scars from it?" I asked.

"No, no, no. Like I said, the bites will be tiny, to look at under a microscope. That's how tiny." His voice was as sweet as sugar.

"I guess we could agree to it then." I looked at Sue, who still didn't look as if she was convinced. "It's your body. You have the final word," I said to her.

"I don't know, Mom. I don't like being prodded. I thought there weren't supposed to be any invasive tests?"

I had forgotten, but she was quite right there. Dr. Greene wasn't so easily dismissed.

"I'd like to do a liver puncture most of all," he said, "but I know that's out of the question. We'll have to find the answers to the questions we have another way, and this is one of them. This bowel biopsy isn't invasive if you take it literally. Yes, the tube's going into your body, but technically we don't cut through any tissue to get in if you understand what I mean. We still stay on the outside, only taking a tiny test sample from the layer between the outside world and you. Like a skin scrape if you like, but on the inside." He pushed his glasses up his nose again.

"And it won't hurt?" Sue asked.

"I've never heard anyone complain about it. You'll have to swallow the tube, which may be uncomfortable, although your throat will get numbed. But no, it shouldn't hurt at all."

Sue bit her bottom lip as she looked at me.

"Your body," was all I said.

"I really don't know," Sue said and stood up. She walked away from us, away from me.

Dr. Greene looked at me from over the rim of his glasses, his stare intense. Without a word, he was commanding me to convince Sue.

I glanced at Sue for a moment, who had turned her back on us, and I asked Dr. Greene, "Will there be a chance that, with the result of your research, you can make Sue normal?"

"Sure," he said. With eyebrows high, he jumped onto the wagon toward approval. "I can't give you any guarantees, of course, but we can certainly look into that. Technology is developing at a tremendous rate. Who knows what will be possible in the near future. What do you say, Sue? If we do this, there may be a chance we find a way for you to be able to eat normal things, like a normal person."

Sue turned around. She studied us for a while and finally sat down. "Okay, I'll let you do this test."

Dr. Greene didn't waste any time. He immediately collected his documents and got up.

"Great. I'll get the paperwork organized and we'll do this tomorrow."

We had the rest of the day off.

Torment

I had taken Sue to swimming lessons when she was little, but when she had begun to show she 'had talent' and attracted attention from the swim instructors, we had stopped going. We hadn't visited a pool for years now. Having seen one during our grand tour had made me yearn to go for a swim. So, I suggested to Sue we go to the pool while we had the chance and she agreed.

We got bathing suits from the store and found our way to the swimming pool. It felt great to be in the water. It gave me a sense of freedom however false it was. We had a ball and our skin was wrinkled by the time we got out. So far, staying at the compound wasn't all that bad.

***

The next morning, we were escorted to the surgery theater. I wasn't allowed in, but they had a room next door with a large window through which I could follow the whole procedure. Before they started, Dr. Greene had me, as Sue's legal guardian, sign some forms to agree to Sue's 'invasive' tests. This hadn't made me any surer about it all, but Dr. Greene explained to me that legal aspects had to be covered before any procedure nowadays.

When the surgeon was ready, he put a wooden block with a hole in it between Sue's teeth. They had sprayed her throat to numb it, and the surgeon pushed a long, thin tube through the hole in the block and into Sue's throat. Once Sue had swallowed it, it looked as if the surgeon was playing a video game, using remote controls to work the tube down Sue's esophagus and past her stomach to get to her small intestine.

The surgeon watched the progression of the tube through Sue's insides on a video screen. He had been so kind to direct the screen in such a way so I could see it as well. I found it amazing how small cameras were nowadays, with such clear imagery. With a small tool at the end of the tube, he took little bites out of Sue's intestine. He did this a couple of times, at various places in her digestive tract, and the whole procedure went without a glitch. Sue was a perfect patient.

When it was done, I took Sue to her room and sat by her side. She said she had a bit of a sore throat. Fortunately, the ice water she was sipping helped to numb the pain when the numbing spray stopped working. As soon as her throat felt a bit better, Sue said she wanted to sleep. I told her I'd go get a cup of coffee in the canteen if she didn't mind. I knew I couldn't do anything for her, and she reassured me she'd be okay. I kissed her cheek and left her room.

As I was walking through the corridors, I tried to remember when they had said the results of the test would be available.

"Hi, Kate."

It was Caleb's voice, and my heart skipped a beat. I heard him take a few large strides and he walked beside me before I had a chance to ignore him.

"Do you mind if I accompany you?" he asked.

Only if you don't bat your eyelids at me.

"Yeah, that's fine," I sighed. I did my best to feign disinterest in order not to give him any ideas. I didn't want a second 'John-situation.'

"How's Sue doing?" he asked.

"She's just had invasive testing. She's doing fine," I answered.

"Oh, what kind of invasive testing?" he asked with what seemed like genuine interest.

We entered the canteen. There weren't many people there as it wasn't lunchtime yet.

"They've taken samples from her intestines," I said as I picked up a serving tray. He did the same.

Why did he get a tray?

"Ah, to find out why she's different," he said knowingly.

You know nothing, Jon Snow.

I glanced sideways at him. It seemed people here knew more than I did, and it irritated me.

"A cappuccino, please," I said to the canteen lady. I

also grabbed some sandwiches for Sue and myself to have later. I didn't know what sandwiches they were as I wasn't particularly concentrating on my food. Instead, I was trying very hard to ignore the closeness of Caleb, who put a single beaker of blood on his tray and stood so close behind me I could feel his breath on my neck.

"She's a half-blood. That's what's different

"Yes, so I've heard. That's exactly what's so exciting about Sue, about her and the other girls." His whole face smiled. It was a bit disconcerting.

"You know about them too, hmm?" I said nonchalantly, trying to prevent him from prying information out of me about Maddy and Milly.

"Yes, the three of them are the first half-bloods ever, you know."

You're joking!

I cleared my throat. "Are they?" I asked, pretending extremely hard not to be surprised.

Why had nobody bothered to tell me this?

"Yes, they never could find an unbitten person to... to mate... with a sucker, or the other way around for that matter."

Is it me or are you blushing?

"You mean an insane person?"

"If that's how you want to put it."

I took a bite from my sandwich, which I absentmindedly had taken out of its wrapper. It had salmon and cream cheese on it and tasted rather nice. I hadn't wanted to eat it right now, but half of my brain had switched to automatic pilot so the other half could focus very hard on ignoring Caleb's closeness, his hypnotic smile, and his dark, intense eyes.

"I would have mated with you if they had given me the choice," Caleb said as he examined his beaker.

I choked on my sandwich.

Excuse me?

"Yeah, right, said he-who-nearly-killed-me," I hissed after I had coughed a piece of bread out of my throat.

He put his beaker down and made a good effort to look sincere.

"I don't know how to say this without sounding corny, Kate, but from the first moment I met you, I knew you were the one for me... and I knew you felt the same." His eyes were locked on mine. I couldn't look away. He leaned forward, his body so close I could feel the heat radiating off it. It made my heart beat faster. He whispered, "You came back for me, didn't you?"

As his words washed over me, so did the memory of my yearning for him during Black October. In an instant, I relived crying myself to sleep every night I wasn't with him. I relived drowning in his beautiful dark eyes as if it was yesterday. Heck, as if it was right now as I was doing it again. My memory went back to the time when I found myself locked in by Caleb in the corner of the school building. He had been standing so close to me, ready to bite me for the first time. How the warmth of his breath had exhilarated me as he dragged his fangs over the skin of my neck. How his presence had been so overwhelming and ecstatic. That moment he had been everything I had ever wanted.

I blinked and broke his stare. I was sure he was gifted with a spell of some sort to make me do what he wanted.

Kate, get a grip on yourself.

"Caleb... I... That was then. Things have changed," I managed to say. My life with Charlie and Sue flashed in front of my eyes. Ten years passed in a fraction of a second. It made me put everything into perspective. "You loved Sasha. You nearly killed me for her. I've moved on. I'm with Charlie now."

I focused on Caleb's hair, his ears, the little hollow at the bottom of his throat. I looked everywhere but at his eyes. They were my kryptonite.

"But you do have feelings for me, don't you? Say it isn't so, and I won't bother you again." His voice was low, his words deliberate. He was trying very hard to make eye contact. He had put his hand over mine. He wasn't holding it, only touching it.

Just the way I like it.

I was lost for words. Emotions rolled over me like a tidal wave. As I once couldn't tell Charlie I didn't love him, I now couldn't get it past my throat to say I didn't have feelings for Caleb. I knew I had to get out of this situation before I said or did something stupid.

I stood up, knocking over my chair, again, and ran from the canteen. I didn't know where to go. I only knew I had to get away from Caleb. I heard him come after me, and I fled into the ladies' toilets on the other side of the corridor. There was nobody there, and I tried to breathe as I stared at myself in the mirror. There were lots of words going through my mind to describe myself.

Liar, traitor.

And those are the nice ones.

The door I had come in through was flung open, and Caleb stood in the door frame. As he walked in with large strides, I turned and tried to speak. Before I had a chance to get my throat to work, he had picked me up and sat me on the countertop. He gently parted my legs and stood so close to me it was almost unbearable. I looked at his compelling eyes as he tenderly took my face in his large hands and kissed me. I couldn't help but give in to the moment and closed my eyes to drown in his presence. His lips were soft and wet, and I kissed him back with fervor. Our mouths opened in sync, one tongue finding the other. They were like snails making love, twisting and turning. Caleb groaned, and my eyes popped open. The sound he made scared me.

What the hell am I doing?

Caleb still had his eyes closed and moved his hands underneath my top, over my back, pressing my body to his. Despite my conscious state of warning, it gave me a feeling of wild exaltation. His lips went to my neck. Now my feelings flickered between ecstasy and fear. I want this man right here and now, but what if he bit me? What if he finished the revenge he didn't get to carry out so many years ago?

Get out, Kate!

To my surprise, he didn't bite me. He only kissed my neck. His lips stroked my skin, his fangs dragging, like that first time. His touch was caring, loving, and arousing. Caleb licked my skin, trailed my jugular all the way up, and sucked my earlobe as he pulled my hair. I put my arms and legs around him, pulling him even closer, pressing him to my sensitive parts. His arms embraced me with want and longing, and his caresses were like a typhoon, wrecking me as if I were a house built of straw. I was nothing against his invisible power.

Suddenly I had to cry. I felt wonderful and awful at the same time. Images of John and Charlie were photo-bombing my thoughts. I didn't want to betray Charlie, but I wanted Caleb so much right there and then. Yet, Caleb's hands on my body reminded me of John's, and it made me feel dirty. This was so unfair. There was no way to feel good about this any which way I turned.

"Caleb, I can't do this," I said as I took his hands from my body. Tears streamed down my face. Caleb saw them, and he frowned, confused. "I love Charlie too much."

Caleb's eyes now welled up with tears as well.

"I have waited for you for ten years, Kate. Ten years," he said under his breath. He kissed me on the lips, his hands again on my face, my neck, one arm moving around my waist. I loved the taste of his lips, the feel of them on mine. Reluctantly, I pulled my face away from his and grabbed both his hands.

"But I can't be with you, can't you see that?" I urged him to understand. "I have a partner and a daughter. I love them both dearly. I can't throw all of that away just like that."

There was hurt, denial, and frustration in his beautiful eyes. It pained me so much to see it. I rested my forehead against his. We both cried. When our bodies began shaking with our sobs, we embraced each other to comfort the pain we both shared.

We stayed like this for a little while until the sobs subsided into heavy breathing. Then, all of a sudden, Caleb let go and strode out of the bathroom. He didn't look back, and I wasn't able to see his face. I could understand if he was angry with me. I had done nothing to show him I didn't care for him, quite the opposite actually, and then I had tortured him by saying he couldn't have me. It had been cruel and inconsiderate. Heaven only knew what state of mind he was in now.

Sue!

Fear for repercussions made me jump down and run back to Sue's room. She was sleeping soundly. I sat down beside her bed, hid my face in my arms, and wept silently.

Setting the Scene

I didn't see Caleb the next day. According to Alex, whom we met at breakfast, his father wasn't feeling very well and was staying in his room. I had to bite my tongue to offer to visit him as I knew this wasn't a good idea. So, I asked Alex to wish him well for me instead.

Sue felt better fast and was back to normal the day after the test. The doctor had advised her to take it easy for at least another day. We were sitting in the lounge reading magazines when Alex came to join us. He was dressed as if he was going for a jog.

"Are you going to the gym?" Sue asked him.

"No, I have combat training in a few minutes," he answered.

"Combat training?" I asked.

"Yeah, jiu-jitsu and karate today," and he made a few action moves. It made Sue laugh. It had the opposite effect on me.

"How long have you been doing that?" I asked. It didn't look like he was a beginner.

"Karate for as long as I can remember. I'm a black belt. I'm officially a green belt in jiu-jitsu as I am under 16, but my instructor says I'm good enough for a blue belt.

"You can stop there, Alex, I have no idea what you are talking about," Sue said.

He looked at her as if she had spoken another language.

"I have always taught Sue to use her brain instead of her body," I explained.

"You've never done any sport?" he asked Sue. He sat down opposite her on the coffee table and looked at her as if she was an oddity.

"Apart from swimming, no, I haven't," Sue said with a smile.

"You must understand," I said, "that Sue has been living amongst the unbitten, trying to blend in. To have Sue doing sports wouldn't have been good camouflage."

"We must get you to the gym then, so you can experience how good it makes you feel," Alex said.

Sue's eyes lit up, and when she turned to me, her eyes were practically begging me.

"Not yet, darling, you need to heal from your surgery first. But later in the week should be good. I'll discuss it with Dr. Greene."

"Great! Looking forward to it already." Alex put his hand on Sue's knee.

Sue didn't say anything. She sat there, beaming back at him. It annoyed the hell out of me.

Get your hands off my daughter.

Alex saw my stare and stood up.

"Well, I have to go. See you guys at dinner," he said

as he left for his training session.

"He's cute," Sue said when Alex was out of earshot.

"The boy's not bad looking," I said as I was still staring in the direction he had gone.

I put my magazine down and moved closer to my daughter. I checked the room. There weren't a lot of people in the lounge, and none of them were close to us.

"Sue," I whispered. "I don't think I ever told you this specifically, but suckers aren't always nice people."

"What do you mean?" Sue asked. "Alex seems pretty nice to me."

"That's exactly what I mean, Sue. The sucker may seem pretty nice to you, but you never know what he's up to."

"Mom, his name's Alex and what in heaven's name are you getting at?" She didn't hide her irritation at my remark.

"Sue, you are a daywalker. The only way for these guys to get out of this prison and blend in with normal people out there is if they are also able to walk in daylight. You, me, Rhona, the twins, we are the key to that. The boy..." Sue grimaced, "Alex... may seem nice, but he may only be out to get the secret of how to become a daywalker. I want you to remember that at all times. Never, ever, tell him how to become a daywalker. The army could have told him if they had wanted to, but if they haven't by now, they must have a pretty good reason for it. Just think of that." I patted her knee and moved back to my original position. Sue stared at the wall in front of her for a moment.

"That's ridiculous. Alex's just a nice guy," she said and continued reading her magazine.

I also resumed reading my magazine. It was about photography. I had been interested in reading it before the boy showed up, but now I found it very hard to focus on the article about shutter-time. I pondered about what I had just told Sue, and whether it could be applied to Caleb.

Would Caleb's advances be his way to get the secret out of me? How would I ever find out his true intentions? What would he gain from knowing the secret? He had been a sucker for so long. I couldn't imagine trying to make him a daywalker now would work anymore. The vaccines only worked for a specific time after the virus exposure. If it hadn't worked for Sue after eight months, it certainly wouldn't work for Caleb after ten years. Had I worried Sue for nothing? Maybe the boy was just a nice guy after all.

I guess only time will tell.

I figured I had to give the boy the benefit of the doubt, for now. The good thing about him, should he and Sue get together, was that Sue could be herself and wouldn't have to live a lie. That is, if they were going to be able to have a life together to speak of at all with him stuck in here and not being a daywalker.

As usual, I was running ahead of myself again. I was

so uptight about my issues with Caleb that I found I was making life too difficult for Sue. I needed to distance myself from her a bit, let Sue get on with her own life. It was hard for me to accept it, but she was nearly an adult and, like her peers, okay, true sixteen-year-olds, needed to have some independence.

***

Otherwise, it was another non-eventful day. No big tests were planned. They only took some blood samples from Sue. This was, they said, to find out how fast she was healing and to track her hormone levels, which appeared to be another study of theirs. Karate Kid didn't seem to have a lot on today either and he and Sue spent most of the afternoon together, playing games or talking about their lives. I kept an eye on them while doing Sudoku puzzles. They got along really well, and I was glad Sue was enjoying herself. It took away the idea we were prisoners. At least, for her.

On Thursday, more blood samples were taken, and they began testing Sue's physical abilities. She had to run on a treadmill while being hooked up to wires and a breath analyzing machine. It looked awful, but she didn't complain about it. Dr. Greene was very pleased with her fitness, especially after we told him she had never worked out.

All this time, I was looking out for Rhona and the

girls, but I didn't see them anywhere. Not in the canteen, not in the corridors, not in the lounges. Nowhere. I wondered if Moore had finally realized they didn't need to be here as they had Sue already.

On Friday morning, Alex rejoined us for breakfast.

"How's your father doing?" I asked. I hadn't seen Caleb around since our painful meeting on Tuesday.

Alex put down his beaker, wiped his lips and frowned.

"He's not doing well," he said. "I've never seen him like this, and I'm very worried. He normally doesn't get sick at all. I can't understand what's wrong with him. Dr. Greene said he would come and look at him tomorrow morning."

"Could he have a virus or something?" Sue asked.

Um, I think it's more of a heart problem.

"No, it doesn't look like that," Alex replied. "He's not drinking, and he's getting weak. Normally he has his share of blood every day, but he refuses to drink a single drop. He also doesn't want to come out of his room. He's staying in bed all day which is so unlike him. I've taken some blood to him, but he doesn't *want* to drink. I have no idea what's wrong with him."

The boy looked mystified. I felt awful for putting him as well as his father through this. I would have to go and talk to Caleb, to bring him to his senses and make him drink.

"I can go and visit him today if you think it won't

upset him too much," I suggested.

And dig my own grave while I'm there.

"Would you?" Alex's face lit up. "He speaks so highly of you, and I'm sure your visit will cheer him up."

"I'll come with you, Mom," Sue said.

I smiled at her, glad she would be chaperoning us.

"Oh, I was hoping I could take you to the pool this afternoon and show you the butterfly stroke," Alex said. He looked down, and I heard him scuff his foot on the floor.

Oh, you're good.

Upon hearing this, Sue looked at me with pleading eyes. I had taught her never to go back on her word. What I hadn't taught her was the butterfly stroke, mainly because I couldn't do it myself. She probably had no idea what it was, but I knew she loved butterflies, and this must have triggered her interest. Apart from the possibility of spending more time with Alex. I took a deep breath and let it out slowly while looking from Sue to the boy and back. I thought of my contemplations the day before and made up my mind.

"It's okay. You go to the pool this afternoon, sweetie," I said.

"Thanks, Mom."

I smiled back at her. Surely, she didn't want to be visiting a sick person if she could spend some more time with the boy. It would also be good for her to get some exercise for a change. It was up to me to make sure I didn't get any.

Just a Visit

After the morning tests and lunch, I sent Sue off to the pool with the boy from Atlantis, and I went back to my room. I stood in the bathroom, leaning on the basin, looking at myself in the mirror.

"Don't fall for him again, Kate. Remember Charlie's words," I spoke to my mirror image. "Go in, tell him to toughen up, and leave. Simple as that." I tried to smile, but it looked more like I had just had nipple clamps applied. "Come on, Kate, you can do this!" I said to myself. "You love Charlie, don't you? Yes, you do, so no feelings for Caleb!"

When I thought I had pepped myself up enough to be able to pull this off, I brushed my hair, brushed my teeth, adjusted my clothes, all in the name of procrastination, and left the safety of my room.

Alex had told me how to get to Caleb's room, and I was there within five minutes. Every time I walked through these corridors, I was amazed at how big this complex was. They had hundreds of suckers living here. A substantial force if they were all trained in martial arts.

I stood in front of Caleb's door and repeated the adjusting of my clothing. I wore only that ugly, yet comfortable, hospital outfit, so there wasn't much to adjust, but I managed to do it.

"You can do this, Kate," I repeated softly to myself. I took a deep breath and knocked on the door.

There was no answer. I knocked again. Still no answer. I became worried and tried the door handle. The door wasn't locked. I popped my head into the room and saw the shape of Caleb lying on the bed, covered by a sheet. He was facing the wall.

"Caleb, are you awake?" I whispered. Silently I hoped he was sleeping. I nearly had the door closed when he spoke.

"Kate, is that you?"

Famous first words.

I opened the door again. "Yeah, I just wanted to say hi and see how you were doing," I replied.

"Please, come in. I'm so glad to see you." He turned around to face me and switched on a night light. I noticed he wasn't wearing any pajamas. My stare tried to find refuge in the ceiling.

Please have mercy on me.

I went into the room, closed the door, and for a moment I kept leaning against it.

His room was dark but orderly. His clothes were folded on the chair, his desk was neat and organized, and there were two large posters on the walls. On the far wall, above his head, was a copy of the painting *The Starry Night*, by Vincent van Gogh. I had never liked that one. I preferred his *Café Terrace at Night* as I found its colors so much warmer.

The other poster, on the wall above the long side of his bed, was a copy of *The Great Wave*, by a Japanese painter. I didn't know the name of the artist, but I had always felt in awe of the painting. I used to have nightmares of tidal waves and of being overshadowed by the water before I drowned. That was before my nightmares turned into memories of Caleb's death. It was strange to see this painting hanging above Caleb's body, combining my two greatest horrors.

I finally let my glance drift down toward Caleb. He was watching me. He hadn't made the effort to sit up. Not good. As I didn't want to displace his neatly folded clothes, I decided to kneel down next to his bed.

"How are you doing?" I asked.

"Much better all of a sudden." He smiled a weak smile. His face had a hollow appearance, and his every movement seemed to take tremendous effort.

"I hear you've not been drinking," I said. "You should keep up your drinking, you know. You'll feel better if you do."

Words you'll never hear at an Alcoholics Anonymous meeting.

He lifted his hand and slowly moved a lock of hair from my face. "All I need is the air that I breathe and to love you," he whispered.

"Caleb, I told you..." I started in protest, but he put

his finger on my lips.

"Listen, it's okay. I've made up my mind. There's no reason for me to continue living if I can't be with you."

That's emotional blackmail!

"Caleb, that's nonsense. You have Alex to live for," I said after I had removed his finger from my lips.

"Alex is leading his own life. I am his father on paper, but to him, I am just another old bloke." Caleb sighed and closed his eyes. His breathing was shallow and fast. "I thought I was doing fine, living the life I have here. Until I saw you." He opened his eyes again. "I knew then it was a lie. It's all a lie."

"But..., but..." I stammered. I tried hard to find words to say. "Can't you pretend you didn't see me? Forget me? I can ask if they can move Sue to another facility, so we don't have to meet. Maybe that would help?"

Caleb took my hand and kissed it weakly, brought it to his heart, and smiled. "Kate, finally having you in my arms again last Tuesday, kissing you, caressing you... That was unforgettable. My life's worthless if I can't be with you. Don't worry, I'll die a happy man with that memory."

This is going nowhere.

"Caleb, you can't mean that." His words shocked me. "You know you can't have me. I told you before..."

"It's okay, Kate," he cut in and held my eyes. "I have made up my mind. If I stop drinking for long enough, I will eventually die. I've heard you drift into a coma before it happens, so I won't feel any pain or anything." His voice got weaker, his breaths shallower and more frequent still. He rolled onto his back and closed his eyes. His skin was as white as... well, as an anemic vampire.

"No! You can't! Don't do this, Caleb!" I yelled. I jumped up and shook his shoulders. He wasn't responding. "Stop doing this! You have to live!"

I was desperate. My eyes scanned the room. Through the open bathroom door, I spotted his razor blade and ran to it. I smashed the plastic on the ceramic of the sink with the glass standing next to the basin and picked up the little metal blade from the fragments. I cut my wrist without hesitation and let the blood drip into the glass. It didn't hurt as much as I thought it would, but it did bleed profusely, which was exactly what I wanted. After tying a small towel over the wound, I hurried back with the glass to Caleb. I lifted his head and held the glass containing my blood to his mouth.

"Drink, Caleb. Drink!" I urged him.

At first he didn't react, and the blood ran from the corner of his mouth. I closed his mouth. It worked. He swallowed. I held the glass to his mouth again, and he began to drink, weakly at first, but getting stronger with every sip.

When the blood in the glass was finished, there was

that familiar glint in his eyes. Every time I had seen it in a sucker, it had scared the shit out of me. I felt like I had turned into Kitty. Caleb abruptly sat up. He grabbed my wounded arm and removed the towel. My body was paralyzed with fear. I let the glass fall out of my hand and a few drops of blood spilled, making a little patch on the sheet. It looked black. Caleb had my arm in both his hands. He slowly opened his mouth, ready to bite me for a third time. His fangs glinted with a mixture of blood and saliva. Survival kicked in and I tried to pull myself loose.

"Caleb, stop! You've got to stop now!" I yelled as I tried to pull my wrist out of his grip.

I freaked out as I couldn't get him to let go of me. He was too strong. My breathing became ragged and my thoughts were desperate for a solution. Realizing I would never be strong enough to make him release his grip on me, I could only think of one thing. With my free hand, I slapped his face.

From one moment to the next, Caleb seemed to come out of a trance. Confused, he looked at me. I must have been a vision of fear. His stare went to my wrist, and he gasped. Shocked, he slumped back onto one elbow. I yanked my arm free of him and hurried to re-tie the towel around it.

"Kate, I'm sorry." Caleb's voice was filled with apology and sadness. He put his hand on my thigh. "I'm so sorry," he said again. His hand slid slightly up. The inside of my leg tingled, and my nostrils took in his scent. My heart skipped a beat.

"I didn't mean to hurt you," he whispered.

My stare dropped from his eyes to his lips, and I felt gravity pull me down.

"I know," I replied barely audible.

Without hesitation, I kissed his blood-smeared lips. Caleb did hesitate, but soon reciprocated the kiss. When he put his arms around me, it was as if he covered me with a warm blanket on a cold night. It was exactly what I needed that very moment. I let him gently roll me over him onto the bed.

"Kate," he said, "I don't want to do this if you don't want to." He sounded sincere, yet full of desire.

The memory of John plagued me. John hadn't asked what I wanted at all. He had only tried to take. John had made assumptions and hadn't taken no for an answer when I had told him to stop. Caleb was so different. He was caring and loving. And I wanted him. I had always wanted to love him, from that very first moment I laid eyes upon him. I had known then and there he was my soul mate. He fitted me as if he were a glove. We were like Yin and Yang. We were meant to be together.

"I do, Caleb. I do want this," I whispered.

Just this once.

As he leaned in to kiss me, I put my hand on his chest, stopping him. "On one condition."

"Which is...?"

God, he has the most beautiful eyes.

"That this will be all you ever ask of me. After this, you won't pursue me again."

He smiled, but his eyes remained sad.

"I promise," he said.

As he moved his body on top of mine, I let the tidal wave of Caleb's love wash over me.

***

Afterward, we lay together without talking, and Caleb fell asleep. He was still weak. I moved slightly away from him, so I could study him better. He was the embodiment of true perfection. My hand caressed his skin. It was beautiful, soft and flawless, apart from the scars where I had shot him. I let my fingers glide toward the ugly marks and regretted ever having mutilated him so. I let my hand follow his body-shape and it felt like caressing a marble statue, every inch artfully chiseled. He was well-proportioned, muscular, and without any chest hair. It was so different from Charlie's body. Thinking about Charlie brought me back to reality. After I absorbed Caleb's body into my memory with all my senses, I silently got up and dressed. I kissed Caleb's forehead and left.

Honesty

The next morning, I sat on the doorstep of the building facing the parking lot, waiting for Charlie. Like the evening before, I had distanced myself from Sue for fear of showing my betrayal of her father. I stood up as soon as the van arrived. When Charlie neared me, I forced a smile on my face. A calm had come upon me on seeing him, but it was short lived. Our welcome kiss didn't feel right. I had made passionate love with Caleb not even twenty-four hours before, and it made me feel such a cheat.

In silence, we went through the security procedures for him to enter the building. I struggled to find what to say to Charlie. I was afraid that every word coming out of my mouth would betray what I had done. I was consumed by guilt, and I was sure Charlie had noticed something was wrong.

When we neared Sue's room, we heard voices. I opened the door and saw Alex lying next to Sue on her bed. They were chatting and smiling. As soon as the boy saw us, he jumped from the bed.

"I'm so sorry. I didn't know you were coming," he apologized.

"Even so, you shouldn't be here, Alex," Charlie said.

His words were short, his voice low. "Sue, get up. We're going to the canteen."

Alex scurried past us and out of sight. The three of us walked to the canteen in silence. Once we sat down with coffee, Sue with blood, Charlie talked first.

"So, what's been happening this week?" he asked. His smile looked as fake as I knew mine was.

I waited for Sue to begin talking. When she didn't, I told Charlie about the tests they had carried out on her. Charlie asked Sue the expected questions. Whether the tube had hurt and how she had experienced the exercise tests. She answered as honestly as she could, but it was clear her mind was elsewhere.

When we finished our drinks, Charlie took a present out of his rucksack and gave it to Sue. She paid him some honest attention now and even gave him a peck on the cheek. Charlie responded with a short smile. Sue tore the wrapper off the little package which appeared to hold an electronic game. I had no idea what it was or how it worked, but Sue was over the moon with it, and she threw her arms around her father's neck.

"Thanks, Dad. This is awesome! Mom, can I go and get it charged?" she said.

"Of course you can. Go ahead. We'll be there a bit later, and you can show me how it works," I smiled.

Charlie took some presents out for me as well.

"You shouldn't have, Smudge," I said. I felt even

guiltier.

"Don't worry. They're just a few little things," he said quietly.

I opened the wrappers and revealed some puzzle books, a novel, and a chocolate bar. It was my favorite brand of chocolate.

"Thanks. Especially for the chocolate. They haven't got much choice of snacks here."

"Let's go for a walk," he said.

He knows.

We put the presents back into Charlie's bag and got up. I didn't want to talk, but I knew we had to. I led him into one of the courtyards. The sun was still low, the courtyard still in shadows. I wished I had brought a cardigan as we sat down on the bench. I did look at Charlie. I knew he could read me like a book. All of a sudden, he grabbed my hand and pulled my sleeve up. I had chosen to wear a long-sleeved shirt today, but there was no fooling Charlie.

"What happened?" he asked as he first looked at my bandaged wrist, then at my face.

"Don't worry, it's just a cut," I said. I tried to say it as casually as I could.

"What happened?" he repeated. I could hear the anguish in his voice.

"I've been with Caleb," I murmured.

I hadn't planned to say it that way. Hell, I hadn't planned to say it at all, but it just came out like that. I didn't even mean it the way I had said it. I hesitated but didn't correct myself. What I had said was the truth, and it was better for the both of us if he found out sooner rather than later. I still didn't look at him. I kept staring in front of me.

Charlie let go of my hand and moved away from me as far as the bench would let him.

"I was afraid that was going to happen," he said, leaning back.

With his move, quite insignificant in itself, a rift tore itself between us, dark and deep. It made me shiver uncontrollably. I felt as if the dark coldness from the abyss reached out to pull me in.

A cardigan wouldn't have helped.

"It wasn't like you think it happened. Caleb was dying. On Tuesday he had said he wanted to be with me, and I had told him I couldn't. He stopped drinking blood after that, and Alex was really worried. I visited him yesterday, to try to convince him to come to his senses. He passed out. I fed him my blood in order to save him... and... and one thing led to another." I sighed and leaned forward, resting my elbows on my knees. I studied the sand grains on the ground between my feet. It was a small distraction but unfortunately not enough to distract me from the pain I felt in my gut.

Charlie didn't say anything. There was only silence.

"But it's over now," I said as I leaned back again, still not making eye contact. "I made him promise me not to pursue me anymore. I was weak, and I'm sorry. I don't know what to say. I only hope that you can forgive me."

Charlie remained silent.

I didn't know what to do. Should I plead with him to take me back? Should I let him be alone, so he could think it over? I felt so incredibly stupid to have jeopardized our relationship, our love, for a one-night-stand.

I wished the ground would open up and swallow me!

I want to get up and scream at the sky!

I sat there and let the tears roll over my cheeks. I hoped Charlie didn't see them. If anybody had the right to cry, it was Charlie. Not me.

Charlie kept quiet for a long time. The suspense of what he was thinking, of what he would decide, was killing me. I didn't want to lose him.

After what seemed like an eternity he spoke.

"I need time."

His words felt like a cool ointment on burning skin. It didn't stop the pain, but it did relieve it a little, at least on the surface. Charlie was still talking to me, and I saw it as a step in the right direction. I was more than grateful. I didn't say anything. If I had tried to speak, I would have sounded like a duck being strangled. We sat there for a while longer until my tears had dried up. I hoped my voice was back.

"Thank you," I whispered.

"Look," Charlie said as he turned to me. "It was bound to happen, one day or another. I wished it had been ten years ago, before we got together, and that it was all over and done with, but I can't have my cake and eat it. I hope he gave you something I couldn't give you, and that it made you happy. As I said before, Kate, I love you to the moon and back, but I feel betrayed, and I need time to deal with it."

"Sure, anything. Please know I still love you."

Silence.

"Let's get back to Sue." He stood up and walked away.

I followed him.

When we neared the canteen, I saw Caleb standing in the corridor talking to another sucker. Caleb saw us coming toward him and changed his stance. The other guy said goodbye and disappeared into the canteen. Caleb awaited us.

Well now, he recovered fast.

Caleb and Charlie meeting was not something I was looking forward to. Not in the best of circumstances, but definitely not now. I quickened my step and put my hand on Charlie's shoulder. I wanted him to know I was true to my word, and that I had put Caleb behind me. Charlie didn't look up but, with a minimum of gesture, shook my hand off. Charlie must have seen Caleb as well. I assumed he tried very hard to ignore him as he didn't seem to react to his presence. As we came closer, Caleb smiled at us.

"You're still here, I see," he said to Charlie.

"Why shouldn't I be?" Charlie replied coldly as we walked on.

Keep on walking, keep on walking.

"Because you're obsolete, my friend." Caleb smiled at Charlie.

What does he mean by that?

Charlie stopped and turned to Caleb. He stayed remarkably calm. "She doesn't want you, Caleb. Get over it."

"Oh, but she did, actually, very much so. And now she's carrying my child."

I thought the ground had opened up beneath me, and five demons were pulling me into hell.

Sinking Ships

My head spun toward Charlie, and he mirrored my shock. I looked back at Caleb. I still couldn't believe my ears.

"That... that's a lie. I can't have any children." I said.

Charlie and I had tried for another child after I had given birth to Sue, but it never happened. Harry had organized tests for us, and it appeared I was just not cut out to become a mother. The doctors had said it had been a miracle I had gotten pregnant with Sue.

"But you gave birth to Sue, didn't you?" Caleb replied, leaning casually against the wall. "Suckers are better at multiplying. Our hormones work their magic differently than normal humans. I can make you ovulate by my presence alone. We are better at everything. Can't wait to find out what Sue's sibling's going to be like, having a sucker father instead of a sucker mother." He laughed.

"You knew this was going to happen!" I spat. "It was all a lie from the beginning. You used me!"

'Don't you see he's using you,' Charlie had said.
I should have listened to him.

I felt anger well up inside me like lava in a volcano about to erupt. I raced toward Caleb. I kicked him, stomped him, tried to scratch him, and screamed at him.

"You bastard! You used me! Wait till Dr. Greene hears about this!"

Charlie ran after me and tried to pull me away from Caleb. His effort was useless as hell hath no fury as I had in that moment. I wanted to kill Caleb for real this time, by any means possible.

Caleb had put his hand on my throat and kept me at arms' length. He was still laughing.

"Dr. Greene you say," he said as he tried to dodge my kicks. "He was the one who suggested it." Caleb laughed even harder when he saw the reaction on our faces. "Like he suggested Alex do Sue. Now that's going to be an interesting outcome; a half-blood daywalker crossed with a pure sucker. I wonder if the child will be a daywalker too."

Charlie let go of me and ran in the direction of Sue's room. Caleb still held me by my throat.

"Let go of me!" I screamed, still kicking him and with my hands trying to get him to undo his vice-like grip on my throat.

"Only if you promise to behave."

"I need to get to Sue!"

"You need to promise first."

"I promise." I stopped fighting, putting my hands behind my back.

He let go of me, and I kicked him as hard as I could

in the nuts. He collapsed on the floor, grabbing his precious jewels.

"I had my fingers crossed, sucker!"

I ran to Sue's room.

"What did you do?" I heard Charlie yell at Sue before I arrived at her room. As I skidded into the doorway, I saw Sue sitting on her bed and Charlie shaking her by the shoulders. Sue looked petrified.

"I didn't tell him, honestly!" Sue cried.

Crap. She thinks it's about telling Alex about how to become a daywalker.

"Charlie, you're scaring her," I said as I hurried into the room.

Sue had been lucky to have had a very secure and protected upbringing. She wasn't used to yelling parents.

Or seductive men for that matter.

I sat down next to Sue and put my arm around her. I kissed her pretty head and turned her toward me.

"Sue, we need you to be honest with us now. It's of great importance. Did you make love to Alex yesterday?" I asked her.

Sue's eyes welled up, and she nodded.

"Did you go all the way?" I had to be one-hundred percent sure.

She nodded again. She must have figured out by our reaction it had been wrong, and she wasn't able to say it. I sighed.

I wanted you to grow up fast, but not this fast, Little Smudge.

I hugged my daughter tightly. Meanwhile, Charlie was freaking out, pacing the room, yelling.

"Those sons of bitches! I knew there was something fishy going on. I should never have let you two come here. How could I have been so stupid!"

He hit the wall with his fist, denting it. He went down on one knee and leaned his forehead against the wall. His body began to shake. Sue stopped crying when her father stopped yelling. It was Charlie who needed me now. I got off the bed, kneeled next to him, and put my arms around him. I shared his grief and frustration. Together we cried.

"Mom, Dad, what's going on?" Sue asked with a quivering voice. Seeing both her parents cry, she took her turn in freaking out.

Charlie and I turned to her, our little Smudge. Tears were streaking down all of our cheeks. Charlie and I wiped our tears and sat down on either side of Sue. We each took one of Sue's hands in ours.

"Little Smudge," I said. "It seems we both have been used in a cruel experiment. We're both pregnant."

Even though no tests were done, and it was way too early for them anyway, I had known Caleb had spoken the truth. I had heard stories of women knowing they were pregnant before it was scientifically possible to know, and I had always dismissed these women as attention-seeking freaks. I knew those stories were true now I felt it myself. It had to be true for Sue as well if Caleb's theory was correct.

Charlie stroked Sue's long blond hair. As if to shake him off, she shook her head.

"No, it can't be. It's not possible. You said so yourself, Mom, when you taught us biology," she said. "It can only happen within a certain time-frame. I'm sure I wasn't within that window, Mom, honestly." She kept shaking her head.

"Shhh, it's okay. You didn't do anything wrong." I put my hand on her cheek to stop her movement. "I'm afraid it doesn't work that way with suckers. I'm so sorry, little Smudge. I didn't know."

I felt like the worst mother ever. How could I have been so stupid to trust that sucker boy? That I had fallen for the charms of Caleb and was ruining my life was my own problem. The fact I had let that sucker boy wreck Sue's was unforgivable. Not only did I have her locked up in this prison, she was now a part of some sort of breeding program.

I put my arms around her and took Charlie's hand in mine. He didn't squeeze it like he normally would have done. I looked at him over Sue's shoulder and found a cold stare.

"We need to get out of here," I said.

Looking for Moore

Charlie looked away and got up.

"Let's find Moore," he said. "He's the one who put you in here. He's the one who should be able to get you out."

The three of us found our way to the offices of the compound. The building was separated by an open space from the suckers' quarters, but as Sue was a daywalker, she had no problem crossing it. We encountered a soldier at the reception desk and surprised, he asked us our business.

"We need to speak to Major Moore, urgently," I said.

"I'm sorry, but you can't," the soldier replied.

Before we were aware that Sue had moved, she was on the other side of the counter and had the man by the throat. Obviously, he had thought he was safe in this building, separated from the suckers by daylight.

"We need to see him now," Sue said as she lifted the man off the floor and he moved his legs in vain.

Our Little Smudge.

She let go of him, so he could speak. He put his hands on his throat, taking a moment before he could talk.

"As I said, you can't. He's not here anymore," he managed.

Charlie and I exchanged glances.

"Where can we find him?" I asked.

"Can't tell you..." He backed off as Sue moved to grab him once again. He spoke quickly before she could reach him. "Nobody can tell you, 'cos nobody knows. He left with the two new test subjects and their mother," he added.

So, blood is thicker than water for Moore.

This was good and bad news. I sought a solution for our current issue.

"Can we speak to Dr. Greene?" I asked.

"Yes. He should be in his room. Let me call him for you."

The soldier watched Sue as his hand went for the phone, but she had no interest in him anymore. She slid over the desk, back to our side. The soldier dialed a number and described us to Dr. Greene. I heard the doctor reply; the soldier confirmed. He put the phone down and told us to wait. Soon, three armed soldiers came to accompany us to Dr. Greene's room. I noted they didn't have their guns out but kept their hands on their holsters.

Dr. Greene stood up as we were shown into his office. It wasn't a big room. It looked even smaller due to the amount of paperwork. Every wall was covered by dark, wooden bookcases, and every horizontal space seemed to be occupied by stacks of books, files, and papers. There was a computer on his desk and a phone, next to more stacks of paperwork. Light entering the room was limited by closed blinds and a stale paper smell filled the room. The whole atmosphere felt oppressive.

"Please sit down," he said and gestured to the two chairs in front of his desk.

"We prefer to stand," I said.

"I prefer you to sit," he replied, and he motioned to the soldiers. The three soldiers took their pistols out of their holsters and aimed them at our heads. Apparently, Dr. Greene thought we couldn't easily attack him if we were seated. Charlie and I took the chairs and Sue sat on the armrest of my chair, away from Charlie.

"What can I do for you?" he asked, looking down at us from his standing position behind his desk, pressing some of the buttons on his keyboard.

"Why?" I asked.

"Why?" he said as he looked at me. He took his glasses off, pulled a handkerchief out of his pocket and began to clean his glasses with it. "I thought that was obvious. Because we could. We were very curious as to the outcome. And, we were extremely lucky you were willing," he smiled as he put his glasses back on.

You don't have to rub it in.

He kept looking at us, but we didn't say anything. None of us were smiling. We waited for him to

143

continue.

"We tried with others, but nobody was willing. Both parties had a problem mating with the... 'enemy', so to speak. Unfortunately, you can't make people fall in love. Money's a powerful tool, but not powerful enough in this case. We think it's something psychological. Apart from the fact there's not much you can do with money here." He finally sat down. "You two coming here, however," and he pointed at Sue and me, "was like hitting the jackpot. Two in one go; we couldn't believe our luck. As soon as I heard you were coming, I manipulated Caleb into getting to you. Over the years he has talked a lot about you. He told us you had a strong mind and that you were his ideal partner. And you cooperated so beautifully."

So it really was you who did the scheming.

This conversation wasn't going the way I wanted it. I had to change the subject.

"I don't want it. Sue doesn't want it. I want you to organize getting rid of both of them," I said. Sue turned her head sharply toward me when I said these words. However, whatever she was thinking, I didn't have time to deal with her possible issues at the moment. I kept focused on Greene.

"I'm sorry, but it's not as if you were raped or anything. You volunteered."

"I didn't..." I began, but Greene cut me off.

"Don't tell me you didn't want it, Kate. We have it

all on tape. You want to see it?"

Greene had directed the question at Charlie and turned the computer screen to show Charlie he wasn't bluffing. The video showed Caleb and me, naked, making love in his room. I deduced from the angle the camera must have been in the TV hanging above the wardrobe. Fortunately, Sue couldn't see the images from her position. She tried to see, but I pushed her back.

You are such a bastard, Greene!

Charlie saw the video. He glanced at me, cleared his throat, and quickly looked away, trying to avoid seeing any more unwanted scenes. I felt like I was hung, drawn, and quartered. I hated Greene with every cell in my body for what he'd just done.

You're going to pay for this, asshole. One way or another.

I had already told Charlie what had happened between Caleb and me, but a visual of the event didn't make the situation between us any better. I would have to deal with the consequences of this later, I was sure of it.

"By law, we are entitled to an abortion, Greene. Don't deny us that!" I was angry as hell, and I wasn't going to let Greene off the hook so easily.

"That's only half-true, I'm afraid. I can arrange for you to have an abortion although I urge you to change your mind. Your child will be of vital importance to our national security. You would do your country a great favor. As for Sue, well, you signed that you agreed for her to undergo invasive testing. She has to follow-up on it," he said as if he was casually talking about extending a work contract. I felt the blood drain from my head.

My daughter is NOT a breeding cow!

"I'm taking them home. The tests are over," Charlie said as he stood up.

"I'm afraid you're wrong there. They will take at least another eight months," Greene smiled with a sleazy smile.

Fuck! Fuck! Fuck!

Greene had us by the balls, so to speak. I had signed the papers stating we would stay until the tests were completed. Only now did I realize there was no expiry date that stated when exactly this was. Tears welled up in my eyes. Not because I was sad, but because I was extremely frustrated. I had this incredible urge to jump over the desk and strangle Greene with my bare hands right there and then. I was frustrated with the fact that I was a rational-thinking, law-abiding citizen with the willpower to get these killing-thoughts under control. My knuckles turned white as I balled my fists and kept myself put in the chair.

Charlie turned toward Sue and me, and said, "Let's go."

I agreed there was nothing more to be discussed with Greene. Sue was his prisoner, and there was nothing we could do about it. I took a deep breath before I got up, and the three of us walked out.

Getting Help

Back in Sue's room, I blew a fuse. This time it was me pacing the room, and I uttered every ugly word I had learned from Rhona. I didn't care Sue was there, I had to vent my anger. Most of all I was angry at myself. I was angry about my weaknesses. My unwillingness to kill John. My stupidity to wait for the army to come and take my daughter away instead of taking her to safety, saving her from this madness. And my greatest weakness of all, to fall for Caleb again. The only strength I seemed to have was hurting Charlie.

As always.

"Let's all go for a breath of fresh air," Charlie said.

His tone made me look up at him. He motioned with his head toward Sue. She was sitting on the bed, knees pulled up, biting her nails. Unfortunately, she had copied my bad habit over the years.

"Good idea. Come on Sue, let's go for a walk." We went into one of the courtyards.

"We can't trust anything or anybody," Charlie said. He sat us down on the bench and stood in front of us. "Group hug," he said. We put our heads together and huddled as if we were rugby players.

"Hold your positions," he whispered. "That way, if

there are any secret cameras, they can't read our lips." Sue and I did as Charlie asked. "I'm going to get the both of you out of here, one way or another," he whispered.

"How?" Sue asked.

"I don't know yet."

"You need to get help," I told Charlie.

"I know, but who can I go to?"

"Go to Julie," I said. "She can contact Maxine. Maybe her Navy husband can get us the help we need. Like a good army lawyer. I'm sure it's illegal what they are doing to us."

"I was thinking of Harry," Charlie replied. "If he knows where the girls are, he'll likely know where Moore is. He may have contacts to help us."

"That's a good idea too," I agreed. "Try both. Remember, the army has a lot at stake here. They may follow your every move and tap your cell. Be very careful of what you say when contacting anybody."

"I will," Charlie said. "I'll go now and be back as soon as I can. I love you."

My eyes sought his after he said those three little words. I knew he had meant Sue and me both and that he had said it out of habit. Charlie cast his eyes down when he noticed me staring at him.

We stopped huddling, and I gave Charlie a short hug after he had hugged Sue. No matter what had happened, he was still my rock to cling to. I would be totally lost without him. I wondered if somebody could have two soul mates. I knew Caleb was one. There was no way I could deny that. Whatever he had been commanded or agreed to do, his actions spoke a different language. Then again, being with Charlie was everything else I needed. His presence had an effect on me nobody else had. He kept me sane and compelled me to look to the future. He was my sunshine on the darkest of days, and I was sure I couldn't survive without him.

We said goodbye to Charlie at the security checkpoint. I kept my fingers crossed they would let him back in next time. If they were to stop him from visiting us... I didn't know what I would do for sure, but I think I would seriously be contemplating murder.

Sue and I walked back to the corridor where our rooms were. We didn't talk, just walked arm in arm. I struggled with my thoughts. I hoped to have a good talk with Sue about her reaction during the conversation with Greene when we were back in my room. When we turned the last corner, I saw that sucker boy waiting in front of Sue's door. Sue also saw him and stopped walking. Her eyes teared up.

"Don't worry, Little Smudge. I'll deal with him," I whispered to her. I gave her a kiss on the cheek and continued toward Sue's door.

"Kate," Alex began as I neared him. "I just heard what happened between you and father. I..."

"Don't," I said. "Just leave. I also just heard what happened between you and Sue. Your father has ruined my life as you have ruined Sue's. You've done your duty. Now let us be."

I stood in front of him with my hands on my hips, trying to block his view of Sue as much as I could. As he was so much taller than I was, it didn't have any effect. Alex looked at Sue, and I threw a glance back at her. She had turned around. From her shuddering body movement, it was clear she was crying.

"Kate, I didn't mean to hurt her," Alex said.

I turned back to him. Pain was written all over his face, and he was shifting his weight from one foot to the other.

Of course, and I have to believe that.

"Cut the bullshit, boy. Get out of my way and out of Sue's life," I hissed at him.

"Kate, you have to believe me," he threw back at me, his face a contortion of desperation.

My face, in turn, was one of hatred.

Before I knew what was happening, he grabbed me with both hands by my top and pushed me against the wall. My heart raced in my throat. What was the boy going to do? I saw him check the camera hanging from the ceiling of the corridor and he adjusted me, so it couldn't see our faces.

"I'm in love with Sue, Kate. Whether you want to believe it or not."

"I don't want you anywhere near her again. We don't trust suckers anymore."

He kept hold of me. He had me on my tippy toes, his mouth close to my face. He hesitated about saying something.

"Kate... I'm not a sucker. I am a half-blood, like Sue!" he whispered. His eyes were darting from my left eye to my right one and back again. His face was too close to mine to look into both my eyes at the same time. I was doing the same thing. I couldn't believe what I was hearing.

Can you say that again, please?

My facial expression changed into one of disbelief.

"What?" I said, demanding an explanation. He kept holding me away from the camera but let me down a bit.

"It's true. My mother was unbitten," he continued to whisper. "When she found out she was carrying a half-blood, she committed suicide. However, she was far enough into the pregnancy at the time that they could save me. Afterward, they stopped doing experiments like these, until Dr. Greene came to the scene recently."

I don't know what to believe anymore.

"I really don't see what difference it makes," I said to him.

Why didn't Caleb tell me the truth?
Oh yeah, I forgot, he's a sucker. Duh!

152

I decided I wasn't going to be played anymore. I pushed Alex away from me, and he let go of my top. I opened Sue's door.

"Go away!" I said to him.

He turned his head toward Sue, who hadn't moved.

"I'll go as I don't want to upset Sue even more right now, but I do love her, and I will be back. I want the best for her and the baby." He turned on his heel and left. When the boy had disappeared out of sight, I called Sue, and we went inside. Her eyes were red and swollen from crying.

"Sit down, honey," I said to her as I closed the door. I gave her a tissue.

"What did he say?" she asked me after she blew her nose.

"Lots of things. I have to think about it," I said and paced the room, silently this time.

I couldn't work out Alex's words. He had said he was a half-blood, like Sue. But I had only seen him drink blood. True, half-bloods could get by on blood alone, like Sue could. She only ate meat because she could, and it was easier for us to get. But why did Caleb think Alex was a pure sucker? Surely, he must have noticed Alex's mother had been a normal human. Then again, he hadn't been conscious when Alex was conceived. But then why hadn't they told Caleb? Would he not have accepted Alex otherwise? If so, why then would he accept my child? It would be a half-blood as well. And, why did Alex want to help all of a sudden? Why only now? Why not before ruining Sue's life? Did he only offer his help so he could pry our escape plans from us? If only I knew.

I decided that, for now, I had to put the issue of Alex on a shelf. He would have to prove his honesty in some way before I could trust him, and I couldn't think of how right now.

Other than killing Caleb for me.

I told Sue I was tired, which I was. Mentally exhausted more like it, but tired nonetheless. She said she was tired too. We hugged, and I went back to my room. I lay on my bed and tried to sleep. All I wanted right now was to escape from this horrible reality.

Communication

I had expected Charlie to return on Sunday, but he didn't. I had no means of finding out what he was doing or what was keeping him, and by the evening I was literally feeling sick with fear. I worried he didn't want to come back to me anymore. Or maybe he did, but they wouldn't let him in. Sue and I spent the day avoiding talking to each other, only indulging in light chit-chat. There was a tension between us I didn't like, but guilt about my affair with Caleb kept me from probing her thoughts. I didn't want her to start asking me questions about my betrayal. So I kept quiet.

On Monday, Sue had to do some more physical tests. At least it kept her mind off things. They probably wanted to get as much information as possible from her before she became too big to move. I didn't pay too much attention to what they were doing as I had a lot of things on my mind. Charlie didn't come on Tuesday either, and the old brick was back to reside in my stomach. I hadn't felt it for years, but it seemed it was as cozy in there as if it had never left. I tried not to look worried for Sue, but I guess she knew I was. I had bitten off all my fingernails and the skin next to them was raw.

We had been lucky to be able to avoid Caleb and his

son so far. As soon as we saw either of them, we made a U-turn and waited until they were gone to get where we were going. Neither of us wanted to deal with the stress of a confrontation.

On Wednesday Charlie arrived at last. He surprised us when he walked into the canteen at lunchtime. As soon as I saw him, I jumped up and hugged him like crazy. The people around us were staring at my display of affection for Charlie, but I didn't care. I was too elated to see him again.

We are still an effective team!

Charlie hugged me back but skipped the welcome kiss.

Or not.

"Shall we go for a walk?" Charlie said after Sue also hugged her Dad, and before we got a chance to sit down.

"Yeah, good idea," I said.

The three of us walked to the entrance of one of the courtyards. I pulled out my card and swiped it through the lock. The light remained red. I swiped my card again, but the result remained the same.

"Here, let me," Sue said. She swiped her card. The lock light still remained red.

"Shit, they've locked us in," I said. I looked up at the ceiling, holding my breath while trying to think of what to do now.

"Can we talk anywhere else?" Charlie asked.

"We can, but there are cameras everywhere," I replied and pouted my lips.

"That sucks," Charlie said. I could see him thinking. "In that case, let's go back to the canteen for now."

Once back there, he rummaged through his rucksack and brought out presents again. For Sue, he brought a new game for her electronic device and a glossy teen magazine. For me, he had more puzzle books; two Sudoku booklets and a crossword one. My mind hadn't been in the mood to do many puzzles during the previous days, so I wasn't spilling over with joy when I opened the parcel, unlike he was.

"This one," and he pointed enthusiastically at one of the Sudoku booklets, "is very interesting." I wasn't mistaken, there was a definite twinkle in his eyes. "You may have to try that one with Sue's help," he said.

I flicked through the pages of the booklet. At first, I didn't see anything special, but as I looked closer, I saw pencil dots in one of the puzzles. I wondered if he had already begun filling it in, thinking he was giving me a second-hand booklet. Suddenly I saw what he had done. My eyebrows went up as I realized what a genius Charlie was. I looked up at him, and I couldn't hide my excitement. He had found a way to silently communicate with us, just in case we weren't able to talk freely. Charlie had used Braille to write in the Sudoku squares.

At home, Sue and I used to have fun leaving

messages around the house in various codes. Braille was one Sue was exceptionally good at. She wasn't good at feeling the dots, as we didn't have any braille books to practice on, but she had a knack for remembering what letters the dots represented. Braille is based on a combination of dots in two columns of three squares each. None, one, or two dots are put in each square. Each combination of dots in the six squares represents a letter. It wasn't rocket-science, but not a lot of people knew it. For Charlie to have hidden it in a Sudoku puzzle was nothing short of brilliant. If someone had flicked through the book, they had probably assumed the dots represented possible puzzle numbers.

I took my chances and kissed Charlie on the mouth. Charlie was taken aback by my sudden move. He didn't push me off him though, and I rejoiced.

"Mom!" Sue said under her breath. She seemed embarrassed for me showing that kind of affection toward her father in public.

"Let's do some crosswords," Charlie said after I let go of him. "Do you still have that other booklet I gave you?" he asked.

I didn't understand what he was getting at. "Yeah, sure, it's in my room," I said.

"Let's go and get it," and he stood up. "Sue, we'll be back shortly, stay here." And the two of us left for my room.

Once there, I opened the drawer of my desk and

retrieved the crossword puzzle booklet.

"Did you do all the puzzles?" Charlie asked.

"No, sorry. I have done some Sudokus, but none of these."

"That's great. Get two pencils and an eraser," he said, and he waited for me to get them. I didn't move.

"How's Sue..." Charlie started.

"Charlie..." I cut him off and shuffled closer to him. I had missed him so much. I wanted to touch him, to be close to him. I wanted to show my love for him.

Charlie took a deep breath.

"Kate..." He sighed.

I stopped. I felt his vibes. He clearly didn't have the same thing on his mind as I did. His expression was apprehensive, with a hint of sorrow.

"I'm sorry, Kate. I'm working hard on forgiving you, but I definitely haven't forgotten yet. You need to give me some more time."

I could see the heartfelt pain that saying these words caused him. The words were also like a dagger in my own heart, but I was the one driving it in. After all, I was the one who had put us in this situation. I wondered if our relationship would ever be the same again. On the surface, everything appeared okay, but it was clear this was far from the truth. And there was nothing I could do to change it.

"I understand," I murmured and turned to rummage in the desk drawer for the pencils and eraser.

I knew exactly where they were, but I needed time to hide my tears. I had made sure my hair had fallen over my face, and I tried to wipe the tears as inconspicuously as I could.

Charlie moved to stand next to me and gently turned me around. I felt naked and exposed now that he could see my tears. I had never been afraid to let Charlie see me cry, but somehow this, too, had changed. He sat me down on the desk chair and wiped my tears away for me.

"It doesn't mean I don't love you anymore," he said tenderly.

My face scrunched up as I began sobbing.

"Are you sad because I still love you?" he asked, unsure.

"No," I said between silent sobs. Charlie handed me a paper tissue from the box on the desk.

"Are you sad because I don't love you?" he asked, even more unsure.

"No!" I said louder.

"Then why are you crying?"

I blew my nose.

"I'm crying because I'm so happy you still love me."

Charlie threw back his head and laughed.

"You're a funny one," he said and put his arms around me. "That's why I love you so much."

I laughed with him, and my tears stopped. Charlie kissed my forehead. Then he told me to splash some water on my face. I cleaned myself up as well as I could in the bathroom, and we went back to Sue, armed with crossword puzzle booklets, pencils, and an eraser.

We decided to move into the red lounge. Charlie picked one of the three-seaters in the corner of the room where the camera above us couldn't point down far enough to see what we were reading or writing. Sue sat on the far side of the couch, playing the new game on her electronic device. Charlie sat close to me, our arms and legs touching. Now and again, I rubbed my foot against his like a friendly nuzzle. I was so happy he didn't pull his foot away.

We were holding one of the puzzle books each. I still had no clue why he was so intent on doing crossword puzzles.

He began filling in the first horizontal word of the first puzzle in his booklet. I peered at the description. In the column for horizontal words, it said; '1. Leg joint (4)'.

He wrote in the empty squares, skipping the black ones to fill the empty squares of the second horizontal word to finish his writing. 'ILOVEYOU,' it spelled.

I finally understood.

'ILOVEYOUTOO' I wrote in the puzzle in my booklet. I smiled at him, and he kissed my hand.

Before I could react, Charlie began writing again, and as he did, I laid my head against his shoulder and closed my eyes.

Thank you.

Charlie tapped my leg. When I opened my eyes, I saw he had finished writing his second sentence. 'IWENTTOSEEJULIE,' he wrote.

'HOWDIDSHEREACT?' I asked in my booklet.

'YOUSHOULDASKHOWIREACTED!'   he wrote back.

I glanced at him with a question on my face. Charlie nodded toward the booklets.

'DOSUDOKU!' he wrote. I was curious now and wondered why he didn't just tell me.

'BUTWEHAVEHELPNOW,' he wrote.

I let this sink in for a moment while I tapped my pencil against my lips. I wouldn't know what sort of help until Sue and I had deciphered the Braille code in the Sudoku booklet as Charlie clearly didn't want to spill the beans.

'DIDYOUSEEHARRY?' I wrote.

'IDID.'

'AND???'

'HEKNOWSWHERETHEYARE,WHEREHEIS,' Charlie wrote.

It took me a moment to realize he was talking about the girls and Major Moore.

'GOINGTOLETTHEMKNOWWHATITOLD HIM,' he added.

The puzzle was full now, and he took the eraser from me and rubbed out all the text. When he was finished, he handed the eraser back to me, and I did the same with my text. There was no more to discuss, for now, so the rest of the time we spent filling in the crosswords properly, hiding our previous entries. Although I couldn't be as intimate with Charlie as I wanted to be, it felt good to be as close as we were, and I enjoyed every second of it.

After dinner, Charlie said goodbye to us. I didn't want him to go so soon, but I knew he had to, to organize things, whatever it was he was planning. He had told me he had taken sick leave from work. Harry had signed a medical certificate stating that Charlie was stressed and needed at least two weeks off. That would hopefully be enough time to organize getting us out. I could only keep my fingers crossed.

More Puzzles

As soon as Charlie had left, I got out the Sudoku booklet he had given me and took Sue to her room. I sat next to her on the bed. I made sure we sat with our backs against the far wall, so no hidden cameras in the TV could see what we were writing.

"Sue, remember the games we used to play with codes?" I asked her.

"Sure," she said, "Why?"

"See if you can crack this one. But don't tell me the answer, write down in pencil what you read," I said. I didn't want to take the risk that our captors would hear what Charlie had so cleverly tried to conceal. For all I knew, they had bugged our rooms with microphones too.

Sue smiled, glad to use her brain again for a change. Ever since the revelation about our pregnancies, she had been very quiet and seemed depressed. It had affected our relationship more negatively than I had thought it would. Over the last few days, I had come to realize she didn't like all the tests she had to do. She only went through them as a necessity. It became clear to me that she had liked being with Alex. He was the one who had pulled her through all this. He had been the ray of sunshine in her life, and it had been taken away from her. Since Charlie's arrival this morning, she had been cheery again, which had surprised me. I hadn't expected her father's visit to have such an effect on her. I was glad for it, though.

Sue took the booklet from me and examined the puzzle. I saw her face light up and knew she had figured it out straight away. Immediately she began to write. I watched, holding my breath, to find out what Charlie had been so excited about.

Sue wrote 'went to see Julie, did not expect to find enlarged community, they have about twenty children, Julie shocked about your situation, everybody agreed to help.'

And that was it. It was indeed exciting news.

"Rub out what you wrote," I said to Sue. "And rub out the dots too."

In the meantime, my mind was racing. Children. Would Julie have a child? Wouldn't she have told me if she did? If Julie didn't mind children, why had she refrained from visiting Sue after that first visit?

Bloody hell, Charlie. This only makes me have more questions.

"Mom," Sue said.

"Write it down!" I said to her. I didn't want her to talk about what we had just found out. I didn't want *them* to find out.

She nodded and wrote, 'I want to keep the baby.'

Oh, hell no!

"What?" I said out loud. "No, Sue, you are not!" I had raised my voice and moved to face her. I grabbed a hold of her upper arms. "This is *not* the time to have a teenager episode."

"But I want to keep it," she said, defying my motherly authority. "You made the decision for me to have an abortion in Dr. Greene's office, but you never asked me. No discussion, no nothing. I can make up my own mind, you know. It's my body."

I so wanted to be able to read her thoughts right now. For the life of me, I couldn't fathom why she wanted to keep it. Would she be saying it only because I hadn't given her a choice?

Serves you right.

I shook my head.

"Sue, you've got to be kidding me! The father... is... a sucker!"

Well, maybe not one-hundred percent.

"So were you when you made me," she said with her nose stuck up in the air.

"Sue... Yes... No! Why?"

I didn't understand it. She had cried when she had seen that sucker boy. I had assumed she was hurt because of the fact he had used her. I had assumed she wasn't head over heels with him, at least not anymore, but maybe I was wrong. Maybe she had cried because she *was* in love with him. This was all too confusing.

Why did she want to keep the baby all of a sudden?

"I don't know. All I know is that I want to keep it. Alex is a good guy," she said.

Huh?

"Sorry, wind that last bit back for me, please. What did you say?" I even made the wind back motion with my fingers.

"Alex is a good guy," she repeated with a dead serious face.

I held my breath until I thought my lungs were going to explode. "Sue, he made you pregnant! On command! He didn't do this of his own free will, Sue!" I couldn't stop myself from yelling at my daughter. I couldn't stop myself from getting angry with her. I knew she was an intelligent girl, but clearly, she wasn't thinking with her brain right now. I jumped off the bed.

I need to put some distance between us before I smack that ridiculous thought out of her head.

I needed to walk around to make more blood flow to my brain, so I could work out an acceptable way for her to see the light.

"Mom, Alex gave me this card," she said and pulled out an envelope from her pocket.

"When?" I asked.

"When you and Dad were getting the puzzle books," she answered.

"Give it to me," I said as I yanked the envelope out

of her hands.

I was angry with myself, for leaving Sue on her own and vulnerable to that sucker boy, and couldn't help myself taking it out on Sue. I opened the envelope and found a strange card inside. It was a folded piece of paper, with bits of newspaper columns glued to all four sides. With a pink highlighter, he had marked letters on the front of the card that spelled out 'I love you' and had drawn a heart around it.

"This doesn't mean anything, Sue. Only that he has the creativity level of a child and too much time on his hands," I said. I really wished for Sue to be happy, but I still didn't trust the fucker.

Pun not intended, but funny in a dry kind of way.

I wasn't going to take anything the boy said or did for granted. I had learned my lesson and wasn't that gullible anymore.

"No, Mom, look better," she said. She smiled.

I examined the card again. I could see the pink markings on the newspaper articles. I studied the articles, inside and out. They were random, with no title or anything. Not about interesting subjects either, mostly politics. I looked at Sue and shrugged my shoulders. I still didn't see more than when I had seen the card the first time.

Sue sighed. "Mom, look at the letters."

I examined the letters. I now noticed some of them were filled in or shadowed over with pencil, ever so slightly. With the light gray of the pencil on the gray newspaper background, it was difficult to see. When I began at the top and lined up the marked letters, going down each line, they began to make words. I couldn't believe it! The boy appeared to be more than a pretty face and a muscled body. I sat down and tried to decipher the message.

It read 'I am so sorry, Sue. I do love you. They made me do it, but my feelings are true. I am not what you think I am. I am like you, a half-blood. I want to be with you and our baby. I will do anything to make it happen. My heart is yours. Alex.' He had used all the sides of the card to highlight the letters he needed to spell out the text.

He even found an x.

I got up and gave the card back to Sue. I stared at the wall opposite me. My mind was blank.

"See!" Sue said.

I didn't know what to say. I didn't know what to think. I needed more time to figure this out.

"We'll talk about it in the morning," I said to her and left.

Another Visit

That night, I couldn't sleep at all. I'd been plagued by nightmares lately, but at least I'd slept. Now, I tossed and turned as too many thoughts went through my mind, giving it no rest whatsoever.

Sue wanted to keep the baby. The words kept reappearing like one of the horses on a merry-go-round. She was way too young to have a child. If only she hadn't met that sucker boy. If only I had taken her away after she bit John. If only I had made the decision to let John die. If only I hadn't taken up John's offer of giving me a lift. If only Sue had been a normal girl.

So many fucking ifs again.

After hours of lying awake, I came to one single conclusion. Caleb was the cause of all my pain and misery. He was the one who had hurt me so badly all those years ago and the repercussions of our meeting kept on coming, pounding me like a sledgehammer. If he hadn't existed, my life would have been so different. Most importantly, Sue would have been a normal human, and I would be living a normal suburban life with my normal suburban family in Bullsbrook at the moment.

I went into a sort of daze. My body took over from

my mind. Even though it was the middle of the night, I got out of bed and dressed. In the bathroom, I stared at my reflection in the mirror for a moment. How I hated this face lately. Not as much as I hated Caleb, but I couldn't deny it was partly my actions that had caused immense pain to the people I loved. I took a deep breath and punched the mirror with all my might. It shattered, and I had to jump back to prevent getting injured by the flying shards of glass. When the dust settled, I studied the broken pieces and picked up a slim, triangular one. It was small enough to fit in my hand but large enough to do substantial damage. I tested the point. It seemed sharp and sturdy. After I carefully wrapped the wide end in toilet paper, I tucked it in the front of my panties, parallel to my leg line. Lifting my leg carefully and wiggling about a bit, I made sure it wasn't stabbing me when I moved.

I left my room and made my way to Caleb's. When I tried the doorknob, I found it unlocked. Quietly I slipped inside. The room was pitch dark, and I heard Caleb's steady breathing coming from his bed.

"Caleb," I whispered. I wanted him to look into my eyes when I killed him again. He woke, and I heard him turn around.

"Kate, what are you doing here? Are you here for me?"

No, I'm here to see Santa.

As he turned the nightlight on, I could see him

smile.

"I am. I can't stand not being with you," I lied.

Caleb kept on smiling and held the sheets up for me to join him in bed. He was only wearing tight undies and seeing his perfect body made me inhale sharply and hold my breath. Memories of touching that athletic body made butterflies appear in my stomach. I slowly walked up to his bed and stood in front of it, but I didn't get in. Instead, moving sensuously, I started taking my top off. When my vision was temporarily limited as I moved the fabric over my face, I felt Caleb's hands touch my exposed body. It gave me goosebumps all over. I dropped the top onto the floor. Caleb now sat on the edge of the bed in front of me, his hands caressing my back. I looked down into his beautiful brown eyes.

Such a shame.

"I thought you didn't want me to touch you anymore," he whispered. He sounded genuinely surprised, a bit flattered. He had a smirk on his face.

I hate that smirk.

"I lied," I lied again.

He moved his hands down to take my pants off. I quickly put my hands over his and kissed him.

"Not yet," I whispered and, to stop him from complaining, playfully bit his ear. He reacted by nuzzling my neck. I shivered from fear and anxiety. Caleb must have noticed, and I hoped he assumed he was the cause of it. He was of course, in a way, just not exactly for the reasons he was probably thinking.

He let his hands trail back up over my back, past my bra, and all the way up to my neck and back down again, his touch as light as a feather. It created ripples of shivers that followed his moves over my body. This time, I wasn't so sure it was from anxiety. When his hands reached my buttocks, he lifted me up and gently set me on his lap.

I smiled as he had put me in a perfect position. He was close enough not to be able to see what I was hiding in my panties, and I was close enough to drive the piece of glass through his chest. I kissed him, trying to distract his mind from the here and now. His scent was driving me wild. One of my hands went from caressing his neck to his chest, over his six-pack, and to his crotch. I felt him become aroused. I moved my other hand into my own panties and pretended to please myself while I was pleasing him. Caleb used his fangs and his soft, sensuous lips to kiss my neck, and continued stroking my back and neck with his hands. I took the piece of mirror in a tight grip and carefully lifted my hand. When his hands moved up to my neck again, I made the most of the moment. I pulled my arm back to get some distance. As I deepened our kiss, I shot my hand forward. To my surprise, Caleb caught my wrist and stopped me just in time as the piece of glass touched his skin. A drop of blood oozed out.

Fuck!

The shock of being caught must have been written on my face.

"You didn't think I wasn't expecting something like this now, did you?" Caleb chuckled. He kept looking at my face as he forced my hand away. I stood up. He squeezed my wrist so hard that I had to drop the piece of mirror.

I was furious and scared at the same time, my heart pounding in my chest and my mouth becoming as dry as the desert. Caleb was still smiling at me, which confused me. I turned to leave.

"It doesn't mean you have to go," he said as he swooped me up and put me gently on his bed. As he slowly moved over me, images of John flashed through my mind.

Holy shit! No way! Not again!

I quickly pulled my knees up and put my feet on his chest. With all my might I pushed him off me.

"Over my dead body!" I yelled as he fell back.

"Ouch, that hurt, Kate," he said as he regained his footing. I had jumped to my feet on the bed and now leaped for the door, but Caleb was faster. He caught me and threw me back on the bed. This time he was on top of me, straddling me before I could raise my legs. "You haven't said sorry yet," he grinned.

I began kicking and screaming. I wasn't going to take this lying down.

Well, not quietly anyway.

Caleb blocked every blow I threw at his head. He laughed, showing off his fangs. He knew I was helpless.

I heard the door open and a sleepy voice said, "Father, what's happening?"

It was that sucker boy of his.

Talk about déjà vu.

A Good Talk

I was pinned down by Caleb on his bed, his actions interrupted by Alex. I had to make the most of the situation. Either Alex was with me or against me and there was only one way to find out.

"Alex, help! Get this monster off of me!" I yelled.

"Go back to your room, son. This is something between Kate and me," Caleb commanded Alex.

"I came here to kill you, you bastard! Alex, if you love Sue, you have to show your loyalty now!"

Caleb flashed fiery eyes at me, and I thought he wouldn't have hesitated to put his fangs in my neck if I hadn't been pregnant with his child. Caleb was holding me by my wrists when all of a sudden, he receded from me. It appeared Alex had pulled him from the bed. He now threw a mighty punch in his father's face. Caleb flew backward and fell to the floor. As he tried to get up, Alex jumped up and kicked his father in the head, karate-kid-style. This time, Caleb didn't get up.

"Did you kill him?" I asked Alex as I crouched on the bed, checking if I could see Caleb breathe.

"No, he's unconscious but alive," Alex answered, looking down on his father.

What a shame.

I jumped off the bed and grabbed the piece of mirror off the floor. I positioned myself on top of Caleb's body and raised the piece with two hands above my head to finish the job. Before I could make the thrust, Alex grabbed my wrists and took the shard out of my hands. He pulled me up and moved me away from Caleb.

"I told you to show your loyalties, boy!"

"He's my father," Alex said calmly.

Those words brought my mind back to reality. I realized what had just happened and trembled from the horror of the crime I had tried to commit. I sat on the bed and covered my face with my hands.

"I'm sorry, Alex. I'm so sorry. I don't know what came over me. Please forgive me." I looked at the unconscious Caleb through my fingers. I seemed to have a subscription on shivers as I couldn't stop them from happening.

"Come on. Let's talk somewhere else," Alex said, and he took me gently by arm, directing me past Caleb. At the door I stopped, realizing I wasn't wearing my top.

"Sorry, I forgot something," I said.

Alex took a moment before letting go of me. I moved back into the room. I felt Alex's eyes following my every move. I stepped over Caleb, picked up my top, and threw it on. On my way back toward the door, I stopped between Caleb's sprawled legs and kicked him hard in the nuts for a second time that week.

"Now I'm ready," I smiled at the boy.

Alex rolled his eyes and guided me out of the room. He took me to a room that appeared unused. Alex told me his room was next to Caleb's, but that it was bugged.

Why am I not surprised?

He closed the door behind us, and I sat on the desk chair.

"I'm afraid I can't offer you anything else to drink but water."

"That's fine," I said. "I'm okay."

"Why did you even try it? You know he's so much stronger than you." Alex sat down on the bed.

"There's no grain of humanity in him, Alex. No sucker cares about who lives or dies. They think they're the best and have no respect for others. He has caused me so much pain so often and in so many ways, I couldn't let him continue ruining other people's lives."

"I know," Alex said.

I squinted at him.

"What do you mean 'I know'?" I couldn't help my hateful tone. "How would you know what I'm talking about?"

"I mean, I know about suckers not having respect for others. As I told you, I am a half-blood. I know plenty of true suckers, I'm surrounded by them all day, and I don't like them. As you said, they think they're better than others. When Doctor Hayley ran the program, he decided to keep the information about me being a half-blood from everybody as he realized early on I wouldn't stand a chance once the others found out, including my father," and he waved his hand in the direction of Caleb's room.

So that's why Caleb didn't know.

"But if Caleb is so against half-bloods, why does he want my child?" I asked.

"Because Dr. Greene wants to build a half-blood, daywalker army," Alex said. "They promised my father his freedom in return for your child. Although I doubt they are ever going to give it to him."

Holy shit. You've got to be kidding me.

"But my child wouldn't be a daywalker. I am not a sucker anymore."

"No, but you have been. They're hoping the vaccination is still lingering in you and that it'll vaccinate the child and make it a daywalker."

I looked at Alex in horror.

"I'm sorry, Alex, but I'm not keeping this child. I don't want it. I don't want anything to do with Caleb anymore. Not now, not ever. I couldn't love this child. It would remind me too much of the monster Caleb is."

Alex snorted.

"They wouldn't let you keep it anyway. They raise the children away from the mothers. They are training them all to become super soldiers, me included, detached from any emotion. That's why I want to help Sue. I want the best for my child and Sue."

"What do you know about the best? You hardly know what's normal." I said it before I could help myself.

"I do watch TV, you know," he chuckled.

Touché.

"But what about you? Are you a daywalker?"

Alex sighed. "No, I'm not. They never vaccinated me."

"I don't understand. If they want to build a daywalker army, why didn't they create daywalkers? They knew how to do it. I told them."

"Dr. Haley had advised against it. He wanted to keep as much control over us as possible. Dr. Greene isn't so strict though, he sees the advantages of having a daywalker army."

There was a hint of happiness in his voice when he said it.

"Surely you're not thinking they'll ever let you leave this place?" I thought out loud.

"I know you don't believe in the sincerity of my love for Sue, and I can't explain it, having only known her for such a short time. But now that she's carrying our child... I only want what's best for them," he said and took a deep breath. "I know I can't be with them out there, not being a daywalker."

He said 'our' child.

I still don't trust him.

I was too tired to think about the information

rationally at the moment.

"I'm sorry," I said. "I'm exhausted. I'm going back to my room. Thank you for saving me from your father." I stood up and walked to the door. I had my hand on the door handle and turned around. "Before I go, I want you to know I still don't trust you. I've had too many bad experiences when I trusted people, particularly suckers. You would have gained it instantly if you had killed your father, but that didn't happen, so...."

Alex moved to speak, but I stopped him.

"Don't worry. I'm glad you didn't as I don't condone killing either. What I tried to do was a... a temporary bout of insanity."

As your mother probably had as well. Suckers seem to have that effect on people.

I opened the door. Halfway out, I turned around to him again.

"If you hurt Sue any more than you already have, I can't guarantee I won't suffer from it again."

Alex gave me a terse nod.

I found my way back to my room, and as I got into bed, I realized I hadn't asked what they had promised the boy if he made Sue pregnant.

Jacky Dahlhaus

Blackmail

Sue and I had breakfast in silence. There were no tests planned today, and we spent the morning in the red lounge. I had wanted to go swimming, but as I was certain that's where Sue's intimacy with Alex had flowered, I sure wasn't going to let her be reminded of that 'good' time and have her fight me even more on the abortion issue. We were sitting in the red comfy chairs, reading, when I couldn't hold it in anymore.

"I tried to kill Caleb last night," I said.

Sue put her magazine down and stared at me.

"You didn't," she said after a while.

"I did. Didn't work, though."

"What? Why? How?" Sue always wanted to know the ins and outs of everything.

"I realized he was the cause of all our trouble." I sighed. "So I tried to get rid of him before he could do any more damage."

"What did you do?"

"I tried to stab him with a piece of mirror. Unfortunately, he was faster than I was. And then he tried to rape me." Sue sucked in air in shock. "Fortunately, Alex showed up at the right moment. He must have heard me scream. His room's next door to

Caleb's. He knocked Caleb out cold with a karate kick. It was awesome. Before I left the room, I kicked Caleb in the nuts."

"Serves him right!" Sue chuckled. "I can't believe you wanted to kill him, though. That's so not you. Especially after what you told me earlier."

"I know. This place is driving me nuts. I sure hope your father can get us out of here soon."

Sue didn't reply, and we went back to reading in silence.

The rest of the morning remained uneventful. I waited for Charlie to come with more news. Sue was waiting to hear more from Alex, but neither Alex nor Charlie showed up, and Sue and I were both rather bored. We watched some TV, but I kept falling asleep. When I saw Caleb in the canteen during lunch, I noticed him walking rather stiffly. I nudged Sue in the ribs and nodded in Caleb's direction. When she saw his awkward walk, she looked at me, and we both suppressed a giggle.

I was glad I had told her what happened. I knew she was going to find out one way or another, and I wanted her to hear it from me, rather than from that sucker boy or anyone else.

After lunch, Alex came looking for us, and he took Sue to the gym to train together. Afterward, when she showed me the karate moves he had taught her, I became eager to learn some of that stuff myself. I had been in defenseless positions too often lately, and I vowed to learn how to defend myself once I was free. For now, I was happy for the boy to teach us what he could. It would also keep my mind off things, like what the hell Charlie was up to.

Friday morning, I was unexpectedly summoned by Dr. Greene. An armed soldier escorted me to his office and remained present during my visit. The doctor still wasn't taking any chances.

"Please, sit down, Kate," he said, friendly as anything as he got out of his chair.

What have you got up your sleeve this time?

"Do you have a date for my abortion?" I asked.

"That's exactly what I wanted to talk to you about, Kate," Greene said as he leaned against the corner of his desk. "I really would like you to reconsider."

"I won't."

"Kate, Kate... you sound as if you've already made up your mind." He smiled.

"I have."

What part of 'no' doesn't he understand?

"Then let me explain to you why this child is so important to your country," he began.

Yeah, why not tell me more of your deranged delusions.

"As you know, Caleb's a true sucker and a prime specimen at that."

One-hundred percent egocentric megalomaniac. I

have to agree with you there.

I nodded.

"You're a very intelligent human being, also a very nice version if I may say so without making you uncomfortable," he said with an even broader smile.

I didn't smile back, so he continued in a more serious tone.

"You were 'vaccinated' by Caleb and became a daywalker. Unfortunately, Dr. Haley never experimented with making daywalkers, and hence we have no data on them other than Sue's. We have no idea whether this 'vaccination' is still working. As you know, there are vaccines that last only a year and there are those that last a lifetime. We have no idea which one of the two this vaccination of yours is. We are hopeful that it words for a lifetime and that your child will be a male daywalker."

"What if it was? You're not suggesting mating siblings, are you?" I joked.

Greene looked at me with a straight face.

You've got to be kidding me!

"You belong in an asylum," I said as I stood up. "First of all, I am not keeping this child and secondly, my daughter's not a breeding cow. You got her pregnant once, but don't think she'll fall for it again. I'm done talking."

"Sit down, Kate," Greene said with less kindness. The soldier at the door unclipped his holster and put his hand on the gun.

I stared at Greene but didn't sit down. I really had heard enough.

"Being able to create an Army of daywalkers would be of vital importance for the national security of our country. For all we know, they already have one in Russia or North Korea. I must stress the importance of your cooperation."

I turned around and walked to the door.

"We have other ways to get you to do what we want," he said, and he left the threat open. This stopped me in my tracks.

Charlie!

I couldn't risk Greene keeping Charlie away from me, or worse, hurting him. I needed to know what he was up to, and how Sue and I could help or prepare our escape. I thought fast and made a decision I hoped I wouldn't regret.

"Okay, I'll think about it." I said reluctantly, without turning around.

"Great, I'll get the paperwork ready!" Greene said cheerfully.

I left.

As I walked back, I breathed through my nostrils and clenched my fists. I didn't want to sign any more paperwork. That's what had us into this bloody mess in the first place. This time, I would have to make sure I read all the fine print. I could later say I had to sign it under duress, which was the truth. For now, I had to carry this unwanted child a bit longer.

The child can't help it, Kate.

Self-defense Lesson

During lunch, I asked Alex if he was free that afternoon.

"I am," he said, frowning. "What do you want to do?"

"I want you to teach Sue and me some self-defense if you don't mind."

Alex's face lit up. "It would be my pleasure," he said.

So, after lunch, we changed into tracksuits and met in the gym. There were plenty of people using the equipment, but the mats were free. Alex seemed pumped up to show off some moves.

"What would you like to start with? Judo, jiu-jitsu, karate?

"How do you get somebody off you once they have pinned you down?" I asked.

Alex smiled a wicked smile as he knew exactly why I had asked. Sue agreed with me that it was a good question as she, too, had seen me helpless in this position.

"Sue, do you want to pretend to be my attacker?" Alex asked.

Sue had no problem with this at all. Alex went to lie on his back on the floor and asked Sue to sit on top of him. She did.

"A bit higher, Sue. Yes, that'll do," I said as she reluctantly moved up to his belly.

"Now try to choke me or something," Alex said.

Without hesitation, Sue kissed him.

"Hey! I don't think he meant that," I said annoyed.

Sue sat up and laughed.

"It would certainly work to get your opponent's mind off thinking about fighting for a moment," Alex said. He glanced at me with a blush on his cheeks. "It would give you an opportunity to punch him in the liver or something, but I'll tell you more about that later. This time, Sue, put your hands around my throat."

Sue did as she was asked. Alex moved quickly and before I knew it, Sue lay on her back and Alex sat on top of her.

"How did you do that so fast?" I asked, neck stuck out.

"It's easy, let me show you." He rolled back onto his back, pulling Sue with him back on top. He showed us how he hooked his arm and leg around Sue's arm and leg on one side, pushing her over from the other, and rolling her onto her back.

"I'd like to give it a try if you don't mind," I said.

"I do mind!" Sue joked.

"Oh, cry-baby. I promise I won't hurt him," I said to her.

I went to lie on the floor and Alex sat over me. He put his hands gently on my throat. Even though his hands hardly touched me, I found it an awkward situation, and I hastily tried to get out of it. I did exactly what he had shown, but no matter how much I pushed or pulled, I couldn't get him to budge one inch as he was too heavy for me. He sat there, grinning, while I struggled. Sue was trying to help me with directions.

"This isn't working," I said after about five minutes of pathetically wriggling under his body.

Alex shrugged. "Yeah, you're right. Maybe you should make sure you never get into this position in the first place."

"How do I do that?" I asked as he helped me up.

"You have to keep your attackers away from you. There are a couple of places on the body that are extremely sensitive. If you are close enough, and there's no way out of the fight, you can try to hit those, before they get a hold of you," Alex said.

"Show us," Sue said eagerly.

"Okay, first is the solar plexus, right below the sternum." He touched the spot on Sue's belly which made Sue collapsed in a giggle.

"I hardly touched you!" Alex said surprised, and he held his hands up in defense. He threw a glance at me, checking whether he had annoyed me again or not.

"It tickles!" Sue said.

"Just don't touch her, Alex, and we'll all be happy,"

I said and smiled. I didn't want him touching my daughter but couldn't help warming to him. He appeared to have his father's charms.

"Okay, so the solar plexus is one," Alex continued more seriously. "A hit in the belly, when they don't expect it, is also always a good one, but it's hard to know if they're prepared or not. There are a couple of hits to the face and throat too, the throat being particularly sensitive, but you'd need a clear shot if you want to do it properly and considerable force. As you are rather small, Kate, I won't bother you with those moves. Instead, you could try to hit your opponent in the ribs, the floating ones in particular. You'll have to come from behind or the side for that one. Another hurtful place to hit someone is—"

"The nuts, I know that one!" I blurted out.

"Mom!" Sue whined, quickly looking around if anybody had heard me.

"Well, it works, you know," I said triumphantly.

"I was going to say the knees," Alex continued. "But you're right, nuts always work a treat. Surprise action is usually best. Your opponent being unconscious helps too."

I laughed.

"When you're going for the knees, you can hit them from the front if they attack you from the back," and he made a backward kick with his leg, "or from the side," and he took a step to stand next to me and faked a kick to my knee. "If you use enough force, they'll probably tear some ligaments, and you'll have prevented them from being able to follow you. The best thing to do afterward is, of course, to run away immediately after you've kicked them."

Sue and I practiced some of the moves under Alex's guidance until we were more confident in them. I sincerely hoped I wouldn't be in a position ever again that required me to use any of these moves, but I thanked the boy nevertheless for showing us.

Next, we all did some cardio work on the machines. I sat on one of the training bikes, and I went full throttle. In no time, sweat was dripping off me. It felt great and helped me get rid of most of my anger.

After dinner, at about 9, I excused myself to Sue and Alex and went to bed early. I desperately needed to catch up on the sleep I had missed lately.

Found Out

It was early Saturday morning, and I was waiting for Charlie at the security point. They didn't let me go out into the parking lot anymore. Why, I don't know. Where was I to go?

I was eager to see Charlie and hear more news. I had no idea if he would come, but I had nothing better to do. I sat on the floor in front of the window and watched the sky. How I missed the fresh air. Being cooped up inside all the time was beginning to take its toll. I was getting crankier by the day. It had been nice to breathe the fresh air in the courtyards, but this was off limits now as well. I appreciated the blue expanse of the sky outside and the freedom it portrayed.

All of a sudden it hit me. We needed to escape by air! If we ever escaped, and this was still a big if, we would easily be tracked if we traveled by road. If we could fly away and stay under the radar, they wouldn't have a clue where to look for us. We couldn't go home of course. We needed to get a hideaway where we could stay safe for a while until we had this mess sorted out legally.

In the distance, I spotted an army van. I waited patiently as the van drove through the gate and parked.

Charlie jumped out, carrying his rucksack over his shoulder, and I stood up. As he walked toward me, I felt myself relax. Charlie always had that effect on me. I had no idea what it was or how he did it but being with him always made me feel at peace.

When he entered the building, I kept on smiling. He smiled back at me, but I could tell from the frown on his face he was wondering what I was smiling about.

"I love you, Smudge," I said when he came through the door.

"Yeah, missed you too," he replied.

There was no missing the fact he didn't say he loved me. I put my hands in my pockets as I wondered if what he had said in my room and written in the puzzle booklet during his last visit, that he loved me, if that had changed now he'd had more time to think about us.

"So, is my fly open?" Charlie asked as he put his rucksack on the belt to go through the X-ray machine.

"What? Why do you ask?" I said with a frown as he walked through the metal detector.

"Because you were smiling when I came in, so either my fly is open, I have something between my teeth, or my hair looks like a pineapple. Which one is it?" he asked as we waited for the soldier to return his bag. Charlie checked his fly, swiped his tongue over his teeth and ruffled his hair to try to sort out all of the named issues in case one of them was the cause of my smile.

I laughed.

"It's bad, isn't it? I knew it. Tell me!" he said impatiently.

"It's nothing," I tried to soothe him, "I'm smiling because I'm happy to see you, you dope!"

Charlie squinted at me.

"Right..."

I knew he still didn't believe me. He was right, of course. I was smiling because I had found a way for us to escape this hell-hole. I hadn't lied though. I was happy to see him as well, but I could hardly tell him of my new escape idea. Not with the soldiers standing right next to us.

Instead of giving Charlie his rucksack back after going through the X-ray machine, as they had done every single time before, the soldier took it off the belt and opened it up. He was taking things out as if he was looking for something.

"Hey, what's going on?" Charlie asked. He threw me a concerned glance.

"Just a routine check," the second soldier said.

Charlie didn't have a lot in his bag. Out came a half-empty water bottle, some snacks for the road, a packet of tissues, and presents. The soldier unceremoniously tore the packaging off them and revealed more puzzle books. He flicked through them and Charlie intently watched him. The soldier didn't look surprised or upset, but he did put the books aside. He put everything back in the rucksack and handed it back to Charlie, except for the books.

"What about those?" Charlie asked, pointing at our presents. "They're gifts. I would like to give them," he said.

"Sorry. They have to remain here for further examination. They will be returned to you as soon as we are done with them," the soldier said.

Charlie threw me another worried glance. I put my arm around his shoulder and guided him away.

"It's okay, darling. I'll get another booklet next time. I still haven't finished the last one you brought me." I tried to sound unfazed. I knew this soldier was only a messenger, and I didn't want to give him any reason to be more suspicious than necessary. It was obvious they had been watching our every move during Charlie's last visit and realized we were secretly communicating through the booklets. They must have picked up on our behavior.

As soon as we were out of earshot, Charlie began cursing under his breath.

"Bloody hell. Why now? Fuck it!"

"What was in it?" I asked.

"Information on our escape plan," he said, hardly moving his lips.

Fuck it indeed.

My stomach wrapped itself around my old companion, the brick. Charlie and I needed to talk, but where was it safe to do so? I wouldn't be surprised if they had my room bugged and Sue's probably as well. The only privacy we seemed to have was in the bathroom.

Lightbulb!

A Change of Plans

As soon as we neared a ladies' toilet, I didn't hesitate. I dragged Charlie by his sleeve toward it. When he realized where we were going, he began to resist. I managed to get him in the entrance doorway where I kissed him passionately. Charlie kissed me back, but when I opened my eyes, I saw his eyes were already wide open. I tried to message him with my facial expression that this had a purpose and that it wasn't sex. I don't think I succeeded. He moved to get back into the corridor. Without saying a word, I grabbed both his hands, so he couldn't hold on to the door frame, and dragged him into the ladies.'

"Kate, I'm not supposed to go in here!" he hissed, his head indicating the ladies' sign.

I looked back at him and still couldn't contain my excitement. I must have given out completely wrong vibes as Charlie kept on trying to go the other way. Fortunately, I persevered and managed to drag him into the ladies', into a cubicle, and shut the door behind us. Once I had him secure, I put my hands behind my back. Our bodies were so close, yet our minds so far apart. I didn't touch him, which calmed him down a bit. I flushed the toilet.

"What was written in the booklet?" I asked as the water made a lot of noise.

It finally dawned on Charlie what I was doing. He waited for the cistern to fill up before he pressed the lever and answered.

"We were going to get you out on Wednesday." The water stopped flushing and Charlie stopped talking. When we could flush again, I pressed the lever.

"How?" I asked.

"By motocross bikes," he answered.

I couldn't imagine how this was going to work. Sue and I couldn't get through the security point as it was manned day and night. So I told him what I'd thought of earlier.

"We need to escape by air, at night, stay under the radar. Flee to an unknown place."

Our communication was short but to the point. Charlie agreed it was a good idea, but that he needed time to arrange this. I reminded him we weren't going anywhere for some time and that things could hardly get any worse. I asked him if he had been able to contact Moore and Charlie replied that he had. He said Moore had only known at the last minute of Greene's plans. It had been the reason he had all of a sudden decided to get his granddaughters out. He'd do anything to help us out as well.

We were soon done discussing the escape. Neither of us flushed the toilet, but neither of us made a move to leave the cubicle either. We stood there, looking at each other. I couldn't stand it anymore, so I closed my eyes, leaned forward, and kissed Charlie on the lips. Butterflies bounced in my belly. It was like a first date, as if I had never kissed his lips before. I leaned back and was so scared to open my eyes to find Charlie looking angry or uncomfortable. He'd said he needed more time. When I finally had the guts to open my eyes, I saw the longing in his and my heart melted. We flew into each other's arms and kissed passionately. There was desire, and longing, and more passion. In our embrace, Charlie and I fell into the corner of the cubicle and we giggled like schoolchildren. Being one with him was all I wanted at that moment.

Charlie's hands went under my shirt, his hands familiar with the territory. He caressed my breasts and made my whole body tingle. My hand went over his crotch and I was not mistaken about his feelings. Charlie lifted my top, moved it over my face.

Uncontrolled, the memory of the night I had tried to kill Caleb flashed in front of my closed eyes. I relived the shivers of feeling Caleb's hands on my skin, which led to the memory of my union with him before. The guilt of my psychological betrayal made all my wants disappear as fast as they had come. All of my sexual desires drained away. Before Charlie could finish taking my top off, I lowered my arms and pulled it down. I moved away from him, avoided his eyes. When I dared a glance at him, he looked confused.

"I'm sorry," I said, "I'm so sorry, but I can't," I tried to explain. I let myself slide down until I sat on the cramped floor space. Charlie kept looking at me, worried and hurt.

"I... thought you wanted this," he said quietly.

I leaned my head back and closed my eyes as I realized how much I'd just hurt him.

Ettu, Brute?

Charlie had set his own feelings aside to accommodate mine, and in return, I had rejected him, hurt him, stabbed him in the back again. There was a bitter taste in my mouth. I hit the cubicle wall with my fist.

Can I please go to rehab to cure my stupidity?

"I know," I said. "I thought I did too, but I can't. Too many things are going through my head right now," I said. "I'm so sorry, Charlie." I put my face in my hands, so I had some time to think about what expression I should have. Should I look guilty, sad, or angry? I had so many feelings rushing through me, I couldn't keep up with them. Charlie had said he needed time to be at peace with what had happened, but it appeared he wasn't the only one who needed time. I stood up and touched his face with my fingertips.

"One day I'm going to get out of this hell-hole and make it all up to you. Everything," I said.

Charlie didn't say anything. He took my hand and

kissed it. I gave him a quick smile and opened the cubicle door.

We left the ladies' toilet not touching each other. If anybody had seen us enter through the corridor-cameras, they would have been completely mystified about what had happened in there.

Booted Out

We met Sue at the canteen. She was there with Alex. Charlie cursed under his breath when he saw them together. I had completely forgotten that Charlie had missed what had happened after he had left on Wednesday. He didn't know about the card that Alex had sent Sue, the stuff that had happened between Caleb and me, and about the talk I had had with Alex. Seeing Charlie and talking about the escape plans had made me forget to tell him all about these things.

"Charlie, it's okay," I tried to calm him. "Alex is okay." I still couldn't get it past my throat to say Alex was a 'good guy.'

Charlie didn't believe me at face value and asked Alex to leave, upon which Alex looked at me. Whether it was for help or permission or whatever, I don't know, but I felt that his continued presence wasn't a good idea.

"Give us some time, Alex," I said. Alex got up, kissed Sue, at which Charlie huffed, and left us.

We sat down. I expected Charlie to ask questions about Sue's tests, but he didn't talk. He looked with concern at Sue. Sue, acting like the typical teenager, went into passive-aggressive mode. She crossed her arms, leaned back, and stared back at her father. She was clearly pissed off because Charlie had sent Alex away.

"Charlie, Alex isn't what he seems," I said, trying to ease the tension. "He's..." and I quickly looked around, spotting one of the cameras pointed directly at us. Before I spoke again, I moved closer to Charlie, my mouth so close to his ear that I hoped the camera couldn't possibly see my lips move.

"Alex is like Sue, a half-blood," I whispered.

At first, Charlie's eyes went big but then narrowed again.

"That doesn't change a thing. He still made Sue pregnant."

So true.

"He's nice, Dad," Sue said, "and I love him."

I thought of telling Charlie about Sue wanting to keep the baby, but I realized this wasn't the right time. Charlie first needed to get to know Alex a bit better. To him, Alex was just a sucker stud, and the possibility of Charlie seeing Alex as a future son-in-law at this very moment in time was as likely as that of a fish being able to ride a bicycle.

I still struggled with the question of how Sue and Alex were ever going to live together, with the boy not being a daywalker. I didn't want Sue to live in eternal darkness as Charlie and I had once experienced. Sue was used to the outside, with lots of colors. She had already complained multiple times about the drab uniforms they had put us in since we arrived here. If she had to live in only artificial light, she would pine away. Hopefully she would forget about Alex after we escaped from here.

You're getting off track, Kate.

Charlie hadn't immediately responded to Sue's comment. Veins stood out on his temples and the color of his face was turning redder by the second. Things weren't good. He was about to explode.

"Oh, well, that's okay then," he said all of a sudden. "Why don't we organize a wedding, and you two can live here for the rest of your lives!" He jumped up and stormed off. I shot Sue an angry glance and hurried after Charlie. I grabbed his arm and spun him around.

"Honey, things have happened since you left," I said.

"A lot of things seem to happen when I'm gone, don't they?" Charlie spat at me, his eyes accusing.

I had never seen him like this. His words were like flying daggers, hurting me all over. I let go of him. He had always been the calm and collected one. The one who helped others, telling them how to deal with situations, pointing out the right path to follow. Never had he been accusing, judging, hurtful. But with that one sentence, that one look, he had been so vicious. He was really losing it, and I couldn't blame him.

So, this is what he had meant with '... and I don't think I can go through this a second time...'

Tears welled up in Charlie's eyes. With brusque

movements, he wiped them away. I gathered he felt out of control, afraid he was losing the two of us. I felt the proverbial knife dig a little further into my chest, the pain unbearable. I dropped to my knees and threw myself around his waist.

"I'm sorry! I'm so sorry," I cried.

Charlie hesitated for a moment before he put his arms around me. Together we cried. I was finally close to Charlie, but this was not the way I had had in mind. Yet it felt good to be in his embrace. His warmth and his closeness were comforting, as was the movement of our bodies in sync with our sobs. Before long, I noticed people were staring at us.

"Come on," I whispered as I wiped my tears and stood up. I took Charlie's hand and guided him to my room. I lay on my bed, pulled him next to me, and hugged him tenderly. Charlie was probably very tired, trying to organize our escape and getting up early to get to us, which didn't help. We needed more time to sort out our emotions and there was no need to talk for now. I caressed Charlie until he was snoring. It didn't take long before the comforting sound sent me to sleep as well.

When I woke up, I felt better, more in control of myself. Charlie was already awake. He smiled at me, and as I smiled back at him, he untangled himself from my arms. He rose and used the bathroom. I was pleased he had waited for me to wake up before getting out of bed. I yawned a big yawn. Charlie returned with a glass of water which he handed to me.

Always taking care of me.

"Thanks."

"So, what's up with Sue and that sucker boy?" he asked as I handed him the empty glass back.

"It seems they are in love." I sighed. "I still don't know if we can trust the boy, but his affections for Sue seem genuine. I have no idea how to test him, other than asking him to kill Caleb for me, which he refused, so—"

"You asked him to kill his father?" Charlie cut in. The light in his eyes flickered.

"Yeah, I did. Sort of..." I recounted my attack on Caleb and how Alex had helped me out and told Charlie about our talk afterward.

"You have a knack of getting yourself into trouble, don't you?" Charlie chuckled after I finished.

"I'm afraid so. I think I have to concur that Sue must get her intelligence from you," I sighed.

"Finally!" Charlie said and poked my side. The origin of Sue's intelligence had been a long-standing discussion between us.

I giggled and tried to get away from his hand. Charlie put his arms around me and hugged me tightly, preventing me from moving away from him.

"I love you, Smudge," I said as I hugged him back.

"I love you too, but don't you ever, ever do

something as stupid as what you just told me. Promise?"

"I promise," I replied. "All I need is to get out of here."

"Yeah, about that..." Charlie sighed.

"Come on," I said and moved under the sheets. I held the sheets up for Charlie who, a little to my surprise, joined me without a word. I guess the fact that I kept my clothes on helped in his decision. With one arm I held my pillow over our heads. It was now pitch black under the sheets, but at least our faces weren't visible, and our whispers were muffled.

"We need to bring the escape forward, Charlie," I said. "If they decipher the code in the puzzle book, they're going to be watching us like hawks. They may not even let you in again."

"I was afraid of that this time already," Charlie admitted. "What did you mean earlier with 'escaping by air'?"

"I meant by helicopter. We can't get to the parking lot through the security point, but we could manage, with Sue's strength, to get onto the roof unseen. If a helicopter could pick us up, we could escape without them being able to follow us."

"Great idea," Charlie whispered. "I'll contact Moore. He should have contacts from his time in Afghanistan who could help with this. I'll do my best to organize it for tomorrow night, 3am. If I can't manage to make it work, I'll try it for the next night and so on."

I frowned but knew Charlie couldn't see that. "Then let's hope they don't find the hole in the roof after the first night."

"Always thinking practically," he said, and I knew he was grinning.

Suddenly, there was a double knock on the door. Charlie and I kept quiet. After about half a minute, there was another knock upon which a soldier barged into the room. Charlie and I sat up in panic, the pillow flying through the air. The soldier stood in the middle of the room.

"You need to leave, sir," he said to Charlie.

"Excuse me, can we have some privacy here," I said to him.

The soldier didn't take any notice of me and repeated his command. Charlie and I exchanged glances and looked back at the soldier. We didn't get up. The soldier put his hand on his holster.

"No! Charlie has unlimited rights to visit me," I said angrily.

"I'm sorry, Ma'am, but there's a security issue. He needs to leave," the soldier repeated.

Shit. They've cracked the code already.

Charlie shrugged, got out of bed, and kissed me.

"I'll be back on Wednesday, don't worry," he said and looked knowingly at me. I smiled. I couldn't wait to get out of this jail tomorrow.

They took Charlie and escorted him back to the van.

I waved from behind the glass although I had no idea if he could see me with the sun's reflection on it. I so hoped he would be able to arrange everything in time.

Lies

The van with Charlie in it disappeared from sight. My feelings of peace disappeared with it. I went back to the canteen to talk to Sue. Her attitude toward her father was unacceptable, and I would have to talk to her about it. Her teenager attitude was too much at the moment. She would have to be a bit more sensitive toward her father. It was the least she could do for him.

At the canteen I looked around for her, but Sue wasn't there anymore. I walked back to her room, chiding myself for not checking it before I had left my own room, but she wasn't there either. I had an idea of where she was, but tried the lounges, the gym, and the pool first, postponing the inevitable. As she wasn't in any of these places, I sighed, and dragged myself to Alex's room. I knocked on his door, and it took a while before it opened. The boy only wore his jogging pants. Sue lay in his bed under the sheets.

Typical teenagers.

It frustrated me to see my daughter under sheets that weren't hers but conceded that not much could happen that hadn't already happened. In a flash, I thought back to the days when Charlie and I had just got together and could find no argument to find the current situation unreasonable.

"I need to talk to Sue," I said to Alex. I did my best not to use an overly stern voice. Nevertheless, I saw Sue pull the sheets over her head. The boy turned to Sue.

"I don't think she wants to talk to you right now," Alex said after he had given Sue the opportunity to respond. He was trying so hard not to take sides.

"Sue, I need to talk to you. Now!" I said more urgently.

"Go away. I don't want to talk," she said from under the sheets.

I sighed and looked back at Alex. Sue was driving me nuts with her behavior, and I wondered if Alex had episodes like these as well. From what I had experienced, he seemed so much more mature.

"Alex, I really need to talk to Sue. Please send her to my room as soon as you can make her leave here." I figured my news about our escape could wait.

"I will, Kate. At least, I'll try," he said.

"Thanks." I turned and left the two turtledoves alone.

I had only taken a few strides away from Alex's room when I saw Caleb turning the corner. I assumed he was returning to his room and, as it was at the dead end of the corridor, I couldn't turn around and go another way. Trying very hard to ignore him, I crossed over to the other side of the corridor. I tried to walk past him while looking at my shoes. Talking to Caleb was the last thing on my mind right now. I didn't want to see him. I didn't want Caleb in my life, period.

Suddenly, I bumped into him. He had crossed the corridor as well in order to be in my path and had let me continue on my collision course. The impact took me by surprise and a little scream escaped my throat before I realized what had happened.

"Are you afraid of me now?" Caleb stood there with his hands in his pockets, a smirk on his face.

Would he smirk just to annoy me?

"Afraid?" I said after I had regained my wits. "Why should I be afraid of you? You should be afraid of me. I tried to kill you twice already, and one of these days it's going to work." I tried to get past him. Caleb blocked my path every which way I turned.

"Me, afraid of you? Don't make me laugh," he chuckled.

"Caleb, get out of my way. You annoy me. I've no idea why you're so happy, but it's irritating."

Caleb stepped aside to let me pass. I hurried away from him as fast as possible. I could feel his eyes following me.

"I am happy because you'll be here with me for another eight months. As soon as our child is born, I'll be free!" he yelled after me.

Oh my god. Idiocy will never go out of style.

I stopped and let out a breath of annoyance. I couldn't believe how stupid Caleb was. Did he really think they were going to let him go? A health hazard, an enemy of the state? Somehow, I felt sorry for him. He was going to spend the rest of his life in confinement. And for what? For being alive, for unwillingly being what he had been made into. I couldn't help myself. Sighing, I turned around and walked back to him, right up close and personal. I looked up at his smirk. The top of my head did not even reach his chin, and he was quite intimidating from my point of view, but I wasn't scared.

"Caleb, they are never going to let you out. You are a threat to society. They don't want another Black October. You represent everything everybody out there hates and fears. There are no suckers out there anymore, and there never will be. All suckers were turned back to normal or have been locked up. Whatever Greene has promised you, it's a lie. You will never leave this place a free man."

Caleb's expression turned into one very similar to the one he'd had when I had shot him ten years ago. His skin turned paler than pale, his eyes jet black.

Who's afraid of Virginia Woolf now?

As I had delivered my message and had nothing more to say, I turned to walk away. I didn't get very far. Caleb grabbed me violently by the arm and whisked me around. His grip was tight. It hurt me. For an instant, I was scared.

"What are you saying? Who told you this?" He

grabbed my other arm as well and shook me as I didn't answer. He stared at me with wild eyes, like the eyes of a tiger pressed into a corner. "Of course I'm getting out. The others have been—"

"Caleb, please. You're hurting me," I cut in. I wasn't afraid he was going to hurt me big time as I was carrying his child, but this didn't mean he couldn't hurt me a little.

To my surprise, Caleb let go of me. He licked his lips and put his hands through his hair. His stare was now darting everywhere, returning to mine again and again, searching for the truth. His last words repeated themselves in my mind. 'The others have been...'

Oh my god, would they have killed suckers that were supposedly have been 'set free'?

"You're lying. It's not true," Caleb said, keeping eye contact now. "Greene told me I'd be free. They said this assignment was the last thing they'd ask of me."

Caleb must have been desperate, and Greene had known it. Greene had figured out that freedom was the only currency holding any value in this place. Caleb had blindly clung to Greene's promise with both hands, and now I had told him he was clinging on to a phantom. If Greene had said this was the last thing they'd ask from him, what did he mean by that? Would they kill Caleb? Dispose of him? A memory of Caleb's eyes full of life as we had collided that first time in the schoolyard flashed in front of me, and I imagined what life must have been like for him before they locked him up. Instantly, I shared the despair Caleb must be feeling after hearing the promise of his freedom was a fake. It was as if somebody knocked the wind out of me.

Caleb was leaning against the wall now, his expression shocked. I didn't want to stay with him, but I couldn't let him be on his own either as I dreaded he would try to take his own life more actively this time.

"Caleb," I said as I put my hand on his shoulder. He looked down at me, and I saw a tear escape from his eye.

"Kate, I can't go on like this. I can't stay here. It drives me crazy. I need to get out! I need to be able to breathe! I want to feel the wind in my hair, I want to see the sea, I... I want to be free..."

Yeah, don't we all.

I guess he saw from my expression I wasn't falling for his act.

"Kate, I'm sorry!" he whispered as he put his hand tenderly on my cheek. "I have no regrets of being with you, but I'm sorry for not telling you what would happen. They tricked me too. We were both used. They promised me I could leave afterward. They said you'd be let go after the baby was born and that I could leave with you. You have to believe me." His eyes were so intense. I found it hard to believe he was lying this time, and my heart ached for him. My mind still refused to accept anything Caleb said though.

"I... Caleb... I don't know what to believe anymore.

You have lied to me too many times. I'm sorry."

Caleb stared at me blankly. He didn't say or do anything. I couldn't place the look on his face. Was it disbelief, anger, frustration? I didn't know what else to say or do, so I turned my back on him for the third time and walked away. After about five paces, I stopped. That last vision of Caleb ate at my soul. I couldn't leave him in this state of mind, whatever it was.

Once a sucker, always a sucker.

I made up my mind and strode back to Caleb. He still stood there, looking blankly into space. He didn't react when I stood in front of him. I put my arm around his waist and pulled him along.

"Come on, let's get you back to your room."

I guided Caleb to his room and sat him on his bed. In the bathroom, I found the glass that once held my blood and filled it with water. Caleb took it from me, but he didn't drink. I actually didn't know if he drank water at all. Caleb lifted his head, and his beautiful eyes regarded me with intense sorrow. My heart broke, and I knew I had to get out before I did something extremely stupid again.

"Wait here," I said and hurried out of his room.

I knocked on Alex's door. I had to knock twice before Alex opened it. When he did appear, he seemed irritated. Obviously, I had chosen a bad time to disturb him and Sue.

"What now, Kate?" he said, his words curt.

"I'm sorry to disturb you, Alex. I wouldn't do this if I didn't think it was urgent, but your father needs you. He needs you now." I waved my hand toward Caleb's room.

I don't know what Alex thought had happened or what I'd done, but without wasting any time, he pushed me aside and ran to Caleb's room. He probably thought I had tried to kill him again. I peeked into Alex's room and saw Sue staring at me from between the sheets.

"I still need to talk to you, Little Smudge," I said and walked away.

Question Time

It wasn't long after when Sue came to see me in my room on the Saturday afternoon. I sat her down and wrote down in my puzzle book Charlie and I had discussed our escape and that we were getting out soon. I didn't tell her the exact way, day, and time as I wasn't sure if she would tell Alex. I still didn't trust the boy one hundred percent. She took it in but didn't ask any questions. I didn't make an effort to continue the conversation, and neither did she. Without a word, she got up and left. I let her. I should have reprimanded her for her behavior toward her father earlier and about her decision to keep the baby, but I was too emotionally drained. It was all too much for me at the moment. I was still too upset about hurting Charlie and preoccupied with Caleb's sorrow.

I spent the rest of the day alone in my room. I lay thinking about getting onto the roof Sunday night. As Sue was much stronger than I was, it would be easier for her to open up the ceiling and get onto the roof. Going up through the ladies' toilet ceiling would be the best option, as it had no cameras and was positioned in the center of a corridor. I didn't know if we would have time to land the helicopter or not, but I guessed as much space as possible would be best. It would be dark, and it was a huge complex. The pilot would need to be able to see our position without wasting any time looking for us. We needed a light. I glanced at the night light but dismissed using it as there wouldn't be an electrical outlet up on the roof. There was a way to make a light that didn't need batteries which I remembered from one of my science lessons. I would have to get a few kitchen items for this. The thought crossed my mind they'd probably lock the kitchen door at night. I had to find a solution for that.

Racking my brain for an answer without finding one, I decided to pin the problem on the board for now. I still had the issue of Sue in the back of my mind. What if she didn't want to come? Nobody had ever given me a manual on how to deal with obstinate teenagers. Did one even exist? I would have to Google it when I got my life back. For now, I hoped Sue would trust my guidance and follow me instead of staying with Alex. I hoped Alex could convince her tomorrow to get out. He had said so himself that he wanted the best for Sue and the baby. Should we take Alex with us?

Shit, do I really want to?

Alex said he was a half-blood, but I still didn't have any proof of it whatsoever. Maybe I could have him eat some meat? But if he had been drinking blood all of his life, would his digestive tract be able to handle that? How else could he prove to me he was what he claimed to be? And even if he did, did it matter? He still wasn't a daywalker, so how could he and Sue be together and live happily ever after?

Next to this, of course, there was the issue of Caleb. What in heaven's name was I to do with him? Why did I have these feelings of responsibility for his well-being? Why did I even contemplate his future? I had tried to kill him twice already, so why did I have second thoughts about leaving him? Had his desperation been an act, or was he for real this time?

So many questions.

The only person I had no questions about was Greene. He was the center of this hell hole. If anybody knew anything about what was going on, it was him.

Second lightbulb moment!

I needed to talk to Greene. He had the answers to most of my questions, at least the ones about Alex and Caleb. He would never tell me voluntarily what I wanted to know, so I had to play my cards right.

***

Sunday morning, after two hours in the gym, I cleaned myself up and went to Greene's office. There were two soldiers at the reception desk, and I couldn't help a corner of my mouth lifting. One of them called Greene, and a soldier escorted me to his office. I had noticed staff didn't have a normal working schedule with weekdays and weekends. They seemed to live on the premises which meant it made Greene available on a Sunday morning. I couldn't imagine him having a wife complaining about it.

"Kate, how nice to see you." His words were as sweet as honey as I entered his office. I suppressed pretending to barf.

"Dr. Greene," I said as I sat down in one of the chairs in front of his desk. In the process, I scanned his worktop for any paperwork that could have contain information which might have been of some interest to me, but it was too hard to do so in such a short time and without looking suspicious.

Apart from the text being upside down.

"Have you made up your mind?" Greene asked as he looked at me with expectation.

"I... have," I replied. I had completely forgotten the abortion issue for a moment and had no clue on how to proceed to get him to spill the information I wanted to hear.

"I'm sorry," I said as I shifted in my seat. "I'm a bit nervous about it all as you can perhaps understand," I was desperate to buy myself some more time, so I could come up with a plan.

"I do understand," he said. I knew he was lying. I was nervous about getting information out of him without being caught, so how could he understand?

Unless I'm too obvious and he's playing the game

along.

"Before I make a final decision," I said, "I would like you to tell me a bit more about what you are doing here. Tell me what you are planning to do with our babies. I want to know more about their fathers and if we are going to have access to our children. That's the sort of stuff I'd like to know."

Greene sat there nodding while I talked. I didn't know if he would answer any of my questions, but any bit of information would be a bonus. When I finished, he took a moment before he spoke.

"Kate, you know I can't tell you everything. This is a highly secret operation and knowing less is better for your own protection. I hope you understand."

I nodded. Over the years, I had been able to catch up on some spy movies and understood that not knowing everything could save your life.

And sometimes it can get you killed because you are of no use.

"But I still would like to know more about the fathers. I want to know if you have used the best breeding stock."

I had no idea from what corner of my brain I retrieved that one. I sounded like a cattle breeder.

Old MacDonald had a farm.

Where some animals were more equal than others.

Greene's smile broadened.

"I'm glad to hear you're beginning to think along the

same lines. I can understand your worries. Please let me lay them to rest when I tell you we used the best."

For a moment I regarded Greene, who kept smiling that slimy smile of his. I tapped the armrest with my fingers and pressed my lips together while my focus shifted to study the blinds behind Greene. There was a minute of uncomfortable silence.

"I won't sign the papers if you don't tell me more," I told him with a poker face. I leaned back, put one leg over the other and crossed my arms. I had no secret ace up my sleeve, so I just had to play tough.

Like a teenager.

"Okay," Greene said. "It doesn't hurt to tell you the following as I am assuming you know most of it already anyway. You know Caleb. He's our prime specimen, but he's getting older and mentally weaker. We only used him for this last assignment because of his connection with you. Your child will be the half-blood we so want for our project."

"What about Alex?" I asked. I had to know.

"Alex is the younger version of Caleb, his son. Your grandchild will be a cross between a half-blood and a sucker. We don't know what the outcome will be. That's what we're hoping to find out."

Mother-fucking shit-faced liar!

I tried very hard not to look shocked.

"Are there any other copies of Alex?" I was sure that if Caleb was such a winner, they would have tried to produce some more.

"Unfortunately, no. Shortly after Alex's mother's death, Dr. Haley destroyed the embryos. We began receiving sucker babies from the outside world, conceived during Black October, and he thought it was unethical to make sucker children while they were available in abundance.

Why breed dogs when the dog pound's full of them?

From Greene's tone of voice, I gathered he didn't agree with Dr. Haley's ethics.

Mutts are not the same as pedigree dogs.

"What about visiting rights? Are any of us going to have any contact with the children?" I asked, remembering Alex had said the children would be taken away from their mothers.

"No, not all of you. Only Alex, as he will be the one training them. That's all I can tell you, Kate."

It was already far more than I had hoped for.

"What about Caleb? What are you going to do with him?"

"He will be... retired," Greene answered.

I didn't like the way he said it. It made my skin crawl.

"I have the papers here," he said as he took them out of his drawer. "Would you like to sign them now?"

"I hope you can understand I would like to study them first, minutely," I said as I put out my hand.

"Of course, take all the time you need."

I took the papers from him and left. I couldn't bring

myself to shake the man's hand.

The Truth

I swore under my breath on the way back to my room.

"Filthy, lying son of a bitch!"

How could I be so stupid to fall for Alex's smooth talk? He sure was his father's son. That's why Caleb didn't know he was a half-blood. Because he wasn't. His one-and-only motivation for sucking up to Sue was to produce more offspring, like a true sucker. How the hell was I going to tell Sue this new information? That would be a tough one. I knew she wouldn't want to listen to me. How I wished Charlie was here with me. He'd know what to do. I needed help, but how to get it?

Oh no, don't even think of going there!

I refused to listen to my common sense and resolutely re-routed to Caleb's room. Once there, I knocked on his door with a steady hand.

"Caleb, are you there?" I asked without giving him the time to respond to the knocks.

He opened the door and, again, appeared genuinely surprised to see me. He looked like shit. His hair was tousled, and it appeared he had slept in his uniform.

"Um, I need to talk to you, urgently," I said.

"Is it not true what you told me yesterday?" Caleb

asked. His eyes were wide open with hope. It pained me to see him like this, and even more so because I couldn't confirm his question.

"No, sorry, that hasn't changed. I need to talk to you about something else."

Caleb frowned but opened the door further to let me in.

"Not here," I said, shifting my weight onto my other foot, "somewhere more private."

He looked back into his room, then frowned wearily at me. I had thought he knew his room was bugged, but now I began doubting this. Looking away into the corridor, I wished I could remember where that empty room was that Alex had taken me too, but I had been too distressed to remember. It may have been bugged as well anyway.

"Um, okay. Let's go to the canteen then," Caleb said.

I didn't know why he suggested the canteen, but I followed him. As we entered it, I realized it was a better place than any other. Even though it was on the early side of lunchtime, the place was buzzing with noise. Yes, there were cameras, but they would never suspect we were having a 'secret' conversation in here. We grabbed ourselves lunch, and I found us a table directly underneath a camera. Once we sat down, and I was sure nobody was paying any attention to us, I began to talk.

"I went to see Greene," I said.

Caleb sucked blood from his beaker through the

straw and waited for me to continue.

"Alex isn't a half-blood," I said with my sandwich in front of my mouth.

Caleb stopped sucking and frowned. "I never said he was."

"No, I know you didn't, but Alex did."

"Why would he say that? He knows his mother was a sucker. We... she and I, had a short relationship after I was told she was pregnant with my child." A blush appeared on Caleb's cheeks. "To comfort each other about being locked up here more than anything else. I honestly tried to make it work, which I couldn't. The affair petered out after a few weeks. She died due to a head injury she got when she slipped in the shower. She was seven months pregnant then. It was a miracle they could save Alex," Caleb said.

Oh, if I could put my hands around that boy sucker's neck now.

"I don't know why he said it," I said. I was becoming more and more agitated about the lying sucker boy. "Probably to make Sue keep the baby, which he has succeeded in doing. She wants to keep the baby."

Caleb looked at me while continuing to suck on his straw. When he finally realized I was expecting a reaction from him, he stopped sucking.

"Wasn't that the whole idea in the first place?"

Can I please have a wall to bang my head against?

"Caleb, we were used, abused! We didn't ask to get

pregnant! But now she wants to keep the fuckin' baby!" I hissed.

Caleb looked at me with a stern face and said, "No need to swear."

I rolled my eyes before I stared at Caleb while holding my breath.

Lord Almighty, please give me strength.

I let my breath out forcefully and decided to change the subject.

"Caleb, Greene also said we're not going to have access to the children after they're born. Only Alex will as he's the one going to train them."

I didn't know if this made any sense to Caleb, but to me, it was obvious he was going to be superfluous. The army didn't have a reputation of keeping people around who were surplus to requirement. I watched Caleb as he put his beaker down and returned my stare with those beautiful, dark brown eyes. They were looking extremely sad, but they showed no despair this time.

"Kate, as I said before, I've made up my mind. If I can't have you, there's no reason for my existence. When you leave here after eight months, I don't care what they do with me." He said it as a matter of fact and continued sipping from his cup.

You've gotta be kidding me.

I put down my sandwich. I couldn't believe what he just said. This wasn't happening, not again. I sat back, blinking. I didn't know what to say, what to think. I didn't know how to deal with somebody who didn't want to live.

Somebody pass me a manual for this one, please.

Caleb chuckled as he put his hand over mine. I was still too overwhelmed with the casualness of his decision to say anything.

"It's okay, Kate. I still have eight more months with you. They have to make sure our child is born okay before they let you leave." He smiled.

Crap. He doesn't know yet I'm not keeping the baby.

Another Perspective

I knew I had to make Caleb see reason, but I couldn't tell him I was planning to have an abortion, not in his current state of mind. I didn't know what his reaction would be.

"Caleb, you can't mean what you just said. It's ridiculous. Why would I be the only reason for you to live?"

I didn't get it. I wasn't that special. I wasn't rich, a photo model, or super-intelligent being.

Did I miss something?

Caleb took my hand in his and kissed it.

"Kate, from the first moment we met, I have been in love with you." His face lit up as if the sun was shining upon it. For a moment, he looked like his old self again. "There's something about you I can't resist. I can't get you out of my head." He wasn't holding my hand tightly. I could take it away if I wanted to, but I didn't. Caleb continued.

"Every waking moment since we met, I have been thinking about you. I even stole Sasha's necklace and told her she must have lost it somewhere in Bullsbrook. It was my only hope of seeing you again as I had no idea what had happened to you or where you had gone. I knew you weren't bitten and wouldn't be with any of the packs. I could only hope you'd come back for me where I had left you. When you did..." he stopped talking for a moment and leaned a little closer to me. His eyes were so incredibly intense. I felt myself drown in their beauty again. "I knew you felt the same for me. It was so hard to stop myself from running to you and kissing you right there and then when I saw you that day."

We'd had this conversation, but hearing it again still shocked me. Again, he said he loved me, always had. I shook my head slowly.

"But you nearly killed me. You almost sucked me dry then," I manage to whisper.

"No! Yes... nearly, but not quite. I was very angry when you sent Sasha into an epileptic seizure, but I didn't want to kill you. Heaven forbid. I bit you because I didn't want to miss the opportunity to turn you properly this time. So I could be with you after I broke up with Sasha," he said. "I'm sorry I got a bit caught up in the act. It was a habit of mine at the time."

He looked away for a moment, embarrassed about his past.

"Then why didn't you take me with you?"

You left me, for the second time.

"Because I had responsibilities. I had a pack of suckers to take care of. I saw the army arrive and Sasha was my best bet to save the suckers who were depending on me. She was my partner. I could only be with you after I broke up with her. I was working very hard on that the very moment you came back. Unfortunately, you interrupted the whole breaking-up scene." He said those last words with his typical smirk on his face.

It all started to make sense now, but I had to make sure.

"You tried to kill me again when I tried to get Julie back."

"No, I didn't."

"Yes, you did," I said, eyes squinting at him. "You came at me with that same smirk you have on your face now."

Caleb sat back. "Am I trying to kill you now?"

"No, but..."

"And I didn't try to kill you then. I only wanted to disarm you. When are you going to get it that I have no ill feelings toward you? Quite the opposite, in fact."

I wasn't going to be convinced by him that easily. I had to know the complete truth this time.

"What about when you laughed at me the other day? When I got angry when you told me I was carrying your child? I felt so used and ridiculed."

"Ah, yes. I'm so sorry about that, Kate. I didn't mean to hurt your feelings. But it was so funny, how your little man tried to bite me with his words, like an annoying insect. I meant to hurt him, not you. And then you acted so wild, scratching and screaming.

Admit it, it was funny." He now had a broad smile on his face, cheekbones raised, eyes glinting. "And then you came to me at night, to kill me. What a night! You liven up my life. That's for sure."

I relived both moments from a distance and had to admit that, from a certain perspective, they were funny.

"Okay, some of it was funny, but not that you tried to rape me. That wasn't funny at all."

The smile instantly disappeared from his face, and he abruptly leaned forward.

"Rape? I never tried to rape you. What kind of a person do you think I am?"

"Caleb, you forced yourself on me after I tried to kill you!" I hissed under my breath, looking around, checking if I was causing a commotion or not. I wasn't.

"That? That was just fooling around," Caleb said. "I toyed a bit with you. All I wanted was for you to apologize to me for trying to murder me and throwing me against the desk. Come on, it was the least you could do. If anything else had happened after that, I wouldn't have objected. But rape? No, no rape. Ever."

My ears were tingling hearing his side of the story. My hand automatically went to my mouth, ready to bite my nails, but before it reached it, my mouth decided on another action. My hand fell back into my lap.

"Why should I believe you?"

He looked at me with those eyes, making my head

spin. Caleb put my hand he was still holding over his heart and solemnly said, "Kate, I have only lied to you once. That was when you asked me not to pursue you after our time together. I had said I was happy being with you only once. That was my only lie for I will always want you. My love for you always has, is, and always will be wholehearted."

His sincerity shattered my defenses.

Have I been wrong all this time?

I believed him now. I finally understood what he had been going through. How misguided had I been to believe he had used me. But whatever his feelings were toward me now, I couldn't accept them.

"Caleb... I... We can never be together. I've told you this before. I'm with Charlie. I love him." I withdrew my hand from his chest and cast my eyes down. What more could I say? It hurt me so much to hurt him, and more words would only be adding fuel to the fire. Guilt was burning me up from the inside.

I'm not hurting Charlie for a change though.

An awkward silence followed that seemed to last forever. I didn't dare to look at him. Finally, he sighed. He patted my leg and spoke.

"I know, Kate. I know now. For the life of me, I can't fathom what you see in him, but I realize you chose him, and I respect your choice. I wish you both the best. I hope life treats you well."

Well, suck me sideways.

I struggled with processing his words. Did he mean what he just said? Will he honestly not pursue me anymore? When I had the guts to look up at him, Caleb was focusing on sipping from his cup, an expression of extreme sadness on his face. I didn't know what to think. He had just bared his soul and said he couldn't go on living without me, yet... he now said goodbye to his love for me as if it was an old friend. Was he having me on again? But then again, what would he gain from that?

"There's... there's only one way you can make me believe your words," I said. I knew I was going to jeopardize our escape, but I had no choice. A glimmer of hope appeared in his eyes. I casually scanned around the canteen. It didn't look as if anybody was listening in on us. I lifted my coffee mug in front of my mouth before I spoke, just in case, and whispered.

"Charlie's going to try to get us out of here. Can you help Sue and me get out, stop Alex preventing us from escaping?"

I studied Caleb's facial features for a sign of treachery. A lift of a lip muscle, a narrowing of an eye, a move of an eyebrow. Anything that would tell me he had been dishonest. Fortunately, nothing hinted at a betrayal. His face went all relaxed and... warm. It was a funny thing to think, but that was what it looked like. As if somebody had given him a teddy bear, a hot cocoa, and a hug.

"Of course, I can do that." He smiled. He picked up my hand and kissed it.

Getting Ready

I had asked Caleb to come to my room at 2am, and he was there on the dot. I was dressed and ready to go.

"We need to get into the kitchen. Do you know if it's locked?" I asked him as we sneaked back into the corridor.

"If you're hungry, there's probably some fruit in the staff lounge," he said.

"Okay, let's go there first." I let Caleb lead the way.

The staff lounge door wasn't locked. The staff didn't appear to have any lockers here, so I supposed there was nothing to steal that suckers wanted to have. There was a fruit bowl on the table, and it contained all sorts of fruit. I picked out the two large oranges. I juggled them as I was thinking.

"Aren't you going to eat them?" Caleb asked. He really thought I was hungry.

"No, I need them for something else," I replied as I put the oranges in the pockets of my shirt. "But I need more and some olive oil and a knife. So we still need to get into the kitchen."

"Follow me," he said and took us into the canteen.

As I expected, the door to the kitchen was closed. There was a number lock on the door and a metal pull-down security shutter above the serving desk.

"Bummer, how are we going to get in?" I asked Caleb.

He grinned and punched his fist through the wall next to the door lock. The wall appeared to be made of gypsum on a wooden frame. I wondered if all walls were made so flimsily and if the suckers had ever tried to break out. Caleb put his arm through the hole, twisted the door lock from the inside, and opened the door. He made a show of presenting the passage to me.

"After you, my dear," he joked.

I laughed and shook my head.

Life's so much more fun when you think outside the box.

In the pantry I found some more oranges. I also picked up a bottle of olive oil and a small, sharp knife from a butcher's block. At the stove, I found a gas lighter. I nearly forgot I needed this as well. Caleb grabbed me a bowl, and I put my loot in it. We went back to my room, thinking nobody had noticed our escapade.

I put the bowl on my desk and sat down. I cut an orange in half and carefully took the flesh out of the skin, leaving the centered stem of white stuff attached to the peel. Caleb, who had sat down on my bed, was watching my every move with interest. I poured some olive oil over the white wick and into the bowl of the orange peel. Then I lit the wick with the lighter. It worked; I had created a candle. I made a show of presenting the organic light decorating my desk.

"Wouldn't it have been easier if you had taken some candles?" he asked.

I stared at him, stunned. "You're allowed to have candles in this place?"

"Of course we are, under supervision of course. We have birthday parties all the time. You should have asked," he grinned. I felt so stupid.

There was a knock on the door. It made me jump up. I grabbed the knife. Caleb had other plans. He hit the light switch next to my bedside and pulled me on top of him on the bed. It happened so fast, I had no idea what he was up to. I hid the knife behind Caleb's body, still holding on to it. A soldier burst into the room, gun at the ready.

"What?" Caleb said angrily at the man.

The soldier hesitated. He hadn't expected to walk in on what looked like a romantic scene.

"Um, the kitchen has been broken into. On the monitors, we saw you two in the corridor..." his words trailed off.

Caleb put his hands up. "Yes, Jerry. I confess. That was us. I'm sorry, but we were in the mood for some romance. Jerry, this is Kate, the woman I've been telling you about for the last ten years. Kate, this is Jerry, the night-watch guy who's been keeping me here for the past ten years."

Jerry and I exchanged courtesies.

"Jerry," Caleb said, "I'm finally having my moment with Kate. I'm so sorry about the kitchen. I'll make up for it tomorrow. But please, could we possibly have some privacy now?" he said with a 'nudge-nudge, wink-wink' attitude.

You sexy devil.

"I don't know, Caleb. You know I have to report it," Jerry replied.

"Oh, come on. Give a desperate man a break. You know how long I've been single. Please? You can take it out of my allowance," Caleb tried again.

To make it all more believable, I kissed Caleb. He didn't object and took the opportunity to return the gesture. The soldier didn't leave. I heard him shuffle uneasily around the room while we continued kissing. I was glad I had grabbed the knife and there was nothing out of place in the room, other than the bowl of oranges.

"Oh, alright," he said. "I'll postpone my report for as long as I can. But you owe me your cinema visit allowance for a month."

Jerry finally left after Caleb solemnly swore he would donate Jerry his cinema visit allowance for the next two months.

"Phew! That was... unexpected," I whispered as I pushed myself off Caleb.

Why have my ears never tingled when you talked

about me?

I didn't get very far as Caleb kept his arms around my body.

"You don't have to move immediately," he said in a low voice.

Um, yes, I do, before more stupid things happen!

"I'm sorry, Caleb, but I do." My eyes went to the knife I was holding. Caleb followed my stare.

"No need," he said and let go of me. I got to my feet. I was glad he wasn't as forceful as he had been that night I had tried to kill him. I had no doubt my room was bugged, so I quickly set out to make more of the orange lights in silence. In the meantime, Caleb sat on the bed. When I had about six orange lights prepared, I took Caleb's hand and pulled him into the bathroom. I used the flushing toilet method to talk to him.

"We need to get to Sue without them noticing," I said.

"Okay, we can't go through the corridor without being seen, so it's the wall or the ceiling. What did you have in mind?" he asked.

I was so glad he was thinking with me here.

"I want to escape through the ceiling, so let's use the wall to get to Sue."

Caleb studied the wall of the bathroom. He put his hands on the tiles next to the new mirror above the sink and let his eyes wander all over the wall. It was tiled from floor to ceiling. Next, he went out into my room.

I followed him and saw he tried to figure out if the bathroom went along the entire length of the room. I quickly pulled him back into the bathroom. I kissed him while I shut the bathroom door. His lips were so soft and kissable. I pulled away to catch my breath and opened my eyes. When I did, Caleb was frowning at me.

"What?" I said.

"I have a problem understanding you, you know?" he said. "One moment you are trying to kill me, the next moment you are kissing me, and this seems to happen over and over again. What is it that you want?" He now had a cheeky grin on his face.

"I'm sorry. I don't know if they have cameras in my room too. I know they have in yours." I let go of him. I turned to look at him via the mirror.

He raised both his eyebrows. "You're kidding?"

"No, I'm not. They showed Charlie," I said. My eyes cast down, tears of anger and frustration welling up with the memory.

One day I'm going to hurt that bastard, Greene.

"I... I'm so sorry, Kate. I didn't know," Caleb whispered. He put his hand on my arm but quickly dropped it when he caught sight of my mood in the mirror. "How did he take it?"

Yeah, let's discuss Charlie's feelings on my cheating on him with you, right now.

I abruptly turned back to face Caleb.

"Caleb, I don't want to discuss this, and certainly

not with you, ever. So let's focus on the fact that we have a helicopter to catch." I didn't want to be rude to Caleb, but I was on a tight schedule here. I popped my head out of the bathroom and checked the alarm clock. We had less than half an hour. I told Caleb to use the shower cubicle to get to Sue's room. He didn't move. He just stood there, looking hurt. I felt bad for being so short-tempered with him, but I didn't have time for discussing feelings right now. I wanted to get out.

"Caleb, please. We have to hurry," I begged.

He took a deep breath and turned around. He positioned himself in the shower cubicle and threw a mighty punch at the tiles. Whether his anger was directed at me, at Charlie, or at the army, I didn't know. I didn't care at that moment.

Most of the tiles he hit came off and fell on the tiled floor, making an awful loud crashing sound. I quickly grabbed a towel and threw it on the shower floor to catch the next tiles falling. Caleb threw a couple more punches and within no time he had made a hole through to Sue's bathroom. When the dust had settled, and we looked through the hole, I saw Alex's face staring back at me.

Shit!

Resistance

The look on Alex's face was one of confusion.

"What's going on?" he asked through the hole.

I didn't answer him. I motioned for Caleb to make the hole bigger. Once it was large enough, I stepped through. Sue stood behind Alex in the doorway of her bathroom, covered in a bedsheet.

"Sue, get dressed. We're getting out," I said to her. I had expected her to move immediately, but she didn't. Her expression was bland, and she focused on Alex's back. My eyes went back to Alex. His expression changed within a millisecond. I was sure I had seen one side of his lip raised and received an instant feel of his contempt for me. However, he had quickly morphed his expression into one of concern. He turned around to Sue.

"Sue, please don't do it. It's not wise, not in your condition," he pleaded.

"Cut the crap, Alex. She's only a few days pregnant. She can do whatever she wants. You said you wanted the best for Sue. Well, that's getting out of this prison, and that's what we're doing."

In the meantime, Caleb had made the hole bigger. I heard him step through behind me.

"Sue, get dressed," I said as I shoved Alex out of the way to get to Sue. Time was of the essence. I felt relieved when Sue turned around, and I saw her get clothes from the wardrobe.

Alex grabbed me by my arm, the strength of his hand like a vice. I winced.

I'll have five nice, blue, temporary tattoos tomorrow.

"Sue isn't going anywhere," he said through his teeth.

If looks could kill, I'd be as dead as a doornail.

All of a sudden, Alex slumped to the floor. Caleb stood behind him, tossing a piece of wood from the wall studs from one hand to the other.

"Thanks, much appreciated," I said to him and let out a sigh of relief.

"I always wanted to hit the arrogant prick," Caleb grinned.

Sue came into the bathroom, dressed, and shrieked when she saw Alex lying on the floor.

"What have you done!" she yelled. She kneeled down next to him and cradled his head. I knew this was going to be hard. I hurried to close her bathroom door.

"Sue," I said, "Alex isn't 'a friendly.' I don't have time to explain, but we need to get out of here. Now!" I turned to Caleb and pointed at the ceiling.

Caleb jumped onto the basin vanity and began creating a hole in the ceiling. In the meantime, Sue was freaking out.

"No, no! Alex is good. He's kind. I don't want to go!" she cried.

I needed her to be quiet but didn't fancy dragging her unconscious body onto the rooftop. I crouched down beside her.

"Little Smudge," I said as understandingly as I possibly could. "Alex is not a half-blood as he said he was. Caleb is his father, and he knows for sure the mother was a sucker. Dr. Greene also said so. Alex is a liar. He only wants your baby for military purposes. You'll never have access to it once it's born."

Sue looked at me, frowning, minutely shaking her head.

"I'm so sorry, Little Smudge," I said as I put my hand on her shoulder.

My words made Sue's anxious face change into one filled with hate. She pushed my hand off her.

"I don't believe you. You only say that because you don't want me to have this baby. You wanted to get rid of it from the beginning."

I pinched the bridge of my nose before I spoke.

I really don't have time for this now.

"We can discuss the baby later," I said sternly. "For now, we need to get onto the roof to catch a helicopter. Your father will be risking his life trying to get you out of here."

A bit of emotional blackmail is a mother's

prerogative.

I hadn't realized Caleb had disappeared through the hole in the ceiling, but, as if on cue, he stuck his head down from it.

"Come on. It's done," he said.

I grabbed Sue by her arm and pushed her up onto the vanity. She didn't exactly co-operate, but she didn't resist either. Mentioning her father had made all the difference. As Caleb grabbed a hold of her to help her up through the hole and onto the roof, I quickly went back into my room and grabbed the bowl with our home-made candles. As an afterthought, I also slipped the contract Greene had given me in my waistband.

Back in Sue's bathroom, I stepped over Alex and climbed onto the vanity. I handed the bowl to Caleb, who moved from sight to hand it to Sue. As my stare drifted down upon Alex's body, I wished I had kicked him in the nuts. I had had enough practice lately to do it really well. Such a pity I didn't have time for frivolities like these at the moment. Caleb's arms appeared through the hole and he lifted me onto the rooftop with ease.

It was slightly windy, but the breeze wasn't too cold. I hoped we didn't need to be up here for too long as it wasn't exactly tropical either. I got busy making the lights. I poured the olive oil into the orange peels, set them alight, and distributed them in a circle around us. The wind made it tricky, but I managed to keep four lights going.

When I was done, I saw Caleb standing on the edge of the building with his arms outstretched and his head thrown back. I grinned.

He's having a Titanic moment.

He was finally enjoying the fresh, outdoor air. I went to stand beside him and joined his admiration of the starry night.

The 'Starry Night' of Van Gogh.

"Isn't it great!" Caleb said. "Feel that breeze, smell the air! I love it!" he said in exultation. "All that's missing is the smell of the sea!"

I didn't agree with him as the smell of the sea meant rotting seaweed and diesel fumes to me, but I felt happy for Caleb to be out at last.

"I've meant to ask you this for a long time," I said. "What did you do before Black October?"

Caleb didn't move, his body a statue enjoying the wind on his face. I waited patiently for his answer as I didn't want to spoil the moment for him.

"I used to be third mate on an oil tanker. I love the sea..." he said as he turned to me. His face was so full of joy. It made me happy to see him so happy. He grabbed my shoulders and said, "Kate, take me with you! Let me get out of here!"

Oh dear.

"Caleb... I... You... can't. It's not... safe..." I faltered.

He had caught me by surprise with his words. I had

been so focused on escaping with Sue that I had forgotten he wanted to be free as well. He tried to reason with me through his eyes, eyes I couldn't refuse. I had only seen them this full of life the first time we met, and a tidal wave of emotions hit me. I didn't know exactly what would happen to him if he stayed, but I knew for sure what would happen if he left. It would be a disaster. Death would follow, one way or another. I couldn't have... didn't want... I couldn't handle having that on my conscience.

Out of nowhere, I heard the crescendo of a motor. Caleb and I both looked up and saw the helicopter. Sue had spotted it too. A flicker of movement from the corner of my eye caught my attention and, with horror, I saw Alex crawling out of the hole onto the rooftop.

I pushed Caleb's hands off me and ran toward Sue. She hadn't noticed Alex yet as she was focusing on the helicopter. I dragged her away from Alex, who was fully onto the rooftop now. He must have rung the alarm as I saw a soldier stick his head through the hole. The soldier looked like Jerry. I glanced back at the helicopter. It was a huge, big, dark monster. The pilot was trying to get close to us without touching down, and the wind it was causing nearly blew me off the roof. I saw Charlie hunched in the side opening, one hand holding onto the inside, the other outstretched to us. Seeing Charlie made my heart jump.

My smile soon faded as I saw worry written all over

Charlie's face. He probably had interpreted the situation all wrong, having seen Caleb clutch my shoulders, and me jerking myself free from his grip.

"Sue, get in!" I yelled at her, trying to get my voice heard over the noise of the rotor blades. Before she could, Alex grabbed Sue's arm.

"Alex!" Sue yelled at him. "Alex, I can't stay! I love you, but you'll have to let me go!"

"You're not going anywhere, stupid cow!" He yanked her from my grip, dragging her back toward the hole.

Alex's harsh reaction was all Sue needed to convince her that my previous words hadn't been a lie. Before I could react, she booted Alex with all her might against the side of his knee, as he so thankfully had taught us. He went down with a scream, and I saw his knee twist in an unnatural position. I kept forgetting Sue was a lot stronger than the average person. Alex still hadn't let go of Sue's wrist. Fortunately, Sue had paid very good attention during Alex's demonstrations of his karate and jiu-jitsu prowess, and, with a fast turn, she twisted her body out of his grip. When she returned to face him, she made use of her momentum and kicked him hard in the head. He went down for a second time tonight.

Somebody's going to have a mother of a headache tomorrow.

Charlie was still in the helicopter urging us to get in.

I saw fear appear in Charlie's eyes as he pulled Sue into the hold of the helicopter. I turned and saw Jerry on top of the roof, his gun aimed at us. I shot my hands up to buy us some time to persuade him from doing anything foolish, but it was too late. I saw him pull the trigger. I felt myself being painfully thrown against the side of the helicopter.

Then it all went black.

Freedom

When I came to, I struggled to breathe. I was lying on my back. My heart felt as if it was being crushed between my spine and my breastbone. I felt gravity move sideways as the helicopter made a break for freedom. It was as if something was on top of me, shifting with the changing point of gravity. When I opened my eyes, I saw it was Caleb's body that was sprawled over mine. I felt the urge to throw up.

Not again!

"Kate, you hurt?" I heard Charlie yell. I didn't know. I couldn't move, but I guessed the centrifugal forces due to the erratic movements of the helicopter and Caleb's heavy body were the cause of it. I saw the search lights from the towers around the camp flicker on the interior of the helicopter, making it harder to get a bearing of what was up and down. I focussed on Caleb's body. It consumed me with horror. I closed my eyes and tried to take deep breaths to keep the bile down. Self-preservation took over after a while, and I checked all my senses to find out if I was hurt. I could move my fingers and toes. If I was injured, I didn't feel it. I smelled blood and felt it on the surface of the helicopter. Warm, sticky blood. Yes, I was nauseated, but I didn't feel myself getting any weaker. I deduced the blood must be coming from Caleb. He must have thrown himself into the line of fire to save my life. This was too much of a sacrifice. I fought to stay conscious.

"Kate, are you hurt?" I heard Charlie yell again.

"No! No, I don't think I am!" I yelled back. When the helicopter finally flew more stably, I pushed Caleb's body off me. As I rolled him over, his eyes opened, and he blinked.

Oh my god, could this guy be immortal?

There was still hope! I hurried to hoist his heavy body up, but there was no motion from his side helping me in my effort. My hands became slippery from the oozing blood. I managed to drag half of Caleb's torso onto my lap as I leaned against the wall of the helicopter hold. I caressed his face. Sue and Charlie watched me, glancing at each other now and again in wonder. I ignored them. This was not the time to explain my feelings for Caleb. I was too busy struggling with the tidal wave myself. I felt lightheaded with the realization I had more love for the man I tried to kill twice than I had ever imagined possible.

Caleb groaned.

"Caleb, stay with me!" I yelled.

He lifted one arm and put his hand on the side of my face as he looked up at me. Blood came out of his mouth. He coughed. I tried to hoist him up a bit higher.

"Caleb!" I cried.

"I... am... free now..." he managed to say. He tried to smile. He coughed again, spattering blood everywhere.

"Caleb!" Tears poured from my eyes. I clutched at him, trying to get him more upright, trying to save his dying body. I didn't want him to go like this. I put my forehead against his, and my hair fell over his face. I cried out loud. I couldn't stop myself.

"Kate..." Caleb struggled to say through his labored breathing.

In heaven's name, get your hair out of his face!

I pushed my hair behind my ears. Caleb's voice was hard to hear, and I tried to read his lips over the loud noise of the rotor blades.

"Kate..., our child..." He coughed. I wiped away the blood coming out of his mouth. "Please... let it live... in freedom."

I looked into his beautiful eyes and saw the light in them fading quickly. I threw a quick glance at Charlie. For support? For rejection of Caleb's request?

Charlie, help me! I don't know what to say!

Charlie's face was tense, but he didn't give me a hint of what he was thinking. I looked back down at Caleb. His hand had slid down next to him, but his eyes hadn't left mine. Those eyes that forever haunted me.

"I will, Caleb. I will," I whispered back. I caressed his face again. How could I show him I still loved him?

Always had, always will.

My tears fell on his face and became caught in the

skin fold of his smile. I smiled back at him. "I love you," I whispered.

There was a last glimmer in his eyes, and it was then the fire in them died for real. I closed his eyes. The realization I would never look into them again sucked my will to live out of me. The grief I felt was so overpowering. Yes, his eyes had haunted me, had given me nightmares, but only now did I realize how much they had meant to me, how much I had loved them. How much I had loved Caleb. How much he had loved me. Wailing, I collapsed over his chest, clutching his dead body. Charlie grabbed me by my arm as Caleb and I began sliding toward the open side of the helicopter as it turned direction. Caleb almost slid away from me, and I frantically flung out my free arm to grab his body. I dragged it to safety, after which I renewed my wailing.

The helicopter resumed a steady flight, and Charlie positioned himself beside me. He plucked me off Caleb's lifeless body and put his arms around me. Charlie was still there for me, picking up the pieces. As always. He was my savior, my rock to cling to in the turmoil of my life. I put my arms around him, and I cried and cried.

Escape

"Hang on, folks, we have company!" the pilot yelled after a few minutes. He began flying lower, dodging obstacles in our path. Charlie and I had to let go of each other and hold on to the helicopter in order not to be thrown out. With one hand, I grabbed on to a hold-on loop, and, with the other, I grabbed Caleb's body. I didn't want him to be lost without a proper funeral. If anything, I owed him that. I noticed Sue hanging half out of the helicopter, trying to see behind us.

"There's only one," she yelled as she, to my great relief, moved her body safely back inside.

Charlie moved closer to the pilot. "How far still?" he asked. I had no idea where they were taking us.

"Twenty minutes," the pilot replied.

Fortunately, it appeared the other helicopter only followed us. No shooting involved. I guessed they only had orders to find out where we were going. Their mission wasn't to retrieve us, the cargo being too precious to be lost during an air attack. Something Jerry appeared not to have been briefed about. We flew for another fifteen to twenty minutes in silence. Now and again, I glanced at Charlie and every time I did, I saw him watching me. It was almost creepy. I could understand why he did it though.

He's probably wondering whether there is still an elephant in the room.

I tried not to think of our relationship. There was nothing I could do about it at the moment. The most important thing right now was to get Sue as far away as possible from Alex, to get her to a safe place where they couldn't find us.

"Hang on, folks!" the pilot yelled. This time he didn't swerve too much when he ducked into a wide tunnel. The wind and noise were incredible. Halfway down the tunnel he set the machine down but kept the rotor-blades going. The following helicopter stayed hovering near the entrance.

We were met by a couple of figures on motocross bikes. They appeared from the dark side of the tunnel as if out of nothing. As they came close, I realized why they were so hard to spot. They were all dressed in black, their bikes and helmets also being matte black. Charlie, Sue, and I jumped out of the helicopter. I began pulling Caleb's body out.

"Kate, we can't take him!" Charlie yelled over the noise of the helicopter.

"I won't leave him behind!" I couldn't explain it, but wild horses couldn't keep me from taking Caleb with me.

Charlie shook his head, and then moved his hands up and down over his face. "Kate..."

One of the black-clad figures came over and took his helmet off. He was a handsome young man. His features were slim and his hair, a red-auburn color, was in need of a good haircut. I guessed he was about Sue's age. The penny dropped.

Ca ching!

The children in Julie's community were suckers! Charlie had mentioned in the Sudoku booklet they had children, and I had assumed they were normal children. How wrong had I been!

"Is there a problem?" the young man asked, subtly showing his fangs when he talked and confirming my thoughts.

"There is." Charlie sighed. "We have a dead body, and Kate wants to bring it." Charlie had never been warm toward Caleb when he was alive, for all the right reasons, and it was clear he wasn't going to change this now that Caleb was dead.

"That's okay, we can deal with it. We anticipated an extra person according to your instructions and brought an extra rider." I turned to Charlie, surprised. Charlie looked down and shuffled his feet. The handsome rider motioned for one of the other riders to come over. Another tall, black-clad figure stepped off his bike and came forward. He didn't take his helmet off, but I noticed this person had even longer hair.

They're a bunch of hippies.

When the rider was close, I realized from the wide

hips and slightly curved chest that this one was actually a female. The first rider stepped toward me and took Caleb out of the helicopter for me. He lifted him as if he was only half the weight. The female helped position Caleb on the guy's back and put Caleb's arms over his shoulders. She produced some plastic ties with which she first tied Caleb's hands together. Then, she tied his feet to the rider's feet. It was almost funny to see him walking bent over with Caleb's dead weight on his back. Once he was back on his bike, the two of them looked normal, as if Caleb was casually hitching a ride with him.

Sleeping, but alive.

That's wishful thinking, Kate.

In the meantime, the female indicated for Charlie, Sue, and me to take a seat on the back of the other bikes. I directed Sue to sit behind the female, Charlie took a seat behind another male rider, and so did I.

Before I put on the helmet they had brought for us, I saluted to the pilot of the helicopter. I didn't have time to thank him properly but wanted to let him know my appreciation for what he had done for us. I made a mental note to seek him out and thank him when all this was over. I would need to thank Major Moore as well as he was probably the one who had arranged the helicopter escape. The pilot saluted back to me. I saw him get a heavy rifle and aim it at the army helicopter. My fear for the other pilot's life was short-lived as our pilot appeared to be an extremely good shot and managed to take out the small rotor. The army helicopter began spinning, and the pilot had no choice but to put his machine on the ground. It wasn't going anywhere anytime soon.

We took off on the motocross bikes, away from the direction we had arrived from. When I glanced back, I saw our pilot exit the tunnel and fly off in another direction. If they had still been following us, they would probably have followed it on a false trail. Before long, the helicopter was out of sight, and we were relieved we weren't being followed by anybody.

Mother and Daughter Talk

The trip on the bikes was long and bumpy. We rode through forests over motocross tracks. Now and again we went over a tarred road, but most of the trip was under the cover of trees. I had no idea in what direction we were traveling. After what seemed like hours, we arrived at the edge of a lake. There stood a large, wooden cabin between the edge of the forest and the sandy shore. As soon as we stopped, the door of the cabin was flung open. A female's frame was lit from behind by the light inside the cabin. I recognized it as Julie instantly. Seeing her brought a lump to my throat. I hadn't realized how much I had missed her these last ten years. I jumped off the bike and took my helmet off as I ran up to her. We hugged, and I cried.

"Thank you so much for doing this for us," I said as I embraced her.

"It's alright, Kate. That's what sisters are for." We were both crying while laughing. We hadn't seen each other for a decade yet it felt as if I had chatted to her only yesterday. Sue and Charlie walked up to us.

"Julie, this is our daughter, Sue," Charlie said.

Sue stuck her hand out to greet Julie, but Julie flung herself around Sue's neck in a big hug. Sue was a bit taken aback by this show of emotion and looked at me for guidance. I nodded encouragingly, and Sue hugged Julie back. Julie was a complete stranger to Sue, so I could understand her hesitation. Julie took Sue's hands in hers and took a step backward.

"Let me have a look at you, you beautiful girl. You're so grown up. I'm so sorry for not being there on your birthdays, Sue," and she turned to me. "I'm so sorry, Kate. If only I had known."

"You're not the only one," I said, gesturing at the bike riders.

"Let's not get comfy on the porch, ladies," Charlie said. "Let's go inside."

Immediately I turned to look for Caleb. The riders had cut him loose and were carrying him toward the porch.

"Where do you want us to put him?" the red-haired rider asked Julie.

"Who's this? What happened?" Julie asked. She rushed to Caleb's body and checked for a pulse.

"He was shot. He's dead," Charlie said before I could answer.

"Oh, I'm sorry to hear that. Put him in the bath, please," Julie said to the riders. I frowned at her. Julie noticed and hitched up her shoulders. "I don't want him to leak on the beds," she said as a matter of fact and went in after them.

No point in arguing that.

I followed everyone inside and made sure Caleb wasn't put in an awkward position in the bath. They left me to it, but Sue joined me. She watched me cross Caleb's arms over his chest and position his head.

"Mom, what's this all about?"

Caleb's head kept falling to one side.

"I have to make sure he looks decent before rigor mortis sets in. I've told you about rigor mortis, haven't I?" Finally, Caleb's head stayed put. I straightened up.

"No, I mean you and Caleb." Sue was biting her nails while she waited for my answer.

"Oh, that. Yeah. I guess I have some explaining to do." I sat down on the edge of the bath and motioned for her to come and sit next to me. I took her hand in mine.

"It appears Caleb has been a good guy all the time. He was victim of circumstances, a pawn in Dr. Green's game. All he ever did was love me, right to the very end." I turned around to look at Caleb's body and seeing his peaceful face, his closed eyes, the eyes I would never see again, reminded me of the ultimate sacrifice he had made, and the grief for him revisited me. I couldn't stop it. The pain was debilitating, making my body sob in heaves. It was an ache I knew could only be healed by time. For now, I would need to learn to endure it. Sue embraced my shaking body as she tried to console me. She said soothing words and stroked my hair.

Woven through the pain for Caleb, I felt happy to

find myself so close to Sue. The distance which had made us strangers to each other these last few days disappeared in this moment. We were mother and daughter once again. It took me a little while before the tears stopped, and I could breathe normally enough to speak.

"Sorry, couldn't help myself there for a moment," I said as I wiped my tears away.

"That's okay, Mom. I understand," Sue said as she rubbed my back.

"I love you, Little Smudge. Dad and I love you so much. We'd never hurt you or make you do something that's not in your interest. I hope you know that."

"I do. I'm sorry for all the things I said to you. I should have listened to you." Sue began crying now, emotions finally catching up with her, and I consoled my daughter.

"Oh, silly girl. We know growing up's hard, especially in these circumstances. I'm sorry you've had to go through all this. I'm hoping it'll all be over soon." I hugged her a little tighter.

"Me, too. I've so had enough of it," she said.

We laughed as I wiped her tears away.

Julie's Story

Together, Sue and I entered the living room. It was a cozy room, with comfy looking couches and red-and-white-checkered curtains and tablecloths. An open fire was ablaze, giving off a lot of heat. The front door had just shut, and I noticed all the black-clad riders, except for the red-haired one, had vanished. As we had walked into the room, the red-haired one had walked past us and had gone into one of the bedrooms. I sat down next to Charlie on the couch and took his hand in mine. He stared at me but didn't take his hand back.

"Where are all the other riders off to?" I asked Julie. I could smell she was making coffee in the open kitchen. I didn't get an immediate reply, so I looked at Charlie. He was still looking at me, still trying to figure me out.

"They are going to patrol the perimeter," Julie said. Just in case you were being followed somehow. They will stay with you until we're absolutely sure you're safe."

While Julie was talking, I felt Charlie squeeze my hand. I glanced at him. There was so much I wanted to tell him, so much I wanted to share with him right now, but it would have to wait. I smiled at him, squeezed his hand back, and leaned slightly closer. He moved minutely closer toward me.

Julie interrupted our non-verbal communication when she handed us our cups. We had to let go of our hands to take the cups from her. She returned to the kitchen and came back with a beaker with, I assumed, blood for Sue and a cup of coffee for herself. When she finally sat down next to Sue, I couldn't contain my curiosity anymore.

"So, sucker children! You have to tell me everything!" I kicked off my shoes and changed position to lean against the side-arm of the couch. I tucked my feet under Charlie's legs to warm them, as they had gotten rather cold during the long motorbike ride. Charlie smiled and put a hand behind one of my ankles. Very subtly, he caressed the skin in the dimple next to my Achilles tendon. I tried not to shiver too obvious. The shivers were caused partly by the caresses, partly by my excitement that Charlie still cared for me.

"It's a long story if you want to hear every single detail. I'll give you the short version for now," Julie began. "As you know, I led an all-girls pack during Black October. When we hunted, we went our own ways. We often hunted together with Duncan's pack and, as is obvious, more than hunting happened. After Black October, the girls and I stuck together and, with all the funds that became available from inheritances, we bought the farm near Bullsbrook. That's where we've been ever since."

"But the children! Tell me more about the children!" I said.

"Now comes the good part," Charlie said and tapped me on my leg. He also turned to Sue with a knowing look. "Listen to this."

Julie smiled and continued her story. "A month after Black October, it was obvious most of the girls were pregnant. By that time, we had been captured by the army. You had told me how you had become a daywalker. Even though we anticipated a vaccine to turn us back to our normal state, I didn't want to take the risk of them not finding one. So, after you half-bit me without Major Moore knowing, I had all the girls half-bite each other."

"No way! So the kids are all daywalkers?" I was stunned.

"Yup! When the babies were born, we had hoped they were normal, that the army's vaccination had cured them too, but unfortunately they were still suckers. However, we did find out my bite had worked as a vaccination against the photo-sensitivity. They could be in sunlight without any ill effects," she beamed.

I couldn't believe my ears. There were others like Sue. I smiled a broad smile at Sue, and my mind pictured a wonderful future for her, with a partner and a relatively normal life.

"Why didn't you ever tell me? Why did you keep it

a secret?" I asked Julie.

"Why didn't you ever tell me about Sue?" Julie replied with an over the top 'look-who's-talking' attitude. I conceded. She continued. "You kept your secret from me for exactly the same reason I kept mine from you. I always thought Sue was a normal child as I had seen you feed her a bottle of milk. I couldn't risk you knowing about our children being suckers. I didn't know how you would react, having played such a big role in eradicating them. How was I to know?"

"Do you have a child? Am I an auntie?" I asked. The question had been on my mind from the moment I had heard there were children.

"No, I haven't," she said without batting an eyelid.

"But... you and Duncan... I thought..." I uttered. I didn't finish my sentence as I didn't want her to talk about something she didn't want to, especially not with Charlie and Sue there. It was a rather private matter. She surprised me when she explained.

"I had to keep Duncan off me with a baseball bat, so to speak. He wanted to, but I didn't. Somehow, somewhere in the back of my mind, I knew there was something wrong about him. Only later did I find out he was a control freak with megalomaniacal tendencies. I am okay with it, though, not having any children of my own I mean. I am too busy running the farm and making sure everybody else is okay. And, as we are a close-knit community, I have enough children around me not to feel left out. But I am sorry I have missed most of your growing-up, Sue." She patted Sue on her knee. "I'm so glad we can catch up now. I have heard a lot from Charlie already, but I can't wait to spend some time with you."

"I'd love to do that too, Aunt Julie, but at the moment I am exhausted," Sue said. "I really would like to catch up on some sleep, if you don't mind."

"Of course not," Julie said. "I know it's been a very long night for you guys. For me too, so let's all get tucked into bed.

Pillow Talk

Julie showed us to our room. Charlie and I got the double bed in the master bedroom while Sue and Julie slept on the couches in the living room. I hugged and kissed Sue goodnight, then turned around to Julie.

"Thanks again, sis, for saving us. You have no idea what it means to me."

"You're welcome, Kate. I love you too." We hugged. I had a lot of hugging to catch up on. Before I left the room, I suddenly remembered a question on my mind.

"Whose cabin's this, if you don't mind me asking?"

"It's Abby and Enrique's. You know, the couple from the Celtic Frog?"

Of course I remembered them well. Charlie and I had often spent our Friday nights in their bar when we had organized Harry and Rhona to babysit Sue. How A&E, as was our nickname for them, knew Julie, I didn't know, but I kept that question for another time. For now, I was happy it didn't belong to someone who could easily be traced back to us and dragged into this horror story.

When I returned to the master bedroom, I found Charlie already tucked in. The bedside light was still on, which only meant one thing, and it wasn't sex. I used the bathroom and saw he had put out pajamas for me. I didn't recognize them. They were new ones and had a Dracula print. It made me smile.

Forever the funny one, Charlie.

Back in the bedroom, I slid between the sheets and cuddled up to Charlie.

As I lay my head on his chest, he put his arm around me and stroked my shoulder tenderly.

"Now please tell me what happened between you and Caleb," he said. There was no jealousy in his voice, no spite, only curiosity. I looked up at him. "I won't let you sleep until you tell me."

I kissed his chest and sighed. "I owe you that. Where should I begin?"

"How about at the beginning?" he suggested.

"Okay, from the beginning it is. I know you're not going to like some parts, or believe any of it, but hear me out please."

"I will," he said and kissed my head.

I had never mentioned my feelings for Caleb to Charlie after Black October. There had been no need to as we both believed Caleb to be dead. Now was the time to bare my soul, without holding back. I was sure that if I didn't tell him now, there would never be another opportunity, he would never understand me fully, and our relationship would never be restored to what it was before.

If it ever could be.

So, I told Charlie all, including the new information I had only gathered these last few days. I told him about my feelings for Caleb, how they had fluctuated over time and how it ended in a tidal wave of love when he gave his life to save mine. Charlie listened without interrupting.

"I never wanted to hurt you. Part of me wished I had never met Caleb, yet part of me is glad that I did."

My throat was swelling from all the emotion, and I found it hard to breathe. I felt Charlie's chest get wet from my tears. Charlie must have felt it too as he put both his arms around me and hugged me tenderly. When he loosened his arms, I lifted my head and our lips found each other. We kissed, a long and passionate kiss. I was so happy and sad at the same time. I was sad because Caleb didn't get to have the future he so deserved to have, and yes, I was happy because Charlie still loved me. After all we had been through, after all I had put him through, he still loved me. But there was one more issue to bring up, one more red-hot poker to torture him with. I broke the contact between our lips.

"Smudge," I said and propped myself up on my elbows, so I could properly look him in the eye. "What about Caleb's child? What about the promise I made?"

I didn't want to tell him whether I wanted to keep the promise or not. I needed to hear his thoughts before I made a decision. I couldn't force this child on him; that would be unfair. I was of the opinion that raising a child is not a decision you make on our own unless you are willing to do it on your own. So I waited for his answer.

"What promise?" Charlie said.

Oh shit, he didn't hear it over the noise of the helicopter, of course.

I had to make a split decision. Would I tell him about Caleb's request or keep quiet about it? I believed I didn't really have a choice if I wanted my relationship with Charlie to work.

"Just before Caleb died, in the helicopter, Caleb asked me to let his child live in freedom. I... I said I would."

Charlie looked away. Time ticked by. After what seemed like forever, he faced me again. "Give me more time to think on it before I give you an answer."

"Don't take eight months," I smiled carefully.

Charlie sighed, and I was afraid I had pushed it too far.

"Don't worry, I won't," he said with a short smile and kissed me.

He turned off the light and fell asleep in no time. It took me longer to fall asleep. We were safe now, but there were still so many things to think about. Lying next to Charlie though, hearing his snoring, felt soothing and familiar. It helped me drift off sooner than I expected.

***

When I awoke, the birds were chirping outside, and the sun shone high through the window. Charlie was lying on his back next to me, still snoring. I watched him breathe and wondered why he still loved me. I softly kissed his shoulder, and he stopped snoring. For a moment, I was afraid I had woken him, but he turned toward me and continued sleeping. I examined his face; his bushy eyebrows, his cute nose, and the stubble on his chin. How I wanted to rasp my nails over it.

Not that I have long enough nails to do so these days.

I became aware Charlie had opened his eyes and was watching me. We didn't move or say anything. Charlie broke the silence after a while.

"Did you ever regret you chose to be with me?"

"Never," I said without hesitation. It was the truth. I blurted the word out without a thought, and I felt the need to explain why. "Of course I have thought about what would've happened if Caleb and I had gotten together ten years ago. But it didn't happen, so there's no use crying over spilled milk. I compare my getting together with Caleb to trying on a pretty dress. For a moment, it looked nice on me. I felt good wearing it, made me feel on top of the world. But I knew I couldn't ever buy it. Given the choice, I'd rather have the jeans I can wear every day of the year, not the dress I could only wear at Christmas. My life with you has been magical. Unlike Caleb, you have stood by me through thick and thin. You never gave up on me. A peace comes over me by just being in your presence. We have the most adorable daughter, and you are a wonderful father. I have never wished for my life to be any different. I love you."

The fact that I had been with Caleb once didn't mean I wanted to spend the rest of my life with him. Never, ever, had it come into my mind to leave Charlie for Caleb. I still racked my brain about why I had cheated on Charlie. I never wanted to hurt him, never wanted to leave him. Charlie didn't say anything. As always, he took it in silently. So I assumed it was my turn.

"Why do you still love me?" I asked. It was a question that had been bugging me ever since my betrayal. I hadn't been able to find an answer, only reasons why not.

Charlie began singing. "You are my sunshine, my only sunshine. You make me happy, when skies are gray..."

I poked him in the ribs, and he laughed.

"Seriously, why?"

"Don't you want me to?" he asked, his face also serious now.

"Of course I do, Smudge. I want you to with all my heart. I just don't understand it."

"I've told you. I fell in love with you the moment I first met you. From that day onward, I've only loved you more and more with every moment I spent in your company. That's a lot of lovin' accumulated over ten years. How in heaven's name can I suddenly stop loving you?"

I pondered his words. It was exactly why I loved him. We had been friends before we became lovers. And every day I had come to know him better, I had grown to love him more and more. With all my heart. My love for Caleb was different. That was more of a primal love, based on instinct. I didn't know Caleb as well as I knew Charlie, yet my love for him was as deep as that for Charlie. How could I have ever loved both of them without hurting the other?

"I know there's stiff competition, but *I'm* not a quitter," Charlie said.

I blinked as I repeated his words in my head. It took a while before they sunk in.

Did he just say what I think he said?

I lifted my head to look at Charlie properly. He seemed serious. Suddenly, he stifled a chuckle, immediately trying to look serious again. His eyes met mine, and it was enough to send us both into a laughing fit. When I had my breathing under control, I playfully slapped his chest.

"You're terrible," I said, trying to sound stern.

"I'm sorry. I couldn't help myself," Charlie said. "I

meant no disrespect." He pulled me close and hugged me tenderly. I let myself be hugged and drank in his closeness. It was another reason why I loved him so much. We had the same sense of humor.

We let go of each other, and I stroked his upper arm. Since our first night in the same bed together it had become our secret message to indicate we wanted the other. I put my hand down and waited for his response. Although he said he loved me, I didn't know if he could make love to me after all that had happened. I wanted him to know I still wanted him. I wanted him to know I was ready for our relationship to resume. If he wasn't, I would wait until he was.

To my surprise, he stroked my arm. I smiled while tears welled up in my eyes. Charlie lifted my chin and smiled the sweetest smile at me.

Our love-making was romantic and full of passion. Even though I cried, I thought I was the luckiest woman alive.

Abby's Story

By the time we came out of the bathroom and were dressed, Sue and Julie were already up. I was grateful Charlie had brought clothing for Sue and me. It meant I didn't have to walk around with Caleb's blood on my clothes, reminding me every minute of the tragic event. We were having a bite to eat when we heard a car arrive and park outside.

Before I could panic, Julie said, "That'll be Abby and Enrique."

I frowned. I didn't want to put any people in more danger than necessary. I had learned my lesson ten years ago.

Why are they coming here, putting themselves in danger? What's the term again? Guilty by association?

"Don't worry," Julie reassured me when I rose from my chair. "They're already involved, out of their own free will, and for longer than you think. They're eager to meet you."

The door opened and, sure enough, Abby and Enrique walked in. Abby was a tall woman, taller than Enrique, who was of average height for a man. She was also what one would call 'a voluptuous' woman, her red, long hair and full lips adding to her attraction. Enrique was quite the opposite. His appearance was plain and could easily be forgotten. I couldn't stop myself from smiling seeing the owners of the A&E. It brought back many good memories of the time Charlie and I had spent in their bar.

At the same time, I was amazed that these people were letting us stay here. Yes, we had known them for ten years, but we had seen them less than once a week and had spoken only a few sentences to them on those evenings, usually comprising an order of beer and some nibbles. Julie had said they were involved, but to what degree? Did they know the whole truth? Did Julie tell them a lie? I would have to guard my words until I knew for sure.

Julie and Abby kissed and hugged. It was obvious they had known each other for a lot longer than these last few days. Then Abby turned to me.

"How are you holding up, love?" she asked as she greeted me with an embrace. "You've been through so much!"

"I'm okay. I'm coping. Thank you for letting us stay here. We appreciate what you're doing for us." I didn't know what else to say.

"It's nothing, darling. We're glad we could help. And this must be Sue," Abby said as she turned to Sue, who was standing half behind me. "You're a gorgeous looking girl! It's a shame your parents had to keep you away from us all these years. Tony's girlfriend would have had some competition." Abby winked at me. "What do you think of our son? Isn't he a hunk?" Her question was directed at Sue.

"Tony?" was all Sue could manage.

"Don't tell me you don't remember him. He's the handsome one! He's probably hiding in his room right now."

There was a moment of awkward silence as everybody re-lived last night.

"Of course, the red hair," I blurted out. "The tall, handsome lad is your son!"

Abby laughed, looking at Enrique who also smiled a broad smile at my words. "Yes, that's the one. And yes, he's our son, but it has nothing to do with my red hair."

"Please sit down first while I make you some coffee," Julie said. "You've had a long drive."

I was perplexed. What story would we be going to hear now? Enrique hugged me too and shook Charlie's hand. We all sat down on the couches, and Abby began telling her story.

"Enrique and I were able to stay in hiding when the sucker attacks happened in Bullsbrook. Our pub's cellar is very well protected against intruders and we were safe, along with a couple of our patrons. When it was all over, life went back to normal, at least for a couple of months. Then one morning, I found this cute little baby, all bundled up, on my doorstep. There was no note, no nothing, only the little babe in its onesie, wrapped in a blanket. I could tell it was a very young baby, only a day or so old.

"As Enrique and I never could conceive one of our own, we were happy to take care of it until we found the parents. But before I could report it, we found out this was no ordinary baby, oh no. It didn't want to drink any milk. Enrique put two and two together and tried to feed it blood from himself. Of course, it would gladly take that, I tell you! This was a sucker child!"

Abby's story-telling was very entertaining. Her voice went up and down with the moods in her sentences and her expressions were almost comical. Her enthusiasm and happiness were very contagious, and I bit my bottom lip to try not to laugh out loud.

"We didn't know what to do. I mean, we serve Bloody Marys but not any real blood. That's when I thought of getting in touch with your lovely sister here. I knew she'd taken over the big farm not long before. I contacted her to find out if she was able to discretely provide me with some cattle blood. I was desperate to keep the little one alive as I thought he was a godsend to us.

"Your sister, however, wasn't born yesterday and soon figured out it was for a sucker baby. She told me I was not alone. It was then that she showed me the crèche they were running at the farm. I couldn't believe my eyes when Julie told me they were sucker babies. Can you imagine? A whole bunch of sucker babies! Our problems were solved. There was, of course, one difference between our Tony and the other babies. Tony's not a daywalker. He can only go out at night."

Enrique put his hand on Abby's back when she mentioned it. It was obvious that Tony's photosensitivity was a burden on their lifestyle. Abby continued.

"During the day, I would keep Tony inside at home. As soon as the sun went down, I would bring him to the farm. The girls were only too happy to take care of him while we were working at the bar."

"And that's the story of how Tony became our son," Enrique said.

"Wow! That's an amazing story. He's one lucky sucker!" I smiled. I meant it. Tony's fate could have been a lot worse. Heaven knows what other people had done with sucker babies. "Are there any others? I mean, besides Tony and the pack girl's children?" I looked from Abby to Julie.

"Not that we know of," Julie said. "But that doesn't mean a thing. We all tried to keep our children a secret. There must be so many more out there, struggling to stay under the radar."

The truth of Julie's words weighed heavily upon me. I knew all too well what it meant to live with a secret sucker child in the house. Our Sue was a daywalker, so life had been relatively easy for us. The challenge of hiding a nightwalker would be exponentially worse.

Something had to be done for these children. They shouldn't be kept in hiding any longer.

Or should they?

"What about their mental state?" I thought out loud.

They all stared at me, frowns and questions on their faces. I had changed the subject a bit too abruptly for them to follow.

"I mean, a lot of suckers are egocentric megalomaniacs. Are the children like that too?"

Julie, Abby, and Enrique continued to stare at me.

"I'm sorry," I said. "Let me explain. Most suckers I knew, Duncan, Sasha, Caleb, Alex…Hell, even you, Julie, you all thought suckers were better than the unbitten, and you wanted to eradicate them. When Sue was little and went to kindergarten, she was a bully, thinking she was superior to the other children. Surely the virus is making your children act the same?"

It was Julie who answered.

"Kate, you know your own daughter. Do you believe she thinks she's better than others?"

I looked at Sue. Sue stared back at me, eyes wide and eyebrows raised. I knew she didn't expect me to say yes.

"No, of course not, but she's a half-blood."

"Well, our children are quite well-behaved too. Remember that we raised them together. They were brought up as equals. And the girls never let them get away with anything. They taught the children to respect them for what they are, their mothers, but also unbitten humans. It's like with all children; you reap what you sow."

"Phew, that's a load off my mind, I was afraid we were heading for another Black October soon," I said as I slumped back in my seat.

Everyone laughed as they apparently thought it was funny.

Cremation

While we cleaned up the breakfast table, I realized we needed to deal with Caleb. His body was beginning to smell. The warm temperatures in the cabin were probably speeding up the decomposition.

"We need to burn Caleb," I said to Charlie.

He nodded. "Yes, he's a real stinker."

I began frowning at Charlie for talking about the dead like that again but couldn't help beginning to giggle. I guess it was my body's natural response to all the stress. When we suggested burning Caleb to the others, they all agreed. We set out to gather as much firewood as possible. The riders, who had been up all night and morning, took the opportunity to use the bed and couches for a nap while we were out. By the time it was late afternoon, we had a decent enough pile of wood on the lake's shore. Charlie and I asked the others, including Sue, to take strategic positions away from the cabin as lookouts, to keep nosey people out. It seemed a rather quiet piece of forest, but people have a tendency to show up at the most inappropriate moments.

The real reason I asked them to leave was that I didn't want them to attend the burning of Caleb, the guy who was supposed to be the enemy. I didn't know how they would react to my falling apart over his death as I was sure was going to happen. I knew Sue would understand, but I didn't want her to witness something as horrible as the burning of a body at her age.

When we were sure we were alone, Charlie and I carried Caleb's body outside and began our attempt to put him onto the funeral pyre. It was a bit of a hassle as the body handled like a mega-sized bag of potatoes. It was heavy and cumbersome. Charlie was short, and I was not tall by any standard, so we struggled to get his tall frame on top of the high stack of wood. I was so glad the others couldn't see us as it was not a pretty sight.

At some stage, Caleb's top half fell over Charlie, who was trying to keep his hips in place as I tried to lift the feet on the top of the stack. It looked as if they were in an intimate No. 69 position. I couldn't suppress a laugh when I saw it, at which Charlie made it very clear he wanted me to move the body immediately, asap, please, thank you very much.

We finally managed to get all parts of Caleb's body on top of the wood stack at the same time. I even climbed the pyre to arrange his arms and legs, so it didn't look as if a giant bird had dropped him on a makeshift nest. Rigor mortis was setting in which made it difficult, but with some determination, I managed.

I was sitting on top of Caleb's body to arrange his arms and head, and when I looked down at Caleb's face,

I thought I saw him smile. I recalled he had been smiling when he died after I had promised him to keep our child. The emotion that accompanied that promise took a hold of me. I collapsed forward onto Caleb's body, engulfed in another breakdown. My forehead touched Caleb's like that day in the ladies' toilet when he declared his love for me. More memories of my time with Caleb came rushing in. They were very vivid and so much more painful than daggers. I let myself go completely as I knew it would be better for the healing process. I wailed and sobbed, tears and snot mixing on my face. After a few minutes, I pulled myself together. I told myself Caleb was gone now, and Charlie was waiting for me. I sat up and breathed deeply a few times. After I wiped the wetness of my face, I leaned forward, and I kissed Caleb's forehead lightly. I took a minute to study his face for the last time. I didn't have a photo of Caleb, and I wanted to be able to describe our child what his or her father looked like. If I was going to keep the baby. That still wasn't decided. I sighed and carefully climbed down.

In the meantime, Charlie had poured fuel around the pyre. I don't know what stank more, Caleb or the fuel. We were now standing next to the pyre, and Charlie handed me the matchbox.

"Are you going to say something?" he asked.

"I suppose I should." I took a deep breath. This was heavy stuff. Together with Maxine and Julie, I had attended the funeral of our parents, but this was so different. Now, together with my lover and father of my child, I was going to burn my other lover and father of my other child.

Awkward!

"Have you thought about it yet?" I asked Charlie without looking at him. I hoped he knew what I was talking about.

"I have," he replied.

I spun around to him, my eyes wide with excitement and anticipation. Every part of me was begging him to tell me his answer. Charlie shrugged.

"I said to you, after you told me you had been with Caleb, that I hoped he gave you something I couldn't give you. Maybe he gave something to the both of us. The two of us can't have any more children. This child isn't mine, but it's half yours and you made it in an act of passion. I'm sure I could love the child."

I didn't know if my heart stopped or pounded twice as fast, but I dropped to my knees and stared at Charlie. He took my face in his hands and kissed me. I had a bit of trouble kissing him back as I couldn't get rid of this huge grin on my face. I also began to cry again.

Geez, I'm such a crybaby these days!

Charlie wiped the tears from my face.

"We're going to have another baby," I whispered and hugged him so tight that we nearly lost our balance.

"Wow, careful!" he said while he tried to get me

back on my feet. "Come on, let's get this over and done with."

I rose to my feet and tried to compose myself. Tears kept on coming, so I gave up trying to wipe them away.

"Dear Lord, Neptune." Charlie turned his head to me when I said that. I quickly glanced at him from the corner of my eyes but continued with my speech. "Please accept Caleb's free spirit. He was a beautiful man in body and mind, caught by misfortune for being in the wrong place at the wrong time. Please... let him know that he was loved... and his spirit will live on in his child... whom we... will love as our own... Amen."

"Amen," Charlie said, barely audible.

My words had come out less and less clear as I struggled to talk. Crying while trying to speak didn't work well. After my speech, I held my hands in front of my face to prevent Charlie from seeing my distorted mouth and quivering lips.

Charlie gently took the matchbox from me and lit the funeral pyre. We both stepped back fast as the flames whooshed through the wood stack. It radiated an enormous amount of heat. Once the flames took hold of the body, there was still plenty of wood to burn. I was glad we didn't need to get more wood to cover a half-burned body.

Charlie took my hand, and we stood there for what seemed like ages. When the body was beyond recognition, and the pyre began to fold in on itself,

Charlie let go of me. He put his hand on my back for a second before walking off into the woods. I heard him get back with the others and go into the cabin. Not long after, the three riders came out of the cabin and departed on their bikes.

I stayed outside with Caleb. I didn't want him to be alone. I knew he was dead and that his body was gone, but still. If there was a god or some sort of spiritual life after we passed away, I wanted to make sure they knew I had cared for Caleb.

Outburst

By the time the fire began dying, it was already dark. I heard sounds of motocross bikes nearing just before I heard the cabin door open. Julie called to me. I turned around and saw her anxious face. The motor sounds appeared to be coming from the three black-clad bike riders. I still didn't know their names. The red-haired one's name was Tony, but nobody had mentioned the names of the others. There was the tall female one, who Sue had hitched a ride with that morning. And then there were the two male ones who had carried Charlie and me.

The riders arrived at the cabin full throttle and made the sand fly up as they braked. One of them took off his helmet. His hair was dark, also half-long like Tony's, his features handsome. I guessed him to be of local Native American descent. I couldn't help wondering if all sucker children were pretty by nature. My wandering thoughts were hauled back to the present as I didn't like the look on his pretty face.

"They're coming!" he yelled.

Holy shit!

I ran inside, following Julie. I heard Abby waking Tony. Sue, Charlie, and I didn't know what to do. We stood in the middle of the room, looking at each other. I didn't want to get any of these other people hurt. When Tony strode into the room, you could feel his presence. Everyone turned to him, and he immediately took control of the situation.

"Sue, Kate, Charlie, get on the bikes," he commanded.

He had this unexplained air of authority about him, and we obeyed him. The Native American rider told Tony that the enemy also rode on motocross bikes.

"Great!" was all Tony said. I thought I saw a smile on his face before he donned his helmet. I wished I was as confident as Tony.

Sue climbed on the back of the Native American rider's bike, and I took a seat behind the girl. I thought it would be best to let Tony be the leader of this escape without the burden of any of us on his bike. Charlie climbed on the bike of the fourth rider. When this one tried to start his motor, it made a pathetic sound and didn't start. The sound of the other motocross bikes came closer and closer. The rider tried a couple more times, but his bike refused to cooperate. My stomach cramped, and dread filled my being.

Charlie jumped off and ran to me. He put his hand on my knee.

"Go! Just go!" he said.

Without further ado, Tony gave the signal, and we sped away, making large sprays of sand. Holding on for dear life to the girl, I turned my head and saw Charlie get smaller and smaller as we got away. So often I had seen Charlie disappear from my life, but it hurt every time.

I had no idea where we were going or what the plan was. We hadn't discussed this situation, assuming we had not been followed on the bikes the night before and thinking they didn't know where we were.

As we turned a corner, I managed another glance backward to check if we were indeed being followed. My heart sank when I saw the riders in the distance. We took a couple more turns through the forest and then, to my surprise, on the top of an outcrop, Tony stopped. The other riders positioned themselves next to Tony. They were waiting for our pursuers to catch up. The woods were dark and misty, and it all gave a spooky feeling. I didn't feel like hanging around there at all. Irritated, I threw open my visor.

"Why are we stopping?" I yelled. "We need to get away!"

Tony didn't move. He waited until the other riders were close. When the six riders came within about ten yards from us, they stopped.

The person who appeared to be the leader of the pursuing posse took his helmet off. It was Alex.

Shit, when did he learn to ride a bike?

And how did his knee heal so fast?

Words that Caleb had said to me in the corridor

suddenly replayed in my head. I had told him he was never getting out and he had said 'the others have been.' Why had I not listened to him then? I turned around to Sue. She had also lifted her visor. Her eyes were narrowed, and it was clear to me, to my great relief, that she didn't have any amorous feelings for Alex anymore.

"Sue, get off that bike and come with us," Alex commanded.

She took off her helmet, shook her hair free.

How is it possible I created such a beautiful being?

"Alex, do I have to beat you up again before you will get the message? I will never be with you again! You don't love me. You only used me to create your fucking army. Why don't you get it into your thick skull that I hate you and won't be a part of your fucking breeding program? I'm not keeping this fucking baby! So fuck off!"

The rider who was carrying her turned his head to look at her. I, too, had to do a double-take of my little girl. During her upbringing, I'd been able to avoid swearing in front of her, despite Rhona's bad influence, but she had picked it up with ease these last few days. She appeared to have a passion for it.

Slightly overdoing it and using a small vocabulary, but nothing a lesson or two can't amend.

"Okay, if that's the way you want it, so be it. You're going to come with us tonight, one way or another. And your bitchy mother too," Alex said, and he moved to put his helmet back on.

Bitchy? You haven't seen me bitchy yet!

Tony decided to remove his helmet.

"Don't be too cocky," he said to Alex.

Tony was not a man of many words, but when he talked, it counted. Alex decided to divert his eyes from Sue and studied Tony. Tony showed off his fangs in a wicked grin. I turned to see Alex's reaction, but the greatest reaction to Tony's revelation came from Alex's followers. Each one of them tried to verify with the other pack members that what they had seen was real. Alex hadn't moved. He had turned a slightly lighter shade of pale, if that was possible, but he didn't show any concern otherwise.

"You are no match for us," Alex said. "We have been trained for combat."

Cocky indeed.

"Not in these woods, not on these tracks," Tony said. He nodded to Sue and put his helmet on. Sue also put her helmet back on.

Before I knew it, we were speeding away from Alex and his pack, who were immediately in hot pursuit.

It appeared Tony and his friends had trained in these woods all of their lives. They knew the track by heart. Every bend, every dip, every branch. I could tell by all the accelerations, breaks, and turns that we made that it wasn't an easy track to follow. I had counted six pursuers, including Alex, and heard two of them crash during the chase.

When we arrived at a clearing at the end of the track, Tony turned his bike around and waited. My rider and Sue's copied. Alex and the three remaining goons stopped at the other side of the clearing. Tony took his helmet off again.

"Two down, four to go," he said to Alex.

I spun my head and saw Alex's face turn bright red. I saw his cheeks move with the air passing through his clenched jaw. He probably never had any real competition at the compound. He jumped off his bike and threw his helmet aside.

"Come on then. You and me! Show me what you've got!" he yelled. He strode to the middle of the clearing, pounding his chest.

I expected Tony not to go for this macho stuff, and that he would lead us out of here now Alex wasn't in a position to follow us immediately. Tony, however, laughed and jumped off his bike.

Why???!!!

Because male testosterone will always win out.

I feared for Tony's life. I was sure he was going to be slaughtered. Alex had been in combat training for years. I had seen proof of it. What was Tony thinking? We had come so far, and now Tony was going to ruin it all with this stupid macho behavior.

As they circled each other, I studied them both. Tony didn't seem insecure at all. He was dressed in his black, leather outfit, looking like a ninja. Alex wore a dark camouflage army outfit. I checked if he carried any weapons but didn't see anything other than a weird metal collar around his neck.

I thought about the three other pursuers. Alex could be distracting Tony to let the others get to us. My gaze shifted to what was happening beyond the two fighters, where the three bike riders were parked next to each other. To my surprise, they were sitting on their bikes, intently watching the fight between Tony and Alex which had commenced in all fury.

Tony wasn't doing badly in the fight. It dawned on me that a sucker kindergarten wasn't the only thing Julie had organized for the children. Tony seemed to be very well trained in martial arts. I didn't know any particular moves but could tell karate from judo. They were using moves from both of them and a heap more. They were chopping, jumping, kicking, pushing, shoving, and wrestling. It was a tough fight, and if I had any money to place a bet, I wouldn't know who to put it on. Tony and Alex appeared to be of equal prowess and strength.

I turned in the hope of getting Sue's attention, but she, like the others, was absorbed in the fight. She had taken her helmet off to see the action better. I wished she hadn't as I hoped we could get out of here before the others noticed.

Suddenly, I heard a heart-piercing scream, and my

head spun back to the fight. I saw Alex twist Tony's arm in what looked like an extremely painful and unnatural way. My heart sank. Tony fell to the ground.

Everything went into slow-motion. Alex let go of Tony and took large strides toward Sue. Sue's rider tried to kick-start his bike. His reaction was too late. Alex grabbed Sue's wrist and yanked her off the bike. The rider tried to grab Sue's arm in an attempt to save her but missed. I saw my baby being dragged away by Alex. Sue struggled with all her might, but she was no match for him. Anger rose inside me, fueled by my hate for this boy. I jumped off the bike and ran after Sue. When I reached her, about halfway down the clearing, I grabbed Alex's free arm. With it, he tried to push me off. His swing, however, was expected. I held on to his arm, pivoted my body upside down while standing on one leg, and hit Alex's throat with a mighty kick. I had paid good attention during his self-defense lesson. Nobody anticipated what happened next.

Alex let go of Sue and me and stumbled backward. There was an audible click. Lights flashed on the collar around Alex's neck. His eyes went alarmingly large. He put both his hands on the collar.

Then his head exploded.

Tracking

When the pressure wave had passed, I scrambled to Sue. We had both fallen away from Alex's body. Like me, she was covered with bits of Alex's head. I was sure I could distinguish parts of his brain. I took off my helmet. After wiping Sue's face clean, I took it in my hands.

"Are you okay, Sue? Are you hurt?" I could hardly hear my own voice over the ringing noise in my ears.

She sat up and pointed at her ears, and I realized she also had been too near to the explosion. Her ears would have been more affected as she hadn't been wearing a helmet. I could only hope it was temporary. I checked over the rest of her body, and when I couldn't see any damage, I threw myself around her neck in a big hug.

Thinking about her safety made me realize there were still three riders to be concerned about. I turned to find them. They had stepped off their bikes and had taken off their helmets. All three of them were touching their collars, having petrified looks on their faces. I knew they weren't going to be a problem to us anymore.

The Native American rider came up to Sue and lent her a hand getting up. He took off his helmet.

"Are you okay?" he asked.

Sue took him in. I did the same but in a motherly way. He had a well-proportioned, muscular body. His expression was kind and worried. I didn't know if Sue could hear him, but she understood his question and nodded. He kept his hand on Sue's arm as he helped me up as well. I thanked him and turned to Tony. He was up again, clutching his shoulder. His arm dangled from his shoulder in an unnatural position. The girl who had been my rider stood opposite him. From the intimacy of their kiss, it appeared she was his.

I decided I had to do something about our pursuers and walked up to the army lads, who were still in shock.

"You have two choices," I said. "Either you go back to where you came from and get your head blown off one of these days," and I made individual eye contact with them to make sure they knew I wasn't kidding, "or you come with us and you can be free men."

They didn't need much persuasion. The three of them agreed to come with us and thanked me for the opportunity.

I turned around to see Sue's rider on a walkie-talkie. He told Julie to come and pick us up. Within ten minutes, she and Charlie arrived in A&E's 4WD terrain wagon.

"Bloody hell, what happened here?" Charlie said when he saw Alex's decapitated body, missing hands, and the blood and gore on Sue and me.

"It was Mom who saved me," Sue said loudly. I was

glad her hearing was coming back. The rider next to her smiled and picked another piece of Alex's brain out of her hair.

"What's your name?" she asked, tucking her hair behind her ear and tipping her head slightly sideways.

"The name's Marlon, my fair lady," he said, and to everybody's surprise he took Sue's hand and kissed it while bowing deeply. Sue looked at me. She was blushing, but I saw that twinkle in her eyes.

Charlie took me by the arm and guided me away from the group for a moment.

"You okay?" he asked me.

"Yeah, I'm fine. Shocked, but I'll live. Poor Alex won't though," I sighed, looking in the direction of his headless body. "Apparently they've been fitted with electronic collars that detonate when they're tampered with. Alex disarmed Tony and dragged Sue away. I kicked him in the throat to stop him, and that's when it happened. The other poor lads are petrified it'll happen to them. It's inhumane. I can't believe they've done this. Surely it's against the law. It's a modern form of slavery."

My hands became fists, and if I had had long nails, I would have made myself bleed. Greene had really crossed another line. This time, I had witnesses.

"But how did they know where to locate us? That's what I don't understand. I am sure we weren't followed from the tunnel," Charlie said.

He had a point. How the hell did they find us?

"A tracker, they must have placed a tracker on us. Could be in our clothes," I said. "Or..." and I turned to look at Sue.

"No!" Charlie said, "You think..."

"It's a possibility," I replied.

I knew it wasn't planted in Sue's gut as the operation had been too long ago for a tracker to be still in her system. Apart from the fact I had followed intently what the surgeon was doing via the screen. They had, however, put numerous needles in her during the time we had been there. One of them could easily have put something in, instead of taking blood out.

I walked back toward Sue and asked her to show me her arms. She said she was fine, so I had to ask again. She frowned but did as I asked. As soon as she had taken her jacket off, I began feeling her skin from her hands up to her wrists, her elbows, and when my search arrived at her upper arms, I found it. There was something hard and elongated under her skin on the inside of her left arm.

"What's this, Sue? Did they tell you when they put it in?" I asked.

"It's... it's a tracker, they said. It tracks my hormone levels, they said."

I looked at Charlie and he didn't hesitate to give me his pocket knife.

"Jules, can you take a picture of this please?" I asked.

Julie was taking photos with her cell phone of Alex's decapitated body. As she turned to us, she asked what I wanted her to photograph. I pointed at Sue's arm, and she began clicking away.

"What are you going to do?" Sue asked rather worried when she saw me pull out the knife blade.

"It's a tracker, Sue, but it doesn't track your hormones. It tracks your whereabouts. That's how they found us. I'm going to take it out, so they can't locate us anymore. Put your teeth together."

Sue did as I asked and clenched poor Marlon's arm when I nicked her skin with the knife. I pushed the little electronic device out. It looked like a capsule with miniature electronics in it. It showed a little flashing light. I gave it to Charlie, who let Julie take photos of it. Charlie put the tracker on a rock and stamped his boot on it. He crushed it completely.

"You better check the lads as well," I said.

Marlon and Charlie went over to them and they were only too willing to be checked. Unfortunately, there weren't any electronic devices on their bodies apart from their collars.

"I'm sure there'll be trackers in the collars," I said.

"This complicates things," Tony said, still holding his arm which was in a normal position now. I had seen the girl pull on his arm moments before. I imagined it would still be very sore. "We can't take them with us now."

We all looked at them. The poor lads were looking desperate.

All dressed up and no place to go.

I didn't like it, but someone had to say it.

"We're sorry guys, but it seems you can't come with us after all. Your collars probably have trackers in them, and we won't be able to get them off right now, not without the possibility of blowing your head off. So, go back to where you came from, for now. We will do everything in our power to get you free. What Greene's doing is wrong, and you shouldn't be prisoners. But go with the flow for now. The only way you can help yourselves is by helping us. Get your fallen buddies from the track and go back."

I knew they didn't really have a choice, but it still surprised me when they agreed. I had expected at least one of them to fall on his knees and beg us to take him with us, but they all got back onto their bikes.

"Wait!" Julie said.

She quickly took some photos of each of their collars. Then they drove off, leaving Alex's remains.

So much for your precious band of brothers, Alex.

We put Alex's body in the back of the wagon, and Charlie and I climbed in the backseat. I was exhausted and leaned my head on Charlie's shoulder. We waited for Sue to get in, but she told us she'd taken up the offer to go back with Marlon. It made me smile. Julie drove us back to the cabin in silence.

Happiness

Back at the cabin, everybody went inside. The threat was gone. Even though I was tired, I decided to stay outside and watch the last remaining glowing logs of Caleb's funeral pyre die out. After a few minutes, Charlie came to stand beside me. He handed me my cardigan. It was the one I had knitted a few years ago with the wool he had given me for Christmas. I gladly took it from him and put it on.

"You ready?" Charlie asked.

"Yeah, almost," I said. "I want to collect his ashes, so I can put him out to sea again.

Charlie looked at me with a question on his face.

"He used to work on a big oil tanker."

"Is that right?"

"Yeah. He told me when we were on the rooftop, just before you picked us up."

Both of us stared into the dying embers.

"Explains the Neptune comment," Charlie said after a while.

I smiled at the memory. Charlie patted me on my butt, turned, and walked back to the cabin. When he returned again, he had a pan and brush with him as well as a roll of aluminum foil and a cake tin.

"A cake tin?" I said.

"Sorry, Abby doesn't want him in her Tupperware. The ashes will be too hot to put in plastic anyway. We'll have to wrap him in foil. For now, of course. It's only a temporary measure." He shrugged as he handed me the pan and brush.

I'm sure he would have collected Caleb's ashes for me, but I probably would have corrected him on which bits of ashes to collect and which not. He knew me too well. I kneeled down, pan and brush in hand. The heat still radiated from the ash. It reminded me of the heat I felt radiating from Caleb's body every time I was near him. I don't know if it was the memory or the heat of the ashes, but tears began streaming down my face. I ignored them completely this time and swiped the brush through the ash, which made it whirl up into the air. Little pieces of Caleb stuck to the tears on my face. It was almost as if he wanted to wipe my tears away. The stream of tears increased. More bits of him clung to my face. This was going to be harder than I thought. I went through the motions while trying not to fall apart. I didn't get all of the ashes, but it would have to do.

Ashes to ashes, dust to dust.

When I stood up, Charlie wrapped the foil over the tin to prevent the ashes from blowing away. As Charlie took the pan and brush from me, he gently pulled me down and kissed me. It was a tender and long kiss. Just lips, but it was exactly what I needed. The tears stopped.

Together, we went inside. Julie came over and gave me a hug as did Abby and Sue. They didn't say anything. I guessed Charlie had explained to them my feelings for Caleb. If he hadn't, the current state of my face would have said it all. I couldn't face talking about it, so I put the cake tin on the countertop in the kitchen and disappeared into the bathroom. I took a couple of deep breaths before I cleaned my face. I didn't want to wipe Caleb from my existence, but I had to move on. He was gone, and Charlie loved me. Sue needed me and there was a new future waiting for us. I cleaned myself up as well as I could and went back into the living room.

Everyone stood around the dining table. Enrique explained to me we had to move as the cabin would probably be compromised by now. Julie was going to take us to the next location. Enrique and Abby would spend a few days at the cabin to dispose of Alex like we did with Caleb and clean up Alex's mess in the woods. Friends were running the pub for them in the meantime.

"Where will we be going?" I asked Enrique.

"I was about to show you all," he said in his French accent as he pulled out a map from his back pocket.

Listen very carefully. I will say this only once.

"This is where we are," Enrique said. He then pointed at another location on the map. "This is where you are going. "Remember the place. Don't write it down on the map or anywhere else, in case you get stopped on the way. It's the holiday place of my parents' neighbors and I don't want to get them into trouble."

"You sure we should go there?" Charlie asked.

"Yes, it's fine. They're too old to use it anymore. Once you get there, you should be okay. You'll be escorted by the kids, in case there's any trouble again. The place is yours for as long as you need it."

We gathered our stuff from the bedrooms and said our goodbyes to Abby and Enrique. I hugged them both and couldn't tell them often enough how grateful I was for their help. Charlie had to push me into the car so we could finally leave.

We drove without speaking. After a few hours without any hold-ups, we arrived at our new destination. Lo-and-behold, it was a caravan park.

Of all places.

We followed the riders and found the caravan we were to use as our home for the unforeseeable future. It was a tiny thing. Julie parked the car in front of it and we went inside. When I flicked on the light, it appeared as small on the inside as it did on the outside. Opposite the door, there was a little kitchenette with a bar fridge under the sink. A cupboard and a toilet/shower were to the left, and to the right, there was a U-shaped bench around a little, square table.

"Where do we sleep?" Sue asked.

"I'll explain that, if you let me in," we heard a voice outside say. We all turned around on our axis. Marlon stood in the light of the caravan. "Julie, you better come out. You won't be sleeping here anyway."

Lucky her.

Marlon swapped places with Julie and he showed us how the table could be lowered between the benches and the cushions rearranged to form a mattress. Sheets and blankets were to be found in the storage under the seats. Sue's 'bed' was above us; it was some sort of pull-out hammock, covering the width of the caravan.

"Okay..." Sue said. She was eying the contraption with suspicion.

"Don't worry, it'll hold. I've slept in it," Marlon smiled.

"If you say so," Sue said. I didn't miss the lingering eye contact between them.

"Where do you guys sleep?" I asked Marlon.

"We're in the caravan three doors down," and he pointed to the left. "Julie and I will keep an eye on you during the day and Shelly and Tony will at night. You'll be safe." He turned his face to Sue when he said the last words. Sue blushed. Marlon left us and closed the door behind him.

Charlie closed the curtains, so we had some privacy. I sat down and thought about our situation. I still couldn't believe there were more suckers like Sue. She wouldn't have to go through life as a freak. I liked Marlon. He was practical, handsome, and just plain adorable. I noticed Sue peek through the curtains in the direction he had gone.

In that instant, I realized I was happy. Even in these cramped quarters, under these circumstances, I was actually happy. Sue had a new love interest, and there was a future for her. I had Caleb's ashes with me and could return him to sea one day. And, last but not least, my relationship with Charlie was still as solid as a rock, and we were embarking on a new journey with a new child on the way. What more could I wish for?

How about a normal life?

Epilogue

We stayed in the caravan for the next three weeks, and they didn't find us again. During that time, we were able to contact a good lawyer whom Maxine had organized for us. The woman was shocked when she heard our story. Major Moore was able, with some help from the inside, to get hold of the army contract I had signed. In it, the lawyer found, in black and white, that I had stated I didn't allow for any tests on Sue she didn't want. Unfortunately, this didn't literally include getting her pregnant as pregnancy wasn't accepted as being a test. We couldn't prove it was part of their plan, at first. Major Moore testified that he took his granddaughters out when he heard of the plan to get the girls pregnant, which was before I fell pregnant, but it was his word against Dr. Greene's. Then I remembered the papers Greene had given me to sign, in which I would agree not to have an abortion and stay until the end of the pregnancy. It also stated I would agree to hand over my child to the care of the army. From the date on these papers, the lawyer could deduce, and convince the jury, that they knew I was going to be pregnant and that there had been a plan for these pregnancies to happen. We also showed the jury the photos we had taken of Sue's tracker implant that had been put inside her without permission, with a lie.

The biggest drive for the jury to convict Greene was, of course, the fact he had issued the sucker lads with detonating collars. The pictures Julie had taken of Alex's mutilated body were very graphic and, even though we were talking about suckers here, the decision had been unanimous that Greene was insane and had to be locked up for life.

Major Moore was acquitted of his crime of going AWOL as there wasn't a jury member who wouldn't do the same in his position. He was reinstated as Major after which he immediately retired.

The trials brought the situation of the sucker children into the media spotlight and began a chain reaction which made more and more sucker children come out of hiding. There was a worldwide debate about their future and in the end, the only condition to their freedom was that they had to be registered. People wanted to know who to point the finger at when somebody was sucked dry, which happened far less often than the usual crimes committed by unbitten humans. Still, people wanted security, which they received when it was proven that DNA testing of the saliva in the victim's puncture wounds would point out the culprit as easily as a fingerprint would. Being a sucker was no longer a reason to live under the radar.

Sue didn't change her mind about having her

pregnancy terminated. Charlie and I took her to an abortion clinic and reassured her she made the right decision. When we came out, Marlon was waiting for her with a bunch of red roses in his hands. Sue's arms flew around his neck, and she kissed him before he could hand the flowers to her. Charlie tried to stop her, but I pulled him back. I convinced him that Sue was a bright girl, and that she wasn't going to make the same mistake twice. I was right. Marlon and Sue became a couple but didn't start a family until ten years later.

Charlie, Sue and I visited the retired helicopter pilot who had saved us from the compound. He told us that Major Moore had saved his life a couple of times in Afghanistan. He was glad he had finally been able to repay his debt. We told him we were very thankful for what he had done for us, and that we would be there for him should he need us in some way.

It was not something I was looking forward to, but we also met up with Rhona and the girls. As soon as Major Moore heard Greene's plans for them, he had walked them outside, told them to get in his car, and had driven off. Just like that. Greene must have then decided to plant a tracker on Sue. We told Harry, Rhona, and the girls our whole story. They were very upset when they heard it. Rhona kept to the background and, unfortunately, our relationship never went back to what it was before.

When I visited Julie on the farm, I realized the

extent of her 'family business.' She ran a major cattle farm, with stud bulls and prize-winning milk cows. The pack-girls worked hard, and the children were also pulling their weight in the work. Next to farming, the children had been taught all sorts of things; from classic high school material to handicrafts, to all sorts of sports, including martial arts and motocross. Sue couldn't wait to catch up on everything. Marlon offered, of course, to help her with that.

Charlie and I were as happy as could be. As we still didn't know if my vaccination status would make my child a daywalker, we asked Tony to 'vaccinate' me, which he thought was an honor.

My pregnancy was uneventful and as soon as we found out it was going to be a boy, I began looking for names. In the end, I decided on Nelson, after Nelson Mandela and an English captain who had kept Napoleon at bay. I think Caleb would have liked the combination of a mariner and a freedom fighter in his son's name. When Nelson was born, and I arrived home from the hospital, I was shocked to find my house filled with visitors. Maxine was there, and Julie of course. But also all Julie's girls, most of their children, Harry and Rhona, Maddy and Milly, and a few of Charlie's friendly colleagues from school. I was so happy I cried. No longer did we have to live a lie, no longer did I have to hide my children. I could finally have the normal life I so wanted.

Well, sort of.

THE END

Releasing A Vampire

Prequel.

Settle into a cozy corner with this novelette and find out about the events that lead up to the action-packed, suspenseful urban fantasy yet funny Suckers Trilogy.

Who created the deadly *Succedaneum* virus? What was it meant to do? How did it escape into the world?

What relationship did Kate have with Charlie before the virus broke out? What was her life like when Black October began? How did Kate deal with her world falling apart?

Living Like A Vampire

Book 1

Kate is trying very hard to stay alive in a world thrown into chaos. Charlie is trying very hard to get Kate to notice him. When Caleb comes to the scene, things change, but is it for the better?

Kate had just begun her new job as a high school science teacher and was looking forward to living a suburban dream life. All her hopes and dreams turn into smoke as a virus turns people into vampires roaming the world in packs and killing everybody they can get their hands on. Together with her friends Sue and Charlie, she hides at a campground. They think they are safe there. They are wrong.

They are attacked by a pack of suckers and Kate has to flee again. She gets separated from her friends, accidentally bumps into a handsome sucker who then mysteriously disappears, after which she has to pretend to be a sucker to stay alive. Having met Caleb, surviving is no longer the only thing on Kate's mind.

Will Kate stay alive and human while pursuing this mysterious stranger?

Pick up this action-packed, fast-paced, suspenseful novel and explore the depths of Kate's emotions as she struggles to make sense of it all.

Killing a Vampire

Book 3

The past is back to haunt Kate. Will her partner survive this evil?

Kate thinks her relationship is on the rocks because of her past infidelity. She's wrought with guilt and wants nothing more than her missing partner back. When the police don't believe there's foul play at hand she's on her own to find him. A horrifying parcel arriving on Kate's doorstep brings the situation to a whole new lever. The police are now willing but can't due to lack of evidence.

There is one person able to help Kate, but everybody warns her not to accept his helping hand. How far is Kate willing to go to save the one she loves?

Killing a Vampire explores the emotional bonds between mother and child, sisters, and lovers. Follow the hints and clues as Kate explores the depth of her emotions while trying to save her love.

Review

Dear Reader,

If you liked reading my novel, please write a review on your favorite book retailer's website. Every review helps me forward as an author (and I love reading them!).

If you really, really like my writing, why not sign up for my newsletter in online magazine form? It contains author interviews, short stories, promos, and freebies. You can sign up for it on the home page of my website (jackydahlhaus.com), and when you do, you'll receive the Prequel novelette to the Suckers trilogy, Releasing A Vampire, for FREE!

With kind regards,

Jacky Dahlhaus

Connect

You can connect with me via:

Email:
jackydahlhaus@gmail.com

Twitter:
https://twitter.com/JackyDahlhaus

Instagram:
https://www.instagram.com/jackydahlhaus/

Facebook:
https://www.facebook.com/Jacky-Dahlhaus-Author-166614624053352/

My Website:
https://jackydahlhaus.com

Thank you so much for reading, and I hope to read your review soon, see your name on my mailing list, and be able to send you updates on my next book!

Jacky Dahlhaus

Acknowledgements

This work wasn't possible without the help of my dear friends from the Suckers Trilogy Launch Team. You know who you are, and I thank you from the bottom of my heart!

A special thanks to Kathleen, my dear American friend who took the time to help me correct my tenses and Americanize the story.

My dear children, thank you for getting off the internet when I asked you to do so when I needed to work on my book cover. I know what a terrible sacrifice it was for you :D.

As always, I would not have been able to do all this work if it hadn't been for the love and patience of my dear husband. You are the rock I cling to. I love you.

Jacky Dahlhaus

About the Author

Jacky Dahlhaus has worked many jobs and tried many hobbies before she realized writing gave her such pleasure. She loves to write paranormal fantasy stories while delving into the human psyche with all its faults and mysteries.

Next to writing novels, Jacky helps indie authors by promoting them on her blog, writes an online newsletter/magazine, runs a writing club for adults and for children at the local library, and is a director for Aberdeenshire Film Productions.

When not busy with the above (which is rare nowadays), Jacky works on renovating her Scottish Victorian home, watches movies with her family, and tries to stop her two Jack Russells from barking for no good reason.

Raising A Vampire is her second novel and the second book in the Suckers trilogy.

jackydahlhaus.com